R·L·H

Ruth Livingston Hill
The Homecoming

R·L·H

Ruth Livingston Hill

The Homecoming

HARVEST HOUSE PUBLISHERS
Eugene, Oregon 97402

THE HOMECOMING

Copyright © 1950 by Ruth H. Munce
(Formerly titled *John Nielson Had a Daughter*)
Published by Harvest House Publishers
Eugene, Oregon 97402

ISBN 0-89081-544-5

Printed in the United States of America.

R·L·H

Ruth Livingston Hill

The Homecoming

Chapter 1

WHEN THE TELEGRAM came, John Nielson was down in the engine room making a final checkup. The handsome yacht on which he was employed had been lying at anchor in Cuba for some weeks. Now it was ready for the run home to New York.

He stopped to wipe his hands thoroughly on a cloth hanging from his pocket before he took the yellow envelope in a gingerly thumb and finger. He gave a wipe to his sweating forehead, too, on the sleeve of his coveralls, at the same time pushing back a thin sandy forelock. He left a smear of black grease down his tired face and across his short crooked nose.

It was excessively hot, even for Cuba. John Nielson wondered why his employer cared to remain so long in the tropics, but that was his business; John's was the engine. John longed for more reasons than the heat to have this trip over with.

There was troubled wonder in his honest blue eyes as he looked down at the telegram. He had few ties, none that he cared about save the little new wife he had taken a month before he sailed on this cruise which had lasted so many months longer than he had expected.

Could it be that something was wrong with Janette? If so, would that hard-hearted half sister of hers take the trouble to let him know? Perhaps this message was just to tell him that Janette was flying south to be with him as she had often threatened she would do if she got lonely. His heart leaped at the thought. Maybe this was to ask him to meet her at a certain time at the airport. That must be it! She had missed him. It thrilled him to think that she cared so much. It was a long time since he had heard from her. He did not even know whether she had stayed in their one room or gone back to live with her sister until his return.

He had met that sister only once, nearly a year ago. That was when he and his little bride had come from the town where they lived a hundred miles away to announce that they had been married. His face burned with the same old humiliation as he recalled the horror in that sister's face when she opened her polished-oak door and saw them standing there, read their joy and guessed the truth.

For a long time she had stood speechless, the color completely drained from her stern face.

Then in a grim flat voice she had said,

"You may as well come in."

John still remembered how she had glanced at their feet and then at the doormat suggestively. He had already wiped his shoes but he did it again to make sure. He remembered how his precious wildflower wife had trembled a bit within his protecting arm, and his own conscience seemed suddenly to have been startled into accusing him, though of what he had not been sure; perhaps of being just plain, homely, honest, sandy-haired John Nielson, without any family in evidence, without any money to speak of, without any great prospects, only a good job as an engineer on a handsome yacht—instead of being the man who owned the yacht.

Myra Fetter had seated them in straight chairs in her dark, magenta parlor as if her half sister Janette were now a guest and not her own flesh and blood although she had lived with her for five years and Myra had tried frantically to bring her up according to her own strict standards. At the top of the list of those standards was cleanliness. Myra reckoned it next to godliness but as the proverb never did state on which side of godliness it was, Myra chose to place it on the far side, above the other virtue. Not a speck of dust nor a scratch marred the high polish of her floors. The chairs were protected with slip covers and lest the slip covers get soiled she made a habit of spreading a towel over them. When she worked she wore an immaculate cotton house dress with a starched apron over it. Her glossy black hair was combed in a stylish upsweep ending in a steep pompadour. There was not a hair out of place; but she wore a hair net to make sure. Her lips were pale and straight and tight; John had a feeling that she placed them so every morning and it would have distressed her to find them at any time untidied by a smile. But her features were good and she might have been a pretty woman like Janette if she had been less severe.

She had seated herself opposite them and looked John up and down. At last she said to Janette,

"Well, who is he?" She used the tone she always had used with Janette when her young sister brought home stray dirty puppies.

Janette's lip trembled but she answered bravely and eagerly,

"Why, you know I have told you about John, Myra. I met him, you remember, at that convention in Chester, that night when you had a sore throat and couldn't go. He was a friend of the Goodwin's. Surely you recall my telling you."

"The Goodwins!" Myra sneered. "Oh! And you thought the Goodwins were more fitted to select your life companion than your own sister?"

Janette wilted.

"That, I believe," went on the hard voice, "was not more than *one month* ago!" Her words were like big shears, cutting through the filmy stuff of their romance ruthlessly.

For reassurance Janette glanced over at her John. His pained eyes met hers, then suddenly the remembrance of their first meeting when they had, as it were, walked into each other's arms and hearts, thrilled them both and a radiant smile of understanding lit up their faces.

Myra Fetter did not fail to see it, and it put a still sharper edge on her voice.

"You had reached the mature age of nineteen at that time, I believe," she stated scathingly to her sister. "And this man," she looked John up and down contemptuously, "is what? Twice that?"

"But I love him, Myra," smiled Janette triumphantly.

Myra sniffed, an indignant, infuriated sniff.

"You love him!" she mocked. "As if you knew what love is! You're nothing but a child, impulsive and scatterbrained. And as if it mattered anyway. Love isn't everything. What *will* people think? And how do you know that the man is fit to marry you? How do you know but he will leave you next week for some other girl? How do you know but he's had a dozen girls already? Can he support you? Tell me, do you know *any*thing about him?"

In flaming misery John Nielson heard his new sister-in-law strip him of honor and integrity. He looked back through his uneventful industrious years and tried to find one thing that he had done that he could take out and show her, something that might deserve honorable mention. His long-dead parents had not been able to give him many worldly advantages, but they had handed down a heritage of decency and honest stability. Now it seemed as if that was not enough. John began to wonder how he had ever dared to take unto himself this charming talented girl who at nineteen had already had two paintings hung in the local art gallery. Why she had ever looked at him was a mystery. But she had, and he knew she loved him. They had understood each other from the instant their eyes met.

He straightened himself and stood up, his humility and courage adorning him in the eyes of his bride. His crooked nose and honest gaze were beautiful to her.

"Madam," he said with gentle self-restraint, "I realize that you must wish to know that your sister is in good hands. Although I am not much to look at and I have no fortune, I have lived a clean life, and Janette is the first and only girl I have loved. I believe I can take care of her and make her happy. I shall not ask you to rely on my word, however. I shall be glad to send you references. I hope that you will make every effort to look into them. Shall we go now, Janette?"

"Wait! Not so fast!" ordered Myra. "I could have this ridiculous marriage annulled, I suppose, since Janette is only nineteen, but I don't approve of that. What's done is done. I will have to make the best of it. Bring in your things and I will make ready your room. We can talk later." She rose to sail upstairs but Janette simply laughed gaily.

"Thank you, no, Myra. John and I have our own place," she answered proudly. "We are going right back to John's room in Chester. He will be away a good deal and then I may come to visit you sometimes, but we shall not be a burden on you. Thank you just the same, Myra."

"Oh!" sniffed Myra again, but it was a sniff of defeat. "Well, you will soon have your fill of that! One room indeed! And in Chester! You may start out by trying to be very independent," she blustered, "but I guess you will both find you have no bed of roses. And you, sir, will discover that it costs quite a good deal more than you realize to keep a wife, and you don't look to me as if you had it in you to make very much!"

"Myra!" blazed Janette. "John is my husband and I will not have you talk to him in that way!"

"Very well, be as independent as you like, but you will see! You will be coming home to roost before long, begging for help. I'm sure I hope you make out better than I expect!"

Her last words were addressed to their backs for the bride and groom had walked quietly out of the house.

It was only one short precious month after that when John had received the news of his employer's intention to take a trip. It had turned out to be a very long trip with unscheduled visits at various South American ports. Letters had not kept up with him very well, and John felt as if that one month of happiness were a dream, he knew so little of what was going on at home. Indeed, he had begun to feel as if he scarcely knew his little-girl wife. He had written faithfully at first, but later on he found it hard to write anything very personal, hearing so rarely from home. He had fallen back on describing the different cities they visited. He sometimes wondered whether Myra's fierce will and her dominating personality could have turned his young wife away from him during his absence. It was three or four months since he had had a letter from Janette. Of course the mail must be trying to follow him. Janette's letters would arrive some time. He sighed heavily as he tore open the telegram. The message crashed against his senses.

"My sister died yesterday. Myra Fetter."

The tight-lipped woman had not even softened the blow by enough details to make up ten words. And she had called Janette "my sister" instead of "your wife" or simply "Janette." Well, that was like her!

The ship suddenly did a whirlwind dance about him, madly screaming the words of the message at him. Died! Died! Your wife is *dead!*

John tried to steady his feet on the engine-room floor. The dials he had been checking seemed to stare coldly at him like the faces of so many Myra Fetters. For an instant he thought the heat had got him at last and he had gone stark crazy. But there were those blue typewritten words against the yellow paper.

Suddenly a terrible trembling seized him. He had not been prepared for anything like this. He looked for a place to sit down but the spotless, efficient engine room had not been prepared for the message either. There was nothing in it but pipes and gears and well-oiled shafts.

With shaking limbs John got himself out to the air on the after deck, and leaning against the rail he mopped his damp forehead again on his sleeve.

Some time that evening he found himself on a plane headed north. Everybody had been pretty nice about it, he thought gratefully. But his mind still felt blank. It was as if he had started on a delightful ride with his dear bride and all of a sudden there had been a blinding crash and an explosion and then all was dark.

Nothing would ever be the same again for him. He had been planning to give up this job and get work at home. Now that would not be necessary. Home life was over for him. There would be no sweet reunion. He began to realize how much he had counted on that.

Almost too soon he found himself at the polished-oak door again, lifting the heavy brass knocker. The rounded surface of brass took his own face and twisted it into a horrible grimace as he waited. Then Myra herself opened the door.

Her eyes were red now with weeping, and John found almost a pity in his heart for this stern grim soul with its hurt pride and disappointment, for she had just lost the only thing that she probably had ever really loved, the sweet young wildflower sister who had, as she had said, thrown herself away on a penniless mechanic whom nobody had ever heard of.

John was dressed in his rumpled brown best but he looked unimpressive after his all-night plane ride. Lines showed deep in his lean tanned face, making him look even older than he was.

Myra stared hard at him a moment before she spoke.

"Oh," she said in a colorless tone. "It's you. I thought maybe you might turn up. Perhaps it's just as well. It will look better, at least."

She led him into the darkened front parlor. It looked just as it had before: heavy, dark, magenta draperies hanging long enough to drag stylishly a little on the floor; family heirlooms all about; a fine old haircloth sofa. John remembered how it had pricked him through his thin summer suit on his former visit. There were several stiff antique chairs, and on the walls oil portraits of forbidding looking ancestors; every possible space was jammed with ornate vases and bric-a-brac. Myra Fetter never tired of telling the story of each, and impressing her guests with the fact that they were all genuine *family* heirlooms.

Then John saw the casket in the corner.

Myra stood aside a few moments in silent distaste of him and allowed this man his right to look into the delicate white face of his bride. Many questions rose to his mind, questions that had been torturing him through all that long night vigil on the plane. What had caused Janette's death? Had she loved him still? Had his last letters reached her? Why had he not heard for so long a time? It would not have been strange if her heart had turned to a younger, more attractive man during his absence. But he could not bring himself to ask anything of this hard forbidding woman. Perhaps her husband Duncan Fetter, whom Janette had mentioned once, would prove to be less formidable.

With a heavy heart he lived again those few blessed weeks they had together, as he dwelt on each lovingly remembered detail of her beautiful face.

But after a few minutes Myra moved up beside him.

"Come to the other room now," she ordered in her dull stern voice.

John hesitated. He felt as if he might not be allowed to look upon his dear wife's form again if he left now, but after all this was Myra Fetter's house, not his, so he followed her heavily.

She seated him on one of a row of stiff antique walnut chairs ranged against the dining-room wall. It seemed as if she was trying to make him as uncomfortable as possible.

John sat down gingerly, lest somehow the dust of his travel might by chance be deposited carelessly upon the handsome gray satin stripes. Just then a gray-looking figure appeared in the doorway leading by a leather cord a bulgy gray wire-haired terrier. Although he was scarcely more than a puppy, the dog's face looked pinched and dissatisfied, as if from too many frustrations regarding bones, or possibly cats, or both.

The man had a thin gray face. He looked as if he had been shut in a book to keep the place long ago and then forgotten. John noticed with some surprise that he was in his stocking feet. He wore thick gray woolen socks.

He cast a furtive look at his wife as if to seek permission to enter while she had company. He must have received a silent reproof, for he caught up the dog hastily and retired.

Then Myra sat herself down on the edge of a stiff chair on the opposite side of the room as if she did not intend to indulge in any lengthy interview.

With a look that seemed to say, "I hope you are satisfied with what you have done to my poor sister," she opened her lips. But it seemed hard for her to speak. John felt again a faint stirring of pity for her. But when she did speak there were no tears evident behind her cold exterior.

"I have arranged everything for the funeral," she announced. Her tone implied that John had no right to make any decisions anyway. And then, as if it were one of the minor details which need not bother him, she added,

"And I will keep the baby."

John started and stared at her. The baby! Had there been a baby in the Fetter family? He tried to think whether Janette had ever mentioned a niece. Then all at once it dawned on him what the woman must mean.

"Baby!" he stammered. He had never thought of such a thing. On the night ride his mind had been filled with wonderings as to what had taken Janette so suddenly, and whether she had been sick long, but the thought of a possible baby had never once entered his mind.

Myra stiffened.

"Yes," Myra opened her pursed lips just enough to let the words through. "Janette's baby. The doctors say that with care it will live. Janette had a bad fall on the ice." She did not mention that the fall was a result of Janette insisting upon starting out to mail a letter to her husband herself, nor did Myra speak of the quarrel that had led up to that. She sat bolt upright and motionless, her thin hands cupped righteously one over the other. This man, from her point of view, was the cause of her sister's death and he should hear as little of the whole matter as she could legally and morally keep from telling him.

But John's head had gone down in his hands, and he was trying to get his breath and accustom himself to the thought of a baby. His baby! His and Janette's. At first it seemed as if an interloper had entered the sacred little paradise he and his bride had shared but all of a sudden it came to him that Janette would have loved the baby. Of course! And he would love it too. It belonged to him and Janette. It was something of Janette that he could keep. He forgot for a moment the grim presence of the tight-lipped woman who sat facing him. Then he looked up with eagerness.

"Where is the baby?"

A frightened look stole like a swift shadow across the woman's face and then disappeared instantly.

"She is in the hospital still. She must remain there for some time yet. There is no need for you to trouble yourself. I will take her. She will need the greatest care."

John Nielson stood up.

"No doubt you mean to be very kind," he said courteously, "but I prefer to take the child myself."

"You!" Myra Fetter hissed the word. "What do you know about babies?"

"Nothing. But I can learn," responded John humbly, with a sad smile.

"Humph!" retorted the woman. "And how would you propose to take care of a baby and work on a boat at the same time? Answer me that?"

"I don't know, yet," said John, speaking slowly as if feeling his way. "It is my problem and there will be a way to work it out."

"Ridiculous!" asserted Myra. "Why make a problem out of it when there is none? Of course I will take my own sister's child. It would certainly look very unfeeling in me if I could not do that much for the girl who was like my own daughter."

John thought that the steely voice might be very near to giving way, but there was no break in it, and the hard cold eyes, set deep in their bony sockets, betrayed no sign of emotion.

"Well, Mrs. Fetter, it doesn't seem to me that this is any occasion for caring what would look well. I intend to take my own baby and take care of her."

Myra's face grew white as death. She knew that John was within his rights. A long moment she sat staring stonily ahead, a gray shadow deepening on her face. Finally she arose with stiff dignity and led the way to the front door.

"The child is in Mercy Hospital," she vouchsafed coldly as he went out, and she closed the door behind him.

John went down the steps with his swarm of questions still unasked. They were not questions about mere funeral arrangements. Janette herself would not be there and so those things could not matter a great deal to him. If Myra Fetter cared about them, and it gave her any satisfaction, all right, let her have her way.

But how was it that he had not heard of the baby before this? Had Janette planned to surprise him? Surely she had told him about it in one of the letters that *must* be following him all over South America. He could not give up his faith in Janette. He sighed and turned his steps toward the city and Mercy Hospital.

But it was not visiting hours and the impregnable doors of the nursery were closed against him, even though he was prepared to prove his identity as the father of a baby there.

So with another heavy sigh he hunted up a cheap hotel in the big city of which Myra's town, Oak Hill, was a fashionable suburb. The thought never occurred to him that Myra had a large house with plenty of room for a guest. He would not have cared to stay there even if she had asked him.

Last night he had been tortured by the question of whether Janette had still loved him. Now the main subject that occupied his mind was, what on earth was he going to do with a baby?

Chapter 2

JOHN AWOKE THE next morning from a restless sleep on a lumpy bed.

He had been puzzling all through his dreams about that baby. The very thought of handling her, and dressing her, terrified him. What if he should drop her? He had heard of such things happening, and sometimes it gave the baby a brain injury for life. Cold sweat crept over him. What should he feed her? He couldn't expect her to live on crackers and cheese as he had often done!

There would be baths, too. Of course she would have to be bathed! What if his hands slipped and he drowned her? Or what if she got to crying and he couldn't stop her? In a panic he arose, possessed with the idea that he must go somewhere to learn how to do all these things. He did not once entertain the thought of hiring someone else to take care of his baby. It was his job and he would do it. Surely there must be a school where one could go. How did young mothers learn?

There were various women, wives of his friends, whom he knew slightly. They all had children, and had brought them up alive, yet those women never seemed to him extraordinarily bright or clever. How had they learned? He could ask them, of course, but they were in his home town a hundred miles away, and he was in a frenzy to begin learning now. The hospital might hand over the baby to him at any time, and *what* would he do with it? Besides he found that he felt a sort of resentment at having anybody else in on this baby. She belonged to him and Janette.

He dressed hurriedly, gulped some coffee at a corner drug

store and started for the hospital again. Surely someone there could help him. He had not noticed the time. It was only quarter of seven when he reached there.

He went up to the desk. Sleepily the night clerk glanced up. The man before her was not handsome enough nor young enough to be interesting. He did not look sick, only harassed. He must be an expectant father. They always came tearing in at unseemly hours.

"Can you tell me where I can go to learn about the care of babies?" asked John seriously.

The woman looked amused.

"You see," explained John carefully, somewhat taken aback at her condescension, "I am going to have to do it myself. I thought there might be some course I could take, or—or something." He had paused, hoping the clerk would help him out, but she had simply continued to smile cynically until he finished speaking. Feeling rather foolish, he stood helpless while the red stole up in his neck.

"You could get one of those booklets the insurance companies put out, I suppose," answered the clerk laconically. "Didn't your wife have one mailed to her? They generally send them out."

"I don't know—that is, my wife—died." John tried to say it in an unemotional tone. He was determined not to keep laying his own heartbreak on other people to bear. It could not possibly mean anything to strangers.

"Oh," said the woman who was accustomed to deaths. "Well, you could probably get one. Most companies have them." Then she turned away.

"When can I see my baby?" he called after her.

"Visiting-hours-for-the-nursery-are-two-to-four," she rattled back.

Two o'clock! There was a great deal for him to learn in the few hours until two. What if they should want to hand the baby over to him right then and there?

He started to hurry out to hunt up an insurance company, but he suddenly realized that they would not be likely to open their doors at seven in the morning just in case some frantic father happened by and wanted instruction in baby care. He hesitated and his anxiety arrested the attention of the superintendent of nurses, happening by. She stopped to ask what he wanted.

She smiled understandingly when he explained, and took him to her office. With a gentleness that would have surprised some of her little trainees, she proceeded to give him a thorough course in baby care in a few sentences. Then she rang for a nurse to bring a copy of his baby's formula, and wrote out for him directions as to how to sterilize the bottles, besides a list of supplies he would need.

John drew a sigh of relief when he withdrew. She had made it seem less complicated than he had feared.

The rest of the morning he spent in his room studying the book he had procured.

The funeral service was at two o'clock. That was an ordeal. Myra had a taste for display that did not appeal to John. The only comforting note in it all for him was in a few words the minister read. He had heard them before but they seemed spoken to his own heart today. "Let not your heart be troubled: ye believe in God, believe also in Me." It was a faraway God who spoke, for John had never dared to draw near to Him, but even distant comfort helped. It took John through the dreary formalities. After they were over, he climbed aboard a bus and set off once more for the hospital.

Up in the corridor he looked around for a nurse to tell him where to find his baby when all at once he heard a voice that sounded strangely familiar, a murmuring crooning voice. It came from a room directly behind him. Some new mother, no doubt, talking to her baby. He thought wistfully how it might have been had he been going to Janette's room to see her with her new baby, and the thought wrung his heart.

"*Precious* 'ittle sweetheart!" came the loving tones. No, thought John, that voice is too old and edgy for the mother of a young baby. Idly curious, he peered through the wide crack at the back of the door. There was no one in the bed. It was made up and the room was bare as if unoccupied. But the thin voice went on trying to coo.

"Darling little girl! *My* little girl. Couldn't you smile just once? I've waited so long for you, sweetheart." There was a sob then. "And now you won't be mine after all. Oh-h-h!"

Unconsciously John leaned forward to see who was speaking and then gasped in utter amazement. There was the thin, stylish figure of Myra Fetter, holding in her bony black crepe arms a little bundle of pink! "Come, little sweetheart, smile at your auntie just once, before he takes you a-waaa-ay!" Then Aunt Myra's stylishly coifed head went down into the pink blanket and her whole gaunt figure shook with sobs.

John stood still, too astonished to stir. Could it be that there was a heart in the woman, after all? He craned his neck to try to see the baby. He wouldn't go in. It would embarrass Myra and himself too. He thought a moment, then he turned and stole quietly down the stairs again and took his way to the train station. If it meant so much to Myra Fetter, he could wait until next week to see his baby. He had thought things over that day and he realized that there were arrangements to be made at home before he brought a baby there. So he compromised by a telephone call to the hospital, arranging to return the next week end for the baby.

John wondered on the long trip home how many other lonely broken hearts there were in the world besides his own. His joy over Janette's love had come to him so unexpectedly after years of hardship and disappointments, and he had actually been with her so little, that the sorrow of losing her was only another greater one added to the rest. He had always tried to take his troubles cheerfully and bravely.

But there was that Fetter woman, now. She had seemed so stern and cold. Was that manner just a cover-up for heartbreak? Her way of trying to be brave? It was like John to give her the benefit of the doubt.

He trudged heavily up the shabby staircase to his room that

he had left so many months ago. It suddenly occurred to him that there would be things there that had belonged to Janette. He unlocked the door with a faint eagerness. He had a feeling that something of Janette herself would still be waiting to welcome him. How long she had stayed there after he left, or how much she had visited at her sister's house he did not know, although she had mentioned in her early letters that Myra had been begging her to come to Oak Hill until her husband returned. He did not resent that. Of course she would have been lonely here in one room, alone in a strange town. Still, she had told him in her first letter that she loved it there because it was his room, and that she seemed closer to him when she was there. Yet he had lived long enough to know that such a feeling did not often last long; companionship generally meant more than sentiment.

Surely, however, some of her things would be here.

He entered and looked about eagerly. The room was immaculately clean, and in perfect order. The brass bed that had been his parents' was made up straight and stiff, covered with his old crinkled blue-and-white striped dimity spread. He noticed that the tear in the corner had been carefully mended. He looked over to the sturdy old golden oak dresser with its narrow, cloudy mirror that had a crack across the top. He had thought that some of Janette's pretty woman's things might still be there. But there was nothing at all on it except a clean white cover.

His desk still had the brass port and starboard lights he had brought home from a fine old boat that was being done over. John had made them into electric lamps and had always liked them. A lot of women might not have cared to live in a room that was so distinctly mannish, but Janette had. She had seemed to love everything there just because it was his.

The one really handsome piece of furniture in the room, the old drop-leaf walnut table, was still standing near the screened corner where the hot plate and minute icebox were. The screen was the only thing that Janette had changed about the room. She had asked him to make the frame and she had decorated it herself. One panel pictured the open sea, with a glorious white gull riding the wind; in the middle one a graceful sloop sailed into view, exulting in its freedom as it rode along; and the third showed the shore line, where a white cottage on a little hill nestled among shading trees, and a brook laughed with some children who played along its banks.

John looked longest at that screen. It seemed to be the only thing that was left to him of Janette. Even the cupboard bore no sign that she had ever been there, or that anyone had lived there in a long, long time. Every scrap of food except a few cans was cleared out and the place was bare.

John sat down in the big wide overstuffed platform rocker, the one chair he had saved from his mother's things because he could remember her rocking him to sleep in her arms in it. He had held Janette in his arms in that big chair many an evening while they both watched the small strip of sky between two buildings and waited for the full moon to rise. He remembered how it had lighted up her beautiful eager face when it had risen above the opposite roof, touching the dusky cloud of her soft hair with reverent fingers. Now he reached out his empty, hungry arms and dropped them again with a moan. He gazed at the little white cottage in the picture and sighed as he realized that that dream never would come true, now.

But John was not one to waste time on his emotions. There was much to be done. At least the joy had been his, an unexpected joy, and in one sense no one could ever take it away.

He got up and looked at the room again with new eyes. Would Janette have thought it the sort of place into which to bring their baby? He tried to think what changes should be made. The nurse at the hospital had made him such a long formidable list of things to get. Baby furniture! Where was he to put it all? He felt bewildered again.

At last he went downstairs to talk to Mrs. O'Leary who lived below him.

She was a motherly woman who had had eleven children, some of whom were constantly coming to visit her with children of their own. If anybody could advise him, she should be able to.

With many expressions of amazement and sympathy she laboriously ascended the stairs with him.

"Ye've no call to be in sech a tizzy, mon," she puffed when she reached his room. "A baby's jist a small person like yerself. I've a bit of an old cradle meself ye can borry if ye like, till ye can get what ye want. Set it here by yer own bed and ye can reach out an' tuck up the wee thing without a bit o' trubble. An' what ilse do ye need? The child'll get as clean in the dishpan as she would in one o' them new-fangled rubber contraptions they charge so much fer."

John gasped and took a look at Mrs. O'Leary's greasy dress and the grime around the back of her neck where the hair made a straggling fringe over it. He decided that he would take pains to secure a brand new bed for his child that very day rather than subject her to a cradle that had seen service for Mrs. O'Leary's eleven and probably a half dozen of her grandchildren into the bargain. As for the dishpan, even "the book" had said that it would be quite all right to use one; but at least he would get a new, clean, white one. Still he did appreciate the good woman's willingness to help out and he felt as if the preparations need not be so elaborate as he had feared.

He hoped to be able to secure night work near home so that he could be there in the daytime, snatching sleep when the baby slept. The superintendent of nurses had told him that babies took two naps a day the first year or two. There would have to be somebody there to look after her at night, and he had vaguely reserved Mrs. O'Leary for that honor. But that was before he took a good look at her. Now she was out of the question.

He thought over all his nearby acquaintances that morning and finally settled upon Miss Mattie Puckett, an impecunious but immaculate elderly spinster. She had been a nurse and though she seemed to John rather prim, he decided that if his baby was anything like her dear impulsive mother, she might need some primness about her. Anyway, Mattie Puckett had always impressed him as utterly conscientious and dependable.

A few days later, after a most gratifying talk with Miss Puckett, and a less gratifying but still satisfactory one with a factory personnel man, John went his way again to the hospital.

As he followed a pretty little starched smiling nurse down the corridor to the nursery, he found his heart pounding strangely. He was amused to think that he was actually frightened of the new little person he was about to meet, terrified at the thought of the responsibility suddenly thrust upon him. But he was determined to see this thing through.

The young nurse dimpled with whimsical amusement at this obviously uninitiated parent; and when she placed in his arms the soft little bundle he had an awful moment when he thought he was going to drop it out of sheer fright.

Then he looked down and caught his breath. For there was a tiny replica of Janette, black hair in a soft downy cloud, sweet lips, a wee nose that had the merest suggestion of upturn and bright black eager eyes that looked alertly up at him and seemed to him to shine in understanding as if she said, "I know who *you* are. My mother told me all about you. You're my father and I'm glad."

With the sudden realization that here was a person with whom he had something in common, one who out of all the world belonged to him and he to her, the awful strain he had been under for the past days, indeed the past months when he had not heard from his wife, seemed to give way and a great sob of relief and joy broke from him, while tears rained down his face.

The little nurse turned reverently away from the holy scene and her own eyes were wet. Not many fathers were stirred like that at sight of their babies, not even new ones. But, of course, his wife was gone, poor man.

Downstairs, John breathlessly stuffed a warm carefully-wrapped baby bottle they gave him into one pocket, and a parcel containing a few spare garments in another, then taking the baby awkwardly in both arms, he hailed a taxi and proudly climbed in headed for the station and home.

On the train he thought again of the harsh-faced woman who had longed to possess his child.

"I can't let you go, though," he whispered tenderly to the little bundle he held close to him so clumsily. "You're mine, after all, mine and your mother's, and she would want you to stay with me, little Janette. You're going to grow up and be just like her, aren't you little girl?"

The baby fixed her bright eyes on him and her determined little rosebud mouth seemed set to say, "Okay, Daddy, we'll work it out together, you and I, and we'll have a lot of fun, won't we?"

Something deeply satisfying seemed to settle somewhere near the region of John's heart and he knew it was there to stay. He had a strange desire to thank somebody for this precious gift. He was not well acquainted with God. Not that he had reason to have anything against Him, but he simply never had taken Him into consideration to any degree. It had always seemed to John that the few people who were in a position to represent God were a weak inconsistent lot, so the worship of God had not interested him. But now those words from Janette's funeral service seemed to be sealed by this gift to him, and his own grateful heart struggled to send a wordless answer out somewhere in space to the One whose care he had never realized before.

John felt utterly unqualified for the great new responsibility of keeping this little soul unspotted. How did it come about that *he* had been chosen for such an honor? For of course this baby seemed to him more lovely, more precious than any other baby that had ever been born.

His heart thrilled again and again as he pressed the warm little body close to his heart, and by the time he reached home he was already wondering how soon he might expect her to begin to talk.

Chapter 3

"HEY, JAN!"

A peculiar long whistle like a bird call, with a trilling loop in the middle of it, ascended to the second story of the dirty yellow brick rooming house where John Nielson still lived with his daughter Janette.

A window at the head of the fire escape opened and down flew Janette, twelve years old now and agile as a cat.

"Coming, Danny," she called blithely. She was a wiry little figure all arms and legs, with two black pigtails attached somewhere near the top. Her sparkling black eyes were as big as ever and her pert little nose was covered with freckles. She was not pretty but John Nielson, who had somehow weathered the years of her babyhood, thought there was no child like her, although he did feel that he would never make up all the sleep he had lost.

Danny Severy, who lived in the dirty yellow brick rooming house across the back alley, adored Jan. She was a year older than he, and she, of all the children down the alley, could think up the most exciting madcap games and outstrip all the rest in running and climbing, and, most fascinating of all, story-telling. As soon as Jan appeared among them each child suddenly found himself a knight or a giant, a fairy or a goblin, taking his part according to the need of the moment created by Jan's fantastic imagination.

The instant Jan's feet touched the ground from the fire escape a swarm of her followers appeared as if by magic, from doorways and corners. The time with Jan was precious, not to be wasted. Her father worked day shifts now, coming home from work at four, and then Jan was theirs no longer. For, much as she enjoyed her play with them, it seemed as if she must have a secret understanding with her father that the time he was at home belonged in a special way to the two of them. Sometimes a picnic they planned might be shared with other children and that was considered a priceless privilege! But more often Jan and her father took long walks alone together down by the river where they never tired of watching the great freighters steaming by, and the busy little river boats tugging their burdens. John would tell his daughter endless stories of the ports the ships had come from or of the cargo that they carried, and Jan's eager mind envisioned each country of which she learned so that no less than the world itself became the four walls of her home, as familiar as her own playground. Sometimes they would walk all the way to the park to hear the band play, and on rare occasions John would buy tickets for a really good concert when he discovered how Jan loved music.

Sometimes, when they were going to hire a boat and go fishing, they would take Danny Severy along, for Danny of all the others could be trusted to use good sense and do as he was told. He was Jan's steady playmate.

Danny lived on the ground floor at the back of the other brick rooming house, the twin to theirs. As a small child Jan used to think he had no parents. Then one night when she and her father were standing at their kitchen window waiting for the ever-thrilling event of moonrise, they had glanced down for a moment from the sky to the sordid alley and caught sight of Danny's father staggering homeward. They could see the fight that took place in the unkempt, dirty, unshaded Severy kitchen. They saw Danny scuttle like a scared kitten into a corner. His mother stood ready with a heavy frying pan but her husband promptly wrested it from her and used it with success on her after she had tried to beat him off with it.

Jan was terrified and shocked. John had had difficulty in keeping her from running down to rescue her little playmate when his father hit him. As time went on however, and Danny learned ways of eluding his parent, Jan grew used to the situation; still she kept a very warm spot in her heart for the boy who seemed so unwanted and neglected. For they never saw the Severys sit down to a meal together. When the boy was hungry he went in and took what he could find. Most of the time his parents were not at home. His mother worked long hours at scrubbing, and spent her evenings at a taproom or gossiping on somebody's doorstep, leaving her own scrubbing undone in order to spend her spare time forgetting her misery.

At intervals the dirty little church nearby would hold a series of revival meetings. Mrs. Severy was always dragged to them by some well-meaning friend who tried in vain to get her husband too, and before the highly emotional strain was over, Mrs. Severy would invariably break down and confess her sins, and go weeping and moaning up the aisle to be prayed over. Danny knew all about it, for he had climbed up outside more than once and watched the whole proceeding. He would observe his mother during succeeding days, but never saw any change in her although the good woman who had persuaded her to go to the meetings had assured him that there would be. So his young heart grew hard and a bitter contempt grew in him for religion as he saw it and emotionalism in any form, although he was still too young to know what that meant.

Danny fairly worshipped Jan, and respected her father. Their home life was the one ray of light in his dark world. He was a bright boy but he did not care for study on its own account and skipped school whenever he found it convenient and politic to do so. The education he received from the Nielsons, both father and daughter, stood him in good stead, but he was far behind Jan in his grades and, as he grew older, sometimes he was ashamed of that and began at intervals to work a little harder. There was an undercurrent of dread in him lest Jan should suddenly soar off on the clouds of her learning and her imaginings and leave him to his dirt and desolation.

For Jan loved study. She ate up her subjects hungrily. She never lacked for novel and interesting ways to fasten facts in her mind.

One winter day her father came home and found her and Danny staring eagerly out the kitchen window, one of Jan's black pigtails pointing west, the other east. She was saying some sort of rhyme over to Danny.

"Oh, Daddy, come here," she called. "Just look! I've found a way to remember the middle states at last. I failed on them yesterday in a test and so did Danny. But we'll get them next time. Here they are outside here all lined up for us, each side of the Mississippi River, see it?" Jan pointed to a long ugly crack in the center of the building on the other side of the alley. It was ominously wide at the bottom and extended almost to the top.

"See," cried Jan, "there's a family for each of the five states each side of the river. All we'll have to do is remember the names of those people who live there. Just hear how they fit! Up there at the top left is lame old Minnie Savage. That one is easy! We'll change her to old Minnie Sota! Then below her are the Joneses, and everybody knows they are always borrowing money and things, so we've called them I-owe-a-lot Jones for Iowa. Miss Emily Mudge below them, will be Miss Ouri Mudge—she'll never know!" giggled Jan. Her father entered into the little game delightedly.

"And old Mr. McArdle, with his long white beard. What will you do with him?"

"Why," she clapped her hands, "that's easy. I'll call him Noah's Ark McArdle, for Arkansas! And I'm going to call Danny's mother Louise Anna Severy for Louisiana. Don't you think she would like that name? Her real name is Anna, anyway. And Daddy! Just listen to this one on the other side of the crack where Lipskys live. Mrs. Ippi Lipsky! Isn't that perfect? And that woman up there who is always sticking her head out of the window and yelling at us not to make so much noise, her head aches. I don't know her name, but I'll call her Mrs. Ill o' Noise!" Jan shouted with glee. "Now all I have to do is think of three more, Daddy. Isn't it *fun?*"

Jan made play of her housework as she did of everything else. John taught her what manners he knew, which were only the simple principles of unselfishness. He always told her the straightforward truth about anything she wanted to know without dulling its edge. He made few rules but he stuck doggedly to the ones he made and he gave Jan to understand very early that he meant what he said. Aside from that he simply let her grow.

Sometimes he looked with troubled eyes at Danny, who had a certain charm beneath his dirt and rags and unkempt mop of hair. He wondered whether it was well for the two to be together so constantly, but he let them alone for he guessed that in time Jan would outgrow and far outstrip Danny; besides he felt infinitely sorry for the lad.

Miss Mattie Puckett had done her work well until such time as she was called from this earth. She had been considerate enough to remain until Jan was ten. Jan had unconsciously picked up from her many ways of daintiness that John would never have thought of teaching her. He noticed them and was grateful. Jan had cried bitterly at the loss of her old nurse, but her elastic spirits had soon helped her to regain her balance.

When Jan was twelve she startled her father one day by asking,

"Daddy, do you believe in God?"

They were standing on a wide bridge over the river watching the last glories of a fading sunset.

John found himself for the first time reluctant to meet those demanding black eyes squarely. Like a good many working men he had a straightforward honesty about his thinking which made him disgusted with the various kinds of religion he had met with. It seemed to him that the ways of many preachers were not in harmony with their doctrine. If the thing preached could not transform the preacher himself how could it help anyone else? So John never went to church. But he looked up to the gigantic painting in the sky before them, and answered, "Why, yes, I suppose—of course I do. Why?"

"Well, a girl in school was talking about God and how her family go to a camp meeting in the summer, and she wanted to know if I was 'saved.' I said saved from what, and she said, 'Don't you even know *that?* Don't you believe in *God?*' I didn't know what to say."

John Nielson thought hard over that one. At last he said, "I guess there are a lot of ways to worship God, Jan. And I don't suppose anybody really knows much about it. Some people get sort of crazy ideas. It's best to let them alone. But there is a God. When you look at that sunset, and all the stars coming up right on time, you know there has to be. And it must be that He is good and wants us to do right. Each one of us has something in us that tells us pretty well what is right and what is wrong. I always figured if we tried to follow that voice and choose right every time, we'd come out all right."

Jan thought a minute. Then she looked straight at her father with clear eyes.

"*Do* you always choose right, Daddy?"

John hesitated, and stammered, "Well, I don't suppose I always have—no. But I try to do my best." Several things in John's life that had not seemed particularly heinous before suddenly loomed large and disgraceful.

"Well, *do* you always do your best?" probed Jan.

John grew red, annoyed that his own daughter's questioning should remind him of those things in his life which he would rather forget. All at once the feeling of inadequacy which he always carried with him stowed away out of sight grew to enormous proportions.

"No, I don't suppose I do," he admitted reluctantly. "I guess everybody *could* do a lot better than they do."

"Well, then," commented Jan bluntly, "I shouldn't think God would give anybody very good marks!"

John stared at his daughter.

"Maybe you're right," he agreed seriously. "But as far as I ever heard, the only thing to do is to keep on trying to do our best. Possibly God has some way to make up for our failures, but if He has, I never heard of it."

Jan looked disappointed.

"Well, I shouldn't think, if He is a really nice God, that He would give us all something we just can't do!" she said.

John sighed. He had always tried faithfully to give a satisfactory answer to his daughter's wonderings, but this seemed to be unanswerable as far as he was concerned. After that conversation, however, he did make an attempt to go to church now and then. But Jan was restless and didn't like it any better than he did so gradually they reverted to their walks on Sunday mornings.

John had never taken Jan to Oak Hill to see her Aunt Myra. He had always intended to do that for it seemed right and proper that he should, but he kept putting it off. He had a strange dread that even yet the woman might find some legal way to keep her niece with her and that eventuality John could not face. But Jan's mother had implied that Myra was very religious. Perhaps Jan ought to have more of that influence in her life.

Myra had written stiffly twice. Once during the first year, when she had evidently hoped that John would be fed up with baby tending, she had offered coldly to take what she called "the burden" from him. Then when Jan was ten years old and Mattie Puckett died she had made the same offer, suggesting that Jan might need "female guidance." She mentioned Jan's age as if she kept constant track of her.

With misgivings and a real pity for the pathetic soul who was evidently hungry for a daughter of her own, John had answered both times with a brief but courteous refusal. Even through the mail he had never felt at ease with Myra Fetter. The birthday letters he had had to write for Jan before she could do it herself, contained only the briefest thanks for the punctual and elaborate gifts Myra always sent. John had never found expression for all those questions that had crowded his mind after Janette's death. And they had never been answered. For although John had written to the post office in every port they had visited on that long yacht trip, and had made every possible inquiry of his former employer, until he almost felt himself to be a nuisance, no letter from his wife had ever turned up. At each disappointment he would sigh and try to forget that his bride must have lost her first love for him. But it was hard not to lay the blame at Myra's door.

One day when Jan was fourteen John took her and Danny to the circus, their first. Danny was fascinated by the clowns and the side shows but Jan sat breathless at sight of the trapeze artists and acrobats. As John watched her feverish excitement he almost regretted having brought her. She had already practiced every conceivable trick, he thought, on the swing he had put up on the high branch of an old oak tree on a vacant lot near their home. But she was seeing new stunts today and she might attempt them, to her misfortune. She was thrilled to her finger tips as she watched them.

But it was when the bicycle riders appeared, riding on their tight ropes high above the tent platform, that Jan's eyes simply blazed with eagerness; she caught her breath and drew her strong fingers into fists in her ecstasy. In imagination her own lithe body was up there balancing along in mid air, not for the sake of the wild applause that swept through the crowd but for the sheer joy of mastering the air.

During all the rest of the show, amid the peanuts and the popcorn and the pink cotton candy, Jan kept that breathlessly eager look behind her eyes, and all she could talk about for days afterward was the feat of the bicycle riders.

It was two weeks later that John, coming home from work one afternoon, saw something that made his hands drip with cold sweat and held his feet as if each weighed a ton.

He had noticed that Jan had been off with Danny several times lately in the afternoons when he came home, but he had thought little of it. In response to his question of where she had been and what she had been doing, she had airily replied,

"Oh, just rooting around the neighborhood. They are tearing down the old apartment house on Ninth Street and we were watching them. They said we could have some boards to play with."

John always took the short way home, through the paved alley which squeezed along between buildings for four blocks and ended in the street where his home was. It was a narrow alley, barely wide enough for small trucks. The fire escapes of all its dreary apartment houses and office buildings zigzagged down its sides.

It was late autumn but the sun had not yet sunk low enough to blind his eyes when John, glancing ahead down the alley, saw what looked like a thin black line drawn across the alley between two fire escapes. It was about fifteen feet above the street in the last block. Drawing nearer he saw it was a long plank. As he looked, a lithe red figure on a bicycle wavered an instant at one end of it then pedalled swiftly across the gap. In terror John let out a gasp and a moan. That was *his daughter*. Now she was reaching with sure hands for the railing of the far platform, holding the bicycle like a horse with firm knees as she stopped, to keep it from plunging down to the alley below.

He forced his heavy feet to run. But before he had gone many steps another figure, wavering more than the first, started out on the precarious plank, reached the middle, and with a cry wavered just too far and fell.

It was Danny. He'd surely be killed, and Jan would be responsible. John almost forgot his terror at Jan's madcap ride and his relief that it was over, in his horror at Danny's tragedy. He was aware too, of just how terrible his daughter Jan would feel. She was always so sympathetic with any hurt thing. She'd not be able to stand the thought that it was she who had done this thing to her friend. For John had no doubt that Jan had been the instigator.

Breathless with horror he reached the spot where the boy lay. A crowd was already gathering. Danny was unconscious and blood was streaming from his head. Jan was leaning over him, her face ghastly white. Characteristically, she did not scream or cry. But the suffering in her eyes was agony even to watch.

A young man with a crown of gold hair was kneeling beside the twisted form beneath the ruined bicycle. Nobody seemed to know where he had come from. He was listening to the heart, feeling for a pulse. He acted as if he knew what he was about, and as none of the others did, he took charge. A car stood panting in the narrow alley. After he had disentangled the twisted bicycle wheels from the boy's limbs and felt of him all over, the young man went to the car and, reaching in, took out a short board and a roll of bandage.

In wonder the horrified crowd watched as he gently drew the head wound together, bandaged it, and then deftly bound one of Danny's legs to the board. There were sympathetic clucks and wails from some in the crowd as they saw him lift the limp form and place it gently in the car. He took a fine soft robe and tucked it gently around Danny. Just an instant his troubled eyes glanced around the crowd as if to ascertain whether there was anyone there to care. But poor Danny's father was at that moment in a taproom six blocks away. His mother was not yet home from work. Mrs. O'Leary had dispatched her youngest to fetch her, and someone else said they would go in search of the father. But when the young man, after looking about that one instant, started to climb into his car, he saw Jan with white face and drawn lips already in it. Her long skinny bare legs stuck out like wires from beneath her short faded red playsuit, and her black pigtails were pointing as usual in different directions. Her strong wiry fingers were locked together to help her control her sobs. She looked even younger than her fourteen years for she still wore the same type of clothes that Mattie Puckett had always bought; John had simply kept on ordering larger and larger sizes.

The young man straightened up when he saw her and started to shake his head. Then he asked:

"Are you his sister?" nodding toward the boy in the back seat.

Jan shook her head and opened her mouth but no words

came. Then her father appeared and climbed in beside her in the front seat. Jan turned to him with a cry of relief. "Oh Daddy!" she wailed.

"Just be quiet, Jan," said her father gently. Then he turned to the stranger. "We will go with him," said John with decision, placing his arm comfortingly about Jan.

A moment more the young man hesitated, obviously disapproving of the presence of the girl. But then he sprang in and starting the motor carefully backed out of the alley and headed for the hospital.

"Is he dead?" Jan wanted to ask. But the words still would not come. She tried to comfort herself with the fact that the man had bandaged Danny's leg and the cut on his head. You didn't bandage dead bodies. She shuddered, and John's arm went close around her warmly.

"Are you a doctor?" he questioned. The stranger looked so very young it seemed a ridiculous question to ask, yet John had been aware of the deftness of his work.

"Not yet," he responded. "I hope to be before long."

Jan turned to glance at him as he answered. She could just catch a glimpse of the lean determined line of his jaw; and she was subconsciously aware of the kindliness and gentleness in his firm lips, and his steady dark blue eyes. The setting sun shone on his bright hair and to her he seemed a ministering angel.

He drove swiftly and skillfully through the late afternoon traffic. Jan had a little feeling of thankfulness that the man who had picked up Danny was like this, if such an awful thing had to happen to Danny at all. She had never given a thought to the chance that Danny might not be able to perform the stunt that she had set him to do and had done herself with fearless elan. Danny had always been game for anything, and being a boy had often done it just a little better than she had. But Jan had not counted on the fact that for years Danny had been undernourished and now that he was beginning to grow faster, that lack was going to show up in many ways. All she knew now was that she had hurt and maybe killed her playmate.

As they neared the hospital the young medical student spoke again.

"Are you his—relatives?" He said it hesitatingly, since the boy was obviously unkempt, and John, even though he had just come from work, was neat in his appearance. John always seemed to have a clean look. And Jan's red plaid cotton playsuit was clean even if it was faded. Also, the young man had not failed to note the fineness of her cream white skin under its freckles, and the patrician tilt to her head. He could not reconcile these two people with the dirty boy.

"Because," he added, "someone will have to sign for him at the hospital."

"We are only neighbors," answered John Nielson. "But I'm afraid his parents wouldn't be much help, poor boy."

The young man frowned understandingly, but said no more about it.

"How did it happen?" he queried. "I saw a plank up on the fire escapes. I thought I had tried some pretty crazy tricks myself, but I never tried that. Surely he wasn't trying to ride across!"

"Yes, he was," added John sadly, turning a look on Jan that was reproachful and yet sympathetic.

With a sob she burst out: "Have I *killed* Danny?"

With tortured eyes she looked up at the stern face of the young man beside her beseeching him to tell her the truth.

"*You!*" he said in a low astounded voice. The road was clear and he turned and looked full at Jan for the first time. "You don't mean to say that *you* got up that crazy stunt!"

Jan's eyes dropped in shame.

Then after a moment she stole a look up at the stranger once more, as if imploring him not to censure her too harshly.

She flushed as she found his eyes upon her again. In a swift glance he seemed to see into the depths of her sorrowful soul. He took in her slender wiry strength, her gangling grace, and her wordless despair, then with an incomprehensible expression he turned back again to his driving without saying anything at all.

Jan felt painfully humiliated. No doubt he thought her utterly scatterbrained. The bicycle act had not seemed to her anything more perilous than many a climb or stunt on the swing that she and Danny had done before. But now she saw that it was a madcap thing to propose. She loathed herself. During the interminable hour that they waited in the hospital before the young doctor came out of the accident room, Jan found herself torn between anxiety for Danny and a fierce desire to exonerate herself in the eyes of the strange young man.

When he came back, his face was serious.

"The boy's leg is broken in two places; three ribs also," he told them. "There is concussion. We cannot tell how bad it is for a day or maybe two. There is *probably* no skull fracture." He said that last sternly, looking hard at Jan as if it were not her fault that there wasn't.

But as her eyes dropped in agony again, his lingered upon her, noting the brave mute way in which she took the news. Most girls he knew would have been crying their eyes out. She was a game little tomboy, but what a daredevil! Then he softened and spoke again with a troubled look.

"It is possible that the boy will not pull through. Do you know whether he is ready to go?" He looked keenly from one to the other of them but seeing only blank bewilderment in either face, he turned away still more troubled.

John stood up, but Jan drew back.

"Oh, Daddy, can't I stay? If Danny should come to, there would be nobody to talk to him. I *have* to tell him I'm sorry!"

"It is not likely the boy will be conscious for some hours at least," the young man said unbendingly. "He will be put in the ward on the third floor and you can come at visiting hours tomorrow. They will give you information at the desk."

Without any more conversation or a glance back at them, he walked away, and Jan had a strange feeling that her best friend had deserted her.

With heavy hearts she and her father took their way home.

Chapter 4

IT WAS A JOYOUS day when at last the doctors gave assurance that Danny would pull through.

During the weeks of his recovery Jan was his faithful companion for as many hours as the hospital would allow. Danny learned to watch the door for her to come, and his beautiful big dark eyes would light up with eagerness. She gave him some of the happiest hours he had ever had. Some of the hard old customers in the ward with him would have been ashamed to admit their interest in the stories she made up for him. Those who were too sick or too deaf to follow her tales took pleasure in watching her piquant little-girl face, and were refreshed by her youth and gaiety. She was quite unconscious of her charm and smiled at all of them as unconcernedly as a child of two.

At first Jan was astonished at the change in Danny's looks.

"Gee, Danny, I hardly knew you!" she exclaimed in admiration the first time she saw him after he had been thoroughly scrubbed and had his hair cut.

He laughed in a shamefaced way but he tucked her precious remark away in a special compartment of his heart.

One day when Jan was in the midst of a story of pirates and buried treasure, the young medical student dropped in to see how Danny was getting along. He was pleased at his progress and he greeted Jan in a gay comradely fashion.

Several times as he joked with Danny, Jan caught the young man's eyes upon her with puzzled interest. She would drop hers in confusion, and then each time he would look away. Afterward she scolded herself for letting her heart get to fluttering so wildly over his glance. She had never felt so when any of the boys she played with had admired her. She felt like a child in his presence and yet she was strangely drawn to him and admired him greatly.

They discovered that his name was Andrew Hightower, and he was expecting to graduate soon and interne in this hospital.

He called Danny his "acrobatic patient."

"They tell me that this is the young lady who got you into trouble," he remarked one day, nodding toward Jan. Jan flushed and twisted in her chair. She could not tell from his tone whether he despised her or whether he was just teasing her.

But Danny flared up in her defense.

"No sir!" he declared with rage. " 'Tweren't Jan's fault. Jan had nuttin' to do with it. She weren't even there!" he lied desperately.

The young man sobered, nodding amusedly with his eyebrows raised. "Oh, I see!" he said with a wink at Jan. Then giving a cheery pat to Danny he said, "You'll soon be well now," and he went off to his classes.

But Jan was a little disappointed in Danny's lack of courtesy.

"You shouldn't 'uv answered him like that, Danny," she reproved. "He's been awful nice to you, you know. He didn't *need* to 'uv stopped that day to fix you up and bring you here at all. And you wouldn't be so well off if he hadn't, 'cause the doctor told Daddy that it was the care you had right off that kept him from having to reset your leg, and maybe kept you from dying."

Danny grunted.

"Okay, okay, may *be*," he agreed grumpily, "but there's no need to get *you* in on this. What's the big idea, anyway?" He suddenly glanced up keenly at her and spoke in a guarded voice. "Have you *fallen* for this guy?"

Jan flashed a look of scorn upon her playmate.

"Oh, for cryin' out loud, Danny!" she sputtered.

But in spite of herself her cheeks burned and she quickly plunged into a wild escapade of the pirates she had introduced into her story the day before. Still Danny kept a suspicious eye upon her for some time.

Danny's father and mother had struggled in once or twice to the hospital to see him. His mother moaned and wrung her hands the first time, and promised in a loud voice to bring Danny all sorts of goodies and presents, but the gifts never materialized, and Mrs. Severy soon departed to drown her own misery in whatever liquor was available at the moment.

His father was silent and gruff on his one visit, and paid little attention to the boy after that.

So John Nielson footed the hospital bills for Danny since he felt that the whole thing had been caused by his daughter's rashness.

Danny recovered quickly but that winter he lost so much time from school that Jan sailed far ahead of him, and he became utterly discouraged. Even after he was well enough to go back to school he stayed away as much as he could without getting into too much difficulty. His voice began to take on a defiant tone, sullen and discontented.

And then, all at once, he started inviting Jan to go with him to shows and cheap entertainments.

Her father looked surprised.

"Do you have a job now, Danny?" he inquired in a kindly way.

Danny assumed a superior expression that seemed to suggest a great deal of information sealed within his own mind which he did not care to release. He shrugged.

"You could call it that," he answered airily.

"What doing?"

"Oh, this and that. Odd jobs, whatever turns up." Danny spoke vaguely and rather crossly as if he resented Mr. Nielson's interest.

John nodded, but looked a little troubled.

"You really ought to have more schooling, Dan," he advised. "Why don't you try to stick it out through high school at least? You have good brains, you know, if you would only use them.

Think how much better off you would be with a good education. I wish I had had more."

For an instant Danny looked wistful. Then he jerked his head impatiently.

"For what?" he demanded scornfully. "White collars run this country too much already. Time us plain people rose up and got our rights. Be a better country."

John Nielson gave him a long slow look.

"Danny Severy, have you been to some of those meetings in the park?"

"If I have, so what?" Danny swaggered.

Jan looked troubled and John hesitatingly began a homily on the principles of American democracy, but Danny only frowned, made an ugly noise and stormed off without answering.

After that John refused permission for Jan to go with him on school nights. He felt reasonably sure of Jan so far, because she was still happy playing ball or climbing trees. But he was troubled about Danny for his own sake, apart from his influence on Jan, for he felt a certain responsibility about him since the boy had been in and out of his house all these years. Somebody ought to do something for him. His parents never had. Oh, he had been provided with an Easter outfit, new from the skin out, every year. The Severys would have been ashamed not to do that, for the sake of their own reputation. It was one of the standards they had retained in their pitifully small list of necessary decencies. But poor Danny had had to get along on that outfit until the next Easter unless some kindhearted neighbor produced a cast-off sweater or an outgrown pair of pants. Many a winter Danny had gone shivering. He stayed at home as little as he possibly could; he hated the emptiness there. No doubt he had absorbed many a street corner harangue during his wandering.

But as time went on John could see that Jan herself was picking up some of Danny's cocksure defiance, and John began to have sleepless nights. It was all very well to try to help

Danny, but what if he harmed his own daughter by allowing this friendship to continue? She would soon be grown up and out of his control. Had he given her principles that would outwear these subtle half truths that were going the rounds? He wondered and trembled. Perhaps he ought to move away from this neighborhood. It had somewhat deteriorated even from what it was when he settled there fifteen years ago. But he was fifty now and feeling his middle age; it seemed a great undertaking to tear up his roots and start in somewhere else. Anyway, where would he find a home at a price he could afford that would not present the very same problems that he faced here? For John had long ago given up hope of making much money—Myra Fetter had been right about that! No, if he had not already instilled right values and principles in his daughter, there was little hope that he could do it anywhere else. For the first time he began to wonder if he had done right in keeping Janette's baby himself.

Then he began to check up on Danny quietly, and grew more and more troubled. But time went on and he could not persuade himself to make a change.

Jan was sixteen and finishing her junior year in high school when, coming home one afternoon with her arms full of books, she noticed a handsome car outside the house. There was no one in it except a stylish looking lady sitting very straight in the back seat "like a dowager duchess" thought Jan with a giggle. Who could she be calling on? Certainly nobody in their building. Probably her liveried chauffeur was merely delivering a message or getting a basket of laundry or some such unromantic errand. Jan did not see any one at the door, and there was no one on the street but a thin oldish looking man in gray with a stout oldish looking dog on leash.

Jan climbed the dingy unpainted stairs and unlocked the door of their apartment. How interesting it would be if some rich stranger should be coming to call on them! But those things only happened in her fancies, never in real life.

Jan threw down her books and unbuttoned her full peasant

skirt letting it billow to the floor. It left her clad in a trim faded little playsuit. She proceeded to fling her hands flat on the floor and her feet up into the air.

Just at that instant there came a knock at the door which Jan had left unlocked. Without a pause it opened and there stood the lady from the big car, gazing in horrified disapproval at Jan whose black eyes widened in amazement at her from somewhere near the floor.

Jan righted herself instantly, but the lady continued to stare, taking in the slight wiry grace of the girl, the pigtails she still wore, facing east and west, in spite of her sixteen years, and the faded old playsuit that was a bit too tight and too short.

Jan started to laugh at first and then she grew a little annoyed at the woman's scrutiny.

The lady opened her mouth to speak but she seemed unable to utter a sound. Jan almost thought she was going to burst into tears, she looked so full of pent-up emotion. Jan simply stood and stared back at her.

At last in a coldly controlled voice the stranger said,

"Of course you do not know me, my dear! I know you, however. I am your Aunt Myra Fetter. I have come to take you away with me."

Jan had been ready to invite the visitor politely to come in, but at her last words Jan gave a little gasp and involuntarily started to shut the door in her face.

"Wait just a moment, my dear!" commanded Myra Fetter. "No doubt I startled you as much as you startled me." She managed a dour smile. "Let me explain. And at least be courteous enough to let me come in and sit down."

She marched past the speechless girl and seated herself in a straight-backed chair beside the drop-leaf walnut table, as if she felt that that article of furniture, being the only really fine piece in the room, was the only one worthy of her propinquity.

She gazed around the room before she spoke again, and took in the two other rooms which John Nielson had acquired since she was last there to get her sister's belongings. She noted with grim grudging satisfaction the cleanliness that reigned throughout, then she looked back at Jan. Her sharp black eyes examined her again but she hid any sign of how she was impressed by her niece.

At last she spoke once more.

"Are you in high school?"

"Yes," answered Jan, still bewildered. As her father had no near relatives she had never been subjected in her childhood to the critical examination that most children have to undergo by adoring kinfolk. It seemed rude to her for this woman to look at her so steadily.

"What year?"

"I have one more year after this."

Aunt Myra's lips relaxed a little in approval.

"You like school, then?"

"Yes."

Jan was still so taken aback that she had lost her usual poise and ready tongue.

"You are athletic." It was a statement of fact.

Jan grinned. "Yes," she admitted. "When you came in I was resting my feet. I work at the dime store after school."

Aunt Myra's lip curled.

"What else are you interested in besides athletics?"

"Oh, music, and the river. I love boats."

"Hm. Music. What kind of music?" asked her aunt apprehensively.

"All kinds, I guess," laughed Jan. "I like the band in the park and *some* radio singers, and best of all, I *love* the orchestra concerts Daddy takes me to sometimes. Now and then there is a good orchestra on the radio, too."

"Do you play?" questioned Aunt Myra.

"Not really well yet," said Jan wistfully. "But I've been studying violin for four years. Daddy has often talked about giving me some really good lessons, but so far I've only taken from the teacher at high school. He teaches all the instruments there are, so Daddy says he can't be very good at any!" Jan laughed again. Her laugh was musical.

Aunt Myra's eyes narrowed.

"Did you choose violin yourself?"

"Yes," replied Jan.

"Why? Don't you know it's the most difficult to learn?"

"Oh," breathed Jan, starry-eyed, "but I just *love* it. It can talk, you know, and it doesn't seem so difficult." She spoke in her fairy-tale voice and her black eyes were alight with dreams. She had no idea that she stirred a thrill in Myra Fetter's well-governed soul, under her stylish quilted black taffeta gown. Myra only said, "Don't fidget so with your fingers when you talk, child. And don't you know it isn't ladylike to put your feet up under you when you sit in a chair?"

The glow faded from Jan's eyes and her cheeks flamed red. She cast a puzzled defiant glance at her aunt while she snapped her bare legs down properly.

Jan wished her father would come home. She scarcely knew how to deal with this strange middle-aged aunt whom she had never seen. She supposed he would have told her to be sure to thank Aunt Myra for all the lovely gifts she had sent her, birthdays and Christmases. So she did it, very stiffly.

Myra nodded.

"It was a pleasure, child." She bit off her words.

They were both silent then, and Jan fidgeted more. She tried her best to think of something polite to say. The clock showed half an hour yet before her father would come home. She had not the slightest idea that her aunt was just as much at a loss for something to say to her teen-age niece.

Myra got up and went to look out of the window. Jan had a feeling that every move her aunt made was for the purpose of checking up on things and disapproving of them.

"Gracious! What a ramshackle building that is across there!" exclaimed Aunt Myra. "It looks as if it might tumble down. I should think your father would be afraid to have you live so near to it! See that great crack!"

Jan got up and glanced out. Then she laughed eagerly.

"Oh, that's the Mississippi River!" she cried.

Aunt Myra turned and looked at her as if she had lost her wits.

Jan laughed, quite naturally again.

"That crack, I mean," she explained lovingly. "That's the dear old crack that helped me learn the middle states." And she went on to tell the names of the people who used to inhabit the various apartments across the way.

While she talked vivaciously, Myra lifted her gold lorgnette and examined Jan at close range. Her face softened and finally, as Jan ceased talking and grew rosy under the scrutiny, her aunt said more gently than she had yet spoken, "You are just like your mother, child."

Jan's face lit up. She sat down again and clasped her hands about her knees, her eyes shining.

"Oh, would you tell me about my mother, please? Daddy has told me all he knew but you must know so many things."

Aunt Myra sighed and settled herself to talk.

Then John's footsteps were heard climbing the stairs wearily.

The gentle look left Myra's face and she stiffened once more folding one kid-gloved hand over the other, and straightening up as if to prepare for battle.

She sat facing the door where the light from the afternoon sun would shine not on her but on John as he came in.

Myra decided he had not changed for the better. He was still the same sandy-haired plain homely unsuccessful nonentity he had always been.

"You needn't look so surprised, Mr. Nielson," she greeted him without stirring. "I'm sure it shouldn't be such a strange thing if I should visit my only niece after sixteen, nearly seventeen years, even if I have not been invited!"

Stupefied, John simply stood in the doorway and stared. An awful foreboding seemed to rise up right there in his own room and threaten him.

"Oh-h!" he stammered.

"No, you weren't expecting me, of course," said Myra dryly, "but I decided that for my niece's sake it was about time that I came. And I can see that I was right. She needs training."

The same old wave of humiliation engulfed John as the cold tones of this woman's voice struck his ears. He had been feeling more and more lately that he had failed in what he had tried to do, and she must have come to tell him so. But he forced himself to stand straight and meet this woman's eye. For Jan's sake he must not let her see her father beaten.

He managed his old comradely smile toward Jan.

"I think Jan's a pretty nice girl, Mrs. Fetter." He tried to speak jocosely.

But Myra had never been jocose. She did not know how to be. Facts were her tools and weapons.

"I didn't mean that she wasn't," she snapped. "She wouldn't be Janette's daughter if she weren't. And at least she looks like Janette although she's terribly dowdy. But nice or not, a girl needs training. Besides, Janette's daughter has no business working in a dime store." Her black eyes cut slashes through John's soul.

He met her look calmly.

"I think a decent job is good experience for a girl," he said.

"Clerking in a dime store is hardly decent," she snapped.

Jan bridled, but John continued to try to keep the discussion on a casual peaceful basis.

"Well," he said looking over at his daughter appraisingly, "Jan has had good schooling, and got good marks. She will graduate from high school next year at seventeen. *I* think that she has done pretty well. And she's not bad to look at, at least her father thinks so!" he laughed weakly. "I don't know just what she is going to turn out to be," he added. "Sometimes she thinks she wants to be a nurse, but right now she leans toward music. The teacher thinks she has exceptional talent. She gets that from her mother, of course." John was never one to take credit for anything himself. He would have been utterly amazed had anyone told him that he himself was artistic, or that the walks they had taken by the river noting this and that beauty of nature, and his long stories of colorful foreign ports, had combined to develop to a high degree his daughter's artistic gift which he so willingly placed to the credit of her mother.

Myra's eyes gleamed narrowly.

"Does she have a good instrument?" Her thin lips opened like a precision machine, just far enough to let her words out, and then chopped them off.

John shrugged. "She is allowed to use the school violin. They rent out instruments for a small fee. I thought to get her a nice one if she turns out to do well enough at it."

Myra turned to Jan.

"Let me hear you play, child."

Jan gasped. There was nothing lately that she loved to do so much as to play her violin. She had found that she could express many longings that had only recently been stirred within her, by simply drawing the bow across the strings slowly, shading her tones from a breath to a deep full sob, and fading again. She had many favorite pieces that she played remarkably well, but she felt that it would be all but impossible to play for this unsympathetic woman. She cast an imploring glance at her father. He evidently wanted her to do as her aunt requested. Although she had begun to feel now and then that it was time for her to order her own life, she was aware that her father was what she would call "on the spot" with this wealthy disapproving relative and perhaps it would help his standing if she would show that she was not so lacking in graces after all. So, rather reluctantly, she produced her violin. It was a crude thing, but it was remarkable what music Jan drew from it.

Myra Fetter, accustomed to the finest in concerts from her youth up, although she had never been able to produce any music herself, was aware that here was unusual talent.

"That was good, child," was all she said however, when Jan had finished. "Mr. Nielson, I came to have a talk with you," she began.

Just then a whistle sounded from the alley and Jan looked beseechingly at her father. He nodded permission for her to go out and she ran off without a word to the guest. Myra Fetter put the little rudeness away in her mind to correct in Jan some day. At the moment she was well pleased not to have the girl around while she transacted her business with the father.

"My niece has unusual talent," she addressed John. He had to repress his indignation over her persistent way of ignoring the fact that Jan was his daughter. He accepted the compliment for her with a nod of his head.

"But as I told you, she needs training. Now I have come today to make you a proposition."

John tried to control a cold shudder.

"As you must be aware, the girl will soon be grown." John bowed his head again. "But she has ways that are not such that a lady can be proud of. A good finishing school is what she needs where she would be thrown with the best people and learn the right ways of doing everything. She wouldn't be bad looking if she were dressed right, either." She spoke as if Jan were an awkward gawk who might trip over her own feet, but John was wise enough to realize that there was some truth in what this woman said.

"Such a personality as hers is going to attract attention from all walks of life and she should be prepared to know how to receive it or reject it as the case might warrant. And as for her musical talent, it would be a crime not to develop that." Her tone set John down as a criminal.

"I am not surprised at her talent," Myra went on, "although I had supposed it might turn to art as Janette's did. However, I am not unprepared for this. I am offering you a chance to have your daughter educated at one of the finest schools in the country—I believe you are aware that Oak Hill holds that reputation—and at the same time I will buy her a really fine violin and see that she has the best teaching that can be had. You are not in a position to do these things for her. I am sure you will not stand in her way." Myra snapped her lips shut as if there was nothing more for her to say.

John sat there gazing in black despair at her. Then he put his head down in his hands and let horror sweep over him. As Myra said, how could he stand in his daughter's way? And yet how could he give her up?

The old, old suspicion took hold of his mind again, that Myra had stolen his little bride's love away from him. If Jan went there to live why wouldn't she do the same with her?

He sat still for some minutes. Finally his sister-in-law grew impatient and barked, "Well?" as if he were a naughty boy to whom she was giving one more chance.

He raised a face, ghastly white, and stammeringly tried to thank Myra. "I'm afraid I'll have to have time to think this thing through, ma'am, if you don't mind. It's a generous offer, I know. But it has come suddenly and I hardly know what to say."

Myra looked coldly away from him out of the window to where Jan's Mississippi River ran crazily down the other building. John felt as if the very chair he sat in was shaking with dread.

"Very well, if you must," she answered coldly. "I shall stay in this city overnight." Her tone expressed disgust at the very city John lived in. "The trip is too long to make before dark now. You can let me know tomorrow. If my niece is to come I should like to know immediately so that arrangements may be made at the school before it is too late."

Myra arose and departed without good-bye, leaving John with the hardest problem he had ever had to face.

Chapter 5

THE HIGHTOWERS LIVED in a lovely rambling house of old stone a few miles out of Chester. It was all on one floor with only an artistic step or two up and down. For Mrs. Hightower was not as young as she had been, and her companion who had done the hardest chores for her for so many years had to spend most of his time now in a wheel chair.

But the house was a happy place. Sunshine flooded the rooms and made them so bright that the flowers outside seemed to be reaching around the edge of the window to peep in and see what made a mere indoors so charming. The carpets were old and worn but they seemed to rest in peace, aware that they had done their duty through the years in softening the steps for weary faithful feet.

The living-room walls were lined with books from top to bottom each side of the wide old fireplace, for the man who sat there in his chair working constantly with his typewriter beside him, loved to be out where the family were instead of being shut up in a den "like a bear!" he said. There were few days when he did not work at his writing, only the times when pain struck him at its worst. Even then his mind was working, for it was then that his most precious thoughts came to send out through paper and ink to others who were in like case. His first book, eagerly awaited by many, had been inscribed, "To all who are suffering, from one who travels the same road." It began: "This is not a message from the highroad of health. We sufferers have all had such messages as those sent us and we have had to close the book and sigh, 'He doesn't understand.' I am writing this while I am still in the dark pit of pain, because I believe that the unspeakable comfort I have found is not meant for me alone, but for all who struggle through with me."

It was no wonder that the publishers had printed on the jacket of the book a portrait of the author, for one look at those steady brave eyes deep with understanding, and that gentle loving smile, had stirred hope in hearts that had long since given up hoping for an answer to their problem of pain. They might well have printed a picture of the writer's wife and named her as co-author. For there was not a twinge or a moment's anxiety which she had not shared with her husband all through the years, and it was her faith in the God of all comfort that had strengthened his own faith.

But it would have been impossible to gather into one picture all the brightness and peace of the home they lived in.

This was not the home that Andrew and his brother had been born in. That one had been a cramped inconvenient parsonage where any and all parishioners had felt free to bring their joys and sorrows at any hour of the day or night. Both Father and Mother Hightower had suffered and rejoiced with their people through the years; but after the older son was killed in the war, the father's health was pronounced gone and he was forced to give up the pastoral work he loved. It was soon after that, when they were wondering where to go next and what to do, that an uncle who had been busier making sure of success in this life than he had been with the next, was precipitated into the next suddenly and it was discovered that he had left everything he had to his beloved nephew Andrew. There were no millions, but there was plenty to live on comfortably.

Andrew promptly bought the old stone house in the country, had it modernized, and established the home there while he went on with his medical studies. His father, for the first time in his life, had leisure to do the writing that he had long been urged to do, and his mother went happily on making the home a joyous spot to all who lived there and those who dropped in to visit.

As for Andrew, his heart was in his work, and he was recognized by his teachers as an outstanding future figure in the medical world. It was rumored that two or three successful surgeons had their eye on him with a view to inviting him to share their success as soon as his training was over, and then to carry on after they would retire. Some said that it was only a question now of which one Andrew would choose to ally himself with.

That rumor was prodding Andrew's mind as he drove into the city for dinner one evening. He was playing with it idly, at the same time half aware of the stiffness of his dress shirt and the press of his broadcloth trousers. For he had dressed carefully this evening. He was on his way to the Sommers' beautiful residence, and he was anxious to look his best.

A silent efficient servitor slid into his car to park it as Andrew got out, and at the front entrance another obsequious uniformed servant ushered him respectfully into the drawing room.

He glanced at his handsome wrist watch, a recent gift from Lucile Sommers. (Andrew would never have spent so much on himself!) He had a sudden fear that in his eagerness he had arrived too soon before the hour set for dinner and that would be a rather unforgivable *faux pas*. These people were so painstakingly correct about everything that he felt uneasy lest he overstep some one of the laws of etiquette. Not that he was unsophisticated, but he was anxious to make a very good impression, and such matters seemed to mean much to them.

His watch showed that he was prompt but not too prompt. Yet it was several minutes before anyone came to welcome him; he began to worry lest his watch was wrong. Just as he was getting himself worked up to real disquietude, his tall blonde hostess appeared, suave in a carefully chosen shade of cordiality.

"This is a pleasure, Doctor Hightower—or may I call you Andrew? You are beginning to seem like one of us, you know, although as a matter of fact I haven't seen much of you myself.

But I feel that I am well acquainted from hearing all the wonderful things Lucile tells me she hears the doctors say about you. Lucile, dear girl, does enjoy her hospital work so much, doesn't she? She has a feeling that she is really doing her bit of good in the world. She has always been such a sympathetic little thing ever since she was a child, wanting to share her old toys with those less fortunate, you know. She really gives a great deal of thought to helping the lower classes. It's so sweet of her, isn't it? I'm quite glad that the war caused the shortage in nurses, really, so that girls in Lucile's position—who would not of course care to do the menial work of nursing—can find their little place to work and do something for the good of humanity! Don't you think so? It's such good experience, you know."

Andrew had little need to do more than bow and smile as his hostess swung the conversation to and fro and up and down. It reminded Andrew of a juggler tossing his balls, constantly pretending to throw you one, which somehow never reached you.

At last she paused and Andrew was beginning to think it was his turn when his attention was attracted by two bright blue eyes below a gorgeous coiffure of golden curls, peeping mischievously around the door.

Andrew's face was suddenly alight as a dainty hand blew him a kiss across the room above his hostess' head, and Mrs. Sommers had to turn to see what had caused his abrupt change in expression. She smiled an indulgent smile at her daughter and as if her duty to her guest was done she excused herself to see to the servants and left the two young people alone together.

Andrew went toward the girl with his arms out, holding her off for an instant in admiration.

She was strikingly beautiful. Her roseleaf skin was set off by the sheerest and palest of soft rosy chiffons in a billow about her bare shoulders and soft bosom. Her red mouth, small like a baby's, was widened by just the right shade of lipstick perfectly applied, and she was smiling now, letting both her enticing dimples beam full at him. It was a provocative smile, just for him. Andrew caught his breath as he always did at sight of her.

He would have drawn her gently to him but she laughingly held him off.

"Not yet, Andy, you'll spoil my face. Wait until after dinner at least! I want to look nice, please, for when the rest come." But as she spoke, she put up her daintily scented little soft hand and stroked his face, watching him archly to see if the caress stirred him as she meant it to. When she saw the deepened hunger in his eyes she laughed coyly and letting her hand slide intimately down his arm she drew him to her side on a soft couch where she continued to let her hands move over him in little possessive pattings that made him long all the more to take her in his arms. When she sat so beside him looking up into his face he always felt that there was nothing in all the world he would not do for her. He was aware that he could rise to heights in his work just for her sake. It was a glorious feeling. Nothing seemed impossible to him when she was near him. But there was a question that he had been meaning to ask her. Perhaps now would be the time. He turned so that he faced her and spoke seriously.

"Darling," he began, "there's something I've been wanting to ask you for weeks—in fact ever since we found out that we cared."

Lucile arched her brows.

"Really, Andy? You look terribly solemn. Can't you put it off? We want to have a good time together." She dimpled.

Just then another of the dinner guests arrived and there was light chatting over cocktails as the rest gathered.

Mrs. Sommers made a great point of reminding the butler to "bring our dear Doctor Hightower his teetotaler drink," and then she laughed gaily, although Lucile looked a trifle annoyed.

"Really, Andy," she said aside to him as they stood near the dining-room door, "it's time you cast aside that silly notion that you'll land in the gutter if you take a little sip with the rest of us now and then. You don't trust yourself as *I* trust you!" she said, looking adoringly up at him.

Andrew looked away with a frown.

"I don't like it and I don't trust *it*, Lucile," he answered. "If you had seen as much as I have of what it can do—"

"Oh, apple sauce, Andy! Don't let's go into that again. All right, be yourself. I love you anyway," she added as she saw him put on what she called his stern look. And again she ran her hand down his arm with the little intimate pressure she knew how to give, that always won from him that worshipful look.

The conversation at dinner was fascinating to Andrew. He had been at the Sommers' only once or twice before and for him there was still an aura of glamor about their palatial home. He had met Lucile at the hospital less than two months ago, but they had made the most of the few dates they had had together. This invitation to dinner indicated that Lucile's family were inclined to accept him and he could not but be pleased. Mrs. Sommers was not a deeply intelligent conversationalist herself, but she was canny enough to invite the people whom her brilliant lawyer husband enjoyed, and to keep her own activities in the field where she knew how to shine; that is, the efficient running of the elaborate establishment they called home. She knew how to oil conversational friction points at just the right moment, and she was a past master at compromise and diplomacy.

The guests at this dinner were older than Andrew, one a judge, another a gray-haired doctor—one of those who had been eyeing Andrew as his successor, in fact—and an Irish merchant in this country on business. The wives of most of them were able to hold up their own end of the repartee and the serious discussions too, so that there was never a lag and Andrew's own keen mind was stimulated to a delightful degree.

And when he caught from time to time the ravishing glance from those blue eyes of Lucile's, he felt that his evening was superlative.

This world where wit and wisdom, intellect and beauty were combined was exhilarating. There were, to be sure, some things about the company of which he did not approve. For instance, their standards on the subject of liquor. Also, he still felt an inward shudder every time he noticed the well-padded judge laying a caressing hand, nonchalantly, on the soft bare arm of the merchant's wife.

"You are so preciously Victorian!" Lucile had teased him on one occasion when he had confided to her his disgust at the way in which some of the doctors and nurses pawed each other.

"Perhaps," he had countered, "but I think such caresses have no meaning—they become dog-eared and lose their personality after they have been passed indiscriminately around from one to another."

That satisfied her since she craved all of his caresses for herself anyway.

Now he stole another glance at Lucile. How exquisite she was, so pure and holy! Sometimes she refused even his kisses although he knew she loved him. It made her seem all the more desirable that she held herself aloof. He could not imagine her letting other lips than his own touch hers, since they had confessed to each other their love.

As he looked he caught another glance from her that seemed meant for a secret between the two of them. His heart thrilled again to think that he of all the personable young men of her acquaintance should be thus honored by this pearl of all girls.

The friendliness of her family was gratifying. And even though he had refused cocktails before dinner, the lights and laughter and the admiration he was receiving from everyone were as exhilarating as wine.

Back in the old stone house that evening there were lights,

too. A good reading lamp by the father's chair, another behind the mother where she sat sewing, and soft firelight playing between them.

But the laughter which often sounded there was still to-night, and Father Hightower kept laying down his book as if it did not hold his interest. Mother Hightower kept glancing up from her work, and her hands would fall restlessly down to her lap, the needle halfway through the sock she was mending.

At last she got up and turned out the lamps and came and sat near her husband.

"You have read so much today, dear, you will ruin your eyes."

He reached for her hand and gave her a loving smile.

Then they both sighed. After a long silence Mother High-tower said,

"Did you say you had met Mr. Sommers once, Father?"

"Yes, some years ago." He spoke as if they had not already gone over all this conversation before. It was as if they were loath to leave the subject lest there might be still some crumb of consolation in it that had escaped them.

"He is a very brilliant man." Ordinarily Mr. Hightower's voice did not sound old. It was usually strong and firm and full of zest for living. But tonight he sounded discouraged, almost as if he wished the man about whom he was speaking were stupid instead of brilliant. "He was prosecution lawyer for that case that poor old Mrs. Wilkins in our church was involved in. It was some years ago, you remember? After her husband died there was some litigation, and she lost everything. I always felt she was not given her rights, but perhaps Sommers was just doing his duty, I don't know." He sighed again.

"Did you ever see the daughter?" asked his wife.

"No, I never did."

"It's strange Andrew doesn't bring her out. You don't suppose he is—ashamed of his home, and us, do you, Father?" Mother Hightower spoke in a low tone that held dread.

"Certainly *not,*" her husband reassured her. "He said he

would sometime, you know. He just hasn't got that far yet."

There was a long speculative pause. Then Mother Hightower continued.

"I saw her picture in the society news one day. She is very beautiful," she sighed again. "But of course you can't tell much about a person from one of those newspaper pictures."

"No," agreed her husband.

Then they were silent a longer time.

"Well, Mother," said the invalid at last, giving his wife's hand a final loving clasp, "I guess we can do as we always have done, leave our boy in the hands of the only One who loves him better than we do. He has always taken pretty good care of Andrew, and I don't think He will stop now, when perhaps Andy needs Him most."

The mother smiled a sweet gentle smile in the firelight. Then she took a deep breath.

"Of course we can trust Him," she agreed. "And yet, Father, I would rather Andrew were—were where David is, than have him marry a girl that would lead him away from the right paths!"

Eric Hightower's arm stole comfortingly around his wife. And then she broke down and sobbed on his shoulder.

Above her sobs came his voice after a moment:

"Lord, we have come to Thee throughout the years with so many problems! We are always asking, asking, asking of Thee. But then we are so poor, and Thou art so *rich!* This time we are asking again for our boy. We believe You have a plan for his life and a work for him to do. Don't let him miss Your best, Lord. We will try to keep our hands off because Andy is yours. We gave him to You long ago. And so You do whatever You want with Him. No matter how it looks to us, we know it will be all right in the end. Thank you, Lord."

Mother Hightower leaned over then and kissed her old lover, smiling again through wet lashes and then she helped him to bed.

It was just about that time that Doctor Endicott, in the

drawing room of the Sommers' mansion, drew Andrew aside and made him a bona fide offer. With characteristic courtesy and poise, Andrew promised to think it over.

"But I did think, sir, that I would like to have a year or two of surgery in Children's Hospital. Don't you think I would be worth more after that?" In all humility Andrew put the question to him.

"Oh, probably," responded Doctor Endicott carelessly, his gray brows raised. "A few years more or less are all right with me. The more training you have, the more figures you can add to your bill!" He laughed. "I just don't want anybody else getting in ahead of me. I think you and I could enjoy working together."

At last, rather breathless from the evening's excitement, Andrew said good night to his host and hostess and received one last languishing look from the blue eyes he constantly sought out. Then he started homeward. He felt almost dizzy from the heights which he seemed to have attained. Of course he must have a talk with Lucile first. He had never yet actually asked her to marry him, nor discussed their future.

There was a vague concern in his mind about another question too, which he had not yet brought out to the light of his conscience and examined. It was like the box of odds and ends from his old desk that he knew he must decide about some day. He had shoved it back in his closet until he would have a convenient time. He had often shoved the question aside but now it tried to nudge itself into his consciousness again as he drew near a church building where he had gone with Lucile to a service last Sunday.

Just then he heard three shots. He jammed on his brakes. This was the south side of town, never a choice neighborhood at best. The church was a historic spot or the Sommers never would have visited it for even one service. Recently a factory had come in with its accompanying cheap hencoop houses. Two old five-story dirty-yellow brick apartment houses reared themselves above the newer, smaller rows of hencoops like two bedraggled old hens amongst the brood of little biddies.

As Andrew idled along the dark narrow street, keeping a sharp lookout, all at once it seemed that he saw a shadowy object slip off a building and slide to the ground. It made no sound and it vanished into the darkness. Then two more lithe shadows slipped stealthily down and disappeared. Andy could see the last one clearly. It was a boy not much more than fourteen or fifteen years old, skinny and wiry. He had an air of assurance and showed practiced skill in his manner of eluding whoever might be pursuing him.

Then Andy heard three more shots and a shout. A policeman ran rubber shod across the street. Then all was still again.

Andy drove on but his heart felt heavy. Such youngsters to be up against the law! He felt infinitely old and wise although he was but a few years farther on than the young scamp he had glimpsed. Where were the parents of those boys? Why did people have children at all if they were only going to let them grow up like weeds? He remembered the boy he had picked up two or three years ago, not far from this very spot. He had often thought of him, and always with a little guilty feeling, for he had intended to look him up again and try to help him. He had been too busy and had put it off, telling his conscience that that boy was not as friendless as some. He had kind neighbors to look after him. Andy gave a wry grin as he recalled the lively girl who had gone to the hospital with them that day. What a game little kid she was! Andy had never forgotten her. She had been so loyal to that boy, too. Well, she should be!

Andy had a sudden fleeting wish that his own beautiful girl had more courage and loyalty. Oh, but Lucile was lovely! She was just what a woman should be, he told himself.

However, the elation of the evening was gone as he drove into the garage at home. He felt utterly weary as he dragged himself to bed.

Chapter 6

"DANNY, WHAT'S THE matter with you lately?"

Jan on her way home from work had caught sight of Danny on the corner and hurried to greet him. It was two months after Aunt Myra's visit, and Jan was working full time at the dime store for the summer.

A courteous but decided refusal of her generous offer had sent Aunt Myra Oak Hillward without delay. Grimly, without even a glance that betrayed her bitter disappointment, she had taken her husband, her dog, and her shiny car and departed for the desolate stone house in Oak Hill. And no gift came at Jan's seventeenth birthday.

John Nielson had spent a sleepless night before he made his decision. In spite of the shining in Jan's wistful eyes over the offer of a violin and good lessons, he had felt that he knew his daughter too well to think that she could be happy in the cold, constrained atmosphere of that house. Besides, he had not yet come to the point where he felt he could give her up.

Jan had bravely swallowed her disappointment about the violin and lived out in fancy instead of fact the romantic life which she imagined a beloved niece of a wealthy Aunt Myra would live. She went patiently through her monotonous days at the dime store, turning every bit of gaudy finery there to gold in her own dreams. But the summer was a dreary one for her; she had so little time for play compared to what she used to have. Also Danny seemed to avoid her.

He did not stir from his lounging attitude against the corner telephone pole as she approached, and he answered her question sullenly.

"Meaning what?" he growled.

"Why don't you come around any more? And every time I see you you act sort of cross."

Danny jerked his head.

"I don't want no parts of a punk!" He sneered.

"Why, Danny Severy!" exclaimed Jan in distress. "What do you mean? When did I ever quit on you? Tell me, have I ever let you down?"

"You ain't done nuttin'."

"Who has, then?"

"Never mine, never mine, skip it."

"Danny, look here. Is it because Daddy wouldn't let me go out on school nights with you?"

"School nights baloney. School's been out two months. You used ta go wid de gang an' now you don't. That's all right. It's your business. We ain't good enough fer you!"

"Danny!" Jan spoke the name gently and sorrowfully. Danny gave a quick look up at her eyes to see how sincere she was, and the old look of loyal camaraderie almost shone again in his big sad hungry brown eyes. Then he hardened again and looked away.

"Danny, listen!" They were in their own alley now, and Jan stopped and turned toward him, laying her firm little hand a moment on the grimy shoulder of his cheap loud suit, unaware of the fierce trembling thrill it gave him.

"Danny, don't you still want to be pals?"

He shrugged. "Could be," he muttered. Then he burst out, "But *you* don't, I tell ya. You got book learnin' an' you got other friends, you got a home, you got—oh, skip it!"

"No, Danny, I don't want to skip it. You have always been my friend and you've done lots of things for me."

"Such as what?" he sneered.

"Taught me how to play ball like a boy, for instance. Remember how you used to rag me for throwing like a girl? And you have got me out of jams many a time. I don't throw away my friends that way, Danny. Listen, if you feel that way, why don't you buck up and get back to school and work, then? Make something of yourself."

He almost snarled. "Yeah. Go ahead, start preachin' again!"

"No, Danny it's not that. But I've always known you could do a lot better than you did. You have good brains. You're working now, aren't you?" Jan scanned his face keenly.

Danny tossed his head. "You can call it that," he responded.

"I thought you must be," Jan praised him with her smile. "Where are you working? Why don't you tell us?"

Danny grunted. "Where? Oh, Thorndyke's, of course." He spit superciliously. Thorndyke's was the city's largest, most exclusive jewelry store.

"Oh, Danny! How wonderful!" exclaimed Jan innocently. Then she caught an ironical expression on his face. "Are you kidding, Danny?" She sounded hurt.

But Danny only laughed, a bitter laugh. "Kidding? Why shouldn't I be working at Thorndyke's?" he demanded angrily.

"Well, anyway I knew you had a job somewhere because you are all dressed up so much of the time now. You look nice, and I'm glad. But I don't see why you can't tell me more about it. Why is it such a secret?"

He kicked the edge of the curbing a few silent minutes.

"People have to be awful good friends to be told things, don't they?" he growled.

Trouble deepened in Jan's eyes.

"You mean you can't trust me any more, Danny?"

"I don't know," he muttered.

"Oh-h-h!"

She sounded so like the little girl of the old days that Danny ventured to look straight in her face. He saw she was genuinely hurt.

"Listen, kid," he said more gently. "You ain't done nuttin'. It's just the way things are in the world. I know I don't amount to nuttin'. I never will. I'm just made that way, I guess. Not good enough fer you. You better have your friends an' I'll have mine. You don't like mine."

"How do you know?" challenged Jan. "I scarcely know them nowadays. Tell me who you think I don't like."

"Well, Pad Hucker, for instance." Danny held her eyes with his to see her reaction.

Jan hesitated. "The Danny I used to know wouldn't have had anything to do with him, but maybe I just don't know him. Do *you* like him?"

Danny gave a furtive frightened glance around, then shook his head almost imperceptibly.

"Well, then, why—" Jan broke off hopelessly.

"Listen here, kid," he said desperately at last, "you know I've always been little and skinny, don't ya?" Jan nodded reluctantly. "Ya know I can't lick some o' these big guys around here? Well, add it up. I live here, don't I? And even if I went somewhere else, it'd be just the same. There's gangs everywhere. Some guys are big enough to rule and some aren't. Well, I'm not. But never you mind, kid. I'll make out. Pad's okay. He's taught me a lot. I'm makin' out." He swaggered a little to cover his embarrassment.

Jan cast about in her mind for a solution to a problem like Danny's. Her impulse would have been to say that her father would help him fight his battles. But of course her father was not always there. And she was not equipped to handle fellows like Pad Hucker. He was sixteen, big and tough with thick black hair. His hands and forearms were red and dirty; they looked like hams.

"Well, Danny, I just want you to know that whatever happens anytime, ever, I'm still your friend. I don't go back on my friends. I'll always do anything I can for you. You know we agreed to stick by each other years ago. You try me and see!"

"Okay," he said after a keen look into her eyes, "maybe I will." His tone seemed to accept her challenge. Then all of a sudden his face went blank and sullen again. Jan, wondering what caused his change in manner, turned and saw Pad Hucker sauntering down from the other end of the alley. She sighed.

"All right," she promised Danny under her breath, "you can

count on me. Good-bye for now, Danny."

But Danny only grunted as if he had not been talking to her at all, and lit a strange-smelling cigarette.

Jan went upstairs feeling depressed. Why did people have to grow up and change? Danny had been such a loyal playmate, and now he seemed so different, so hard, as if he had thrown away all memory of their good times in the past.

She worried over Danny but she said nothing to her father about him because she was aware that her father was not too pleased with him lately anyway.

It was only a day or two later that Danny waylaid her as she came home about five o'clock from the dime store.

It seemed to her that he gave a furtive glance around before he spoke in a low voice. She wondered if he was ashamed to be seen with her. Perhaps his new friends, Pad Hucker, for instance, made fun of him for going with a "brain" as some of the neighborhood boys and girls called Jan.

"Did you mean what you said the other night?" Danny demanded wistfully.

Jan looked brightly at him.

"Sure! Of course I did."

"You mean you'd do somep'n fer me even if I couldn't tell you all about it?"

"You know I would, Danny!" Jan reassured him eagerly, glad to have a chance to show him her loyalty.

"Well, I'm in a jam. I'm 'sposed ta deliver a—a package over on the north side and I can't do it tonight. Never mind why. I got—somep'n else I gotta do. You'll get paid well for it if you'll take it for me." He glanced at her from beneath eyelids that were locked low. It was a cautious, canny glance, and at the same time he cast a swift reconnoitering look up and down the alley.

Jan was just a little bit surprised.

"Why," she hesitated, then caught the instant stiffening in Danny's attitude and sensed that he was ready to throw back her offer of loyalty in her face if she did not respond like a friend. "Why, of course I'll do it. I'd be glad to, Danny."

His features relaxed. "Okay, then," he muttered. "Just don't say anything to anybody about it. This is between us, see? *I'm* supposed to do it but—but there's a reason why I can't, and I don't want to get into trouble."

"That's all right, Danny. You can trust me. I don't squeal, you know that. Where is the package?"

"Sh!" he thrust at her and then suddenly drew her inside his own back doorway. Jan was puzzled. He had never once in all the years invited Jan into his home. She had taken it as a matter of course that he was ashamed of its barrenness, and let it go at that. She had seen enough of it, anyway, from her own kitchen window even though the one unshaded bulb that hung from the Severy kitchen ceiling was dirty and dim.

Inside the door now, however, she met the desolation with a new sense of shock and pity for the boy who had never had a real home.

Jan was doubly aware of the empty silence as Danny stealthily closed the door. She thought he had come in here to get the package, but he produced it from a pocket. A little box, it seemed to be. It was wrapped neatly, but she noticed that the white paper around it was rather soiled. Probably he had carried it all afternoon in his pocket. Thorndyke's would not be proud of the way it looked now, she decided, but she did not mention it.

"Here's the address," said Danny, handing her a slip of paper with a street number but no name. "It's not far from the bus lines, only about two blocks. One of those swell houses down in the northeast section."

"Oh," gasped Jan. "Should I get dressed up?"

"Naw!" replied Danny. "You're all right as you are. It won't make no diffrunce."

"But don't Thorndyke's generally send things in their delivery truck?" questioned Jan, trying to understand the situation.

Danny looked bewildered. Then a sly look came into his eye.

"Oh!—Oh!" he stammered. "Thorndyke's. Well, yes, except special things like this. This is special, you know, *very* valuable. They always send these things by special messenger. Anyway, the lady was in a hurry for it. And Jan, be sure you don't say nothin' to nobody about it. I think the lady didn't want her husband or anybody to know she got it. Maybe it's a surprise— er somethin'."

Jan's eyes gleamed with interest as she slipped the parcel into her purse.

"Oh, how nice," she smiled. "It would be fun to have a lot of money to be able to get surprises for your family, wouldn't it?"

"Yeah, yeah," agreed Danny hastily. "Yeah, it's a surprise, I'm sure. Maybe it's for tonight. Anyway, I was to get it there as soon as I could. So beat it, and—thanks, kid."

"It's okay, Danny. I'm glad to do it. I guess I can get back before time to get dinner for Daddy, can't I?"

"Sure, I should think so," returned Danny uneasily. "It's only a ten minute ride on the bus. I'll be lookin' for ya," he promised.

He did not come out of the house to walk to the corner with her. Jan wished he wouldn't be so mysterious and secretive about what he did these days. But she would show him that she was still his friend. And this was a small thing to do. How exciting to be a special messenger!

On the bus Jan fell to wondering what the little white box contained. It might be a diamond bracelet. Oh no, it was something a woman had ordered for her husband. At least she thought Danny had said that. Maybe it was a handsome wrist watch. Maybe this was his birthday and maybe they had had a quarrel and the woman wanted something especially nice, in a hurry, to show him she was ready to make up. Jan dreamed any number of pleasant dreams on the short ride and felt quite romantic when she got off and walked the two blocks past beautiful mansion-like homes and then turned in at a handsome brick residence, one of the loveliest of all. She was thrilled to be having a part, even so small and synthetic a part, in the lives of the glamorous people who lived in this delightful looking spot. She had had a glimpse of a park-like garden behind the house as the driveway curved up to the porte cochere and her imagination peopled it with gay crowds who would come for the evening birthday party there tonight. She was certain now that that must be the occasion for the gift she bore.

Rather timidly she rang the bell and exulted in the soft chime she heard in response, like the bells of an ancient cathedral of the middle ages.

She had read enough to have formed some idea of the life of wealthy people, and she fully expected to have the door opened slowly and ceremoniously by a resplendently uniformed butler who would look down his nose at the little messenger girl and bow slightly as he received the anxiously awaited package.

Jan had her lips all set to say, "Thorndyke's, sir," as the door opened. She had decided that that was the way a special messenger would speak.

But when the door did open, almost instantly, there was no butler there and when she saw who stood in the doorway, she was so amazed that she simply cried "Oh!" and her hand fluttered up to smooth her hair. She wished that she had waited to change her dress before she came. For it was Andrew Hightower who opened the door.

But the surprise and pleasure in her eyes faded as she saw the look in Andrew's face. She had never seen him look so stern. He stood for an instant as if he had been stunned by a terrific blow. Then suddenly he reached out and grasped her fiercely to drag her into the house.

But even as he did so, two other hands strong as iron clutched her arms from behind. She jerked her head about and saw a dark blue uniform with a formidable silver badge on the coat of it. A policeman! What on earth did they think she had done?

She was not a screaming girl or she would have given them

some trouble. The officer started to propel her down the steps but Andrew Hightower recovered from his shock and stopped him.

"Wait, Mike," Andy managed to say. "There's a mistake here." He gave a short breathless laugh. "This is a friend of mine." He laughed awkwardly again. "Just bringing—something—something I wanted! I'm sorry, old man. I've muffed things this time, I guess." He gave another laugh, sheepishly. "I was sort of surprised myself. You see, I had—forgotten all about—her! You may as well leave now, I guess. There won't be anyone else after this, I'm sure. We may try another time. Sorry!"

The policeman instantly released Jan but he gave the young doctor a quizzical look. Then shaking his head he touched his cap in salute and said, "Okay, Doc, if you say so. It's your party." Then with a laugh he marched off.

Andrew drew Jan into the house. His face was dark and stern, and there was deep sadness in it, too.

She stood trembling in the spacious reception hall, aware of a butler in the background. She was utterly bewildered at the turn of events. Had they been expecting a thief? But Andrew Hightower had exonerated her before the police, why then did he treat her as if she were the thief?

She had automatically handed the little box to him at the door. She saw him open it and glance at it and his face grew even more stern. Perhaps the lady for whom she had brought the package was his mother! But *why* should he be so angry at *her*?

The grim young man took her firmly by the arm, saying, "Come with me." His voice had a threat in it.

She drew back, beginning to be a little frightened.

At that he held her more tightly and said in little more than a whisper,

"Do as I say if you don't want to get into worse trouble!"

Gasping with fear now, Jan went with him out the big front door which the butler closed noiselessly behind them. They went down the steps to Andy's car.

He shoved Jan in the near side of the car which happened to be the driver's side and pushed her past the wheel to the other seat. He did not release his hold on her arm as he climbed in and started the car. Not until he had shifted into high and they were going at a good fast pace, away from the city, did he take his hand from her arm. Even then he kept a weather eye on her as if he half expected that she might attempt to open the far door and jump out.

Chapter 7

THEY RODE A MILE or two out into the country and Jan grew more and more bewildered and frightened. But her pride and her great respect for this young man would not let her speak first. At last Andy began.

"How long have you been doing this?" he demanded grimly.

Jan turned wide eyes upon him.

"Doing *what?*" she asked, her voice rising in a desperate query.

Andy turned and looked hard at her. He slowed down his speed as he spoke so that he could look full at her. Her black hair, which she still wore in short quaint childish pigtails, shone glossy where the bright rays of the afternoon sun touched it. Her big black eyes looked innocently up at him with a hurt look. In spite of all the incriminating evidence he found it hard to mistrust her. He found himself admiring the brave set of her quivering sensitive lips.

"Delivering little packages like that one," he said.

Jan gave a trembly giggle.

"What on earth is so terrible about doing that? I never did it before, but you act as if I were a thief or something!"

She sounded near to tears and he had a foolish desire to put his arms about her and comfort her. After all she was only a child! But he made himself speak sternly.

"Do you mean that you really don't know what was in that package?"

"Why, no, not exactly. In fact—" Jan hesitated. She had a feeling that anything she said might incriminate her, like a prisoner in court. "In fact, I really don't know at all. I was told—that is, I guess I wasn't really told, but I sort of thought it was a watch or a ring or something like that. I was given to understand that it was very valuable and that it must get there tonight." Her voice was high and thin with fright and bewilderment.

"Who told you that?"

Andy had stopped the car now and was looking straight at her. She quailed under that stern look in his eyes. She started to tell him that it was just Danny who had told her, but she remembered in time that Danny had been afraid for some reason that he would get into trouble. He had taught her never to mention names of people if she could help it. She looked away evasively.

"The—the messenger who was to have brought it," she answered vaguely.

Her captor looked more severe than ever.

"Don't you know who sent you with that box?"

His accusing tone put Jan on the defense. Jan frowned. Maybe there really was some sort of thievery connected with this thing. Then all of a sudden she blurted, "I don't see why there is all this fuss about it! What are you asking me all these questions for? What do you have to do with it anyway? Was it your mother's present I brought? Or what *is* the score?" And then a big tear did overflow and run down her cheek. She wouldn't even deign to notice it, however, by brushing it away. What a little soldier she was!

"Look here! Do you belong to one of the kid gangs in the city? Or did one of them send you?"

Jan cast him a wary glance. She *must not* let Danny down. "Why—no, not exactly."

Andy looked out through the dusty windshield at the quivering heat waves that rose from his engine hood. How could he tell whether this madcap girl was telling him the truth or not? It seemed impossible that she could have done what she had knowingly, and almost as impossible that she did not know.

In shielding her from the law he had made himself appear

like either a fool or an accomplice before the officer whom he himself had set on guard. And he had let himself in for a whale of a lot of trouble if this girl was lying to him. He had trusted her on the spur of the moment because he had taken a liking to her a year or two ago when she had stuck by her friend and owned up to her part in the accident. He had sized up her father, too, as a good honest man and dependable citizen. But it was quite possible that, in the intervening time, if not before, she had been drawn into crime that she was scarcely aware of. Or perhaps she had found out what it was and was afraid to back out. He drew a deep breath. He wished he had never asked that policeman to come there this afternoon. He wished that Doctor Endicott had never gone on vacation and asked him to take over the case of the woman in the big brick house.

He looked again at the pure clear profile of the girl who sat motionless waiting for him to explain. It seemed out of the question that she knew what she had done.

Silently Andy followed a habit of years and cried out in his heart for help.

"Oh, God, show me what to say to this girl. She is scarcely more than a child. But You know what a daredevil she is! She would try anything. If she has done wrong, make me strong to condemn the wrong and do what I ought to do. If not, make me sure, Lord, and don't let me harm her."

Andy turned his deep dark blue eyes back to Jan and she was relieved to see a gentleness there that she had not seen before.

"What is your name?" he asked first. "I don't remember."

"Janette Nielson," she replied, wonderingly, yet still on her guard.

"Well, Janette, I'm going to tell you what was in that package. But first I want to tell you a story. It is the story of a beautiful, wealthy, brilliant woman. She was happily married and had two handsome little boys. But a few years ago she began to have terrible headaches. She went to one doctor after another and no one could cure the headaches. Finally she had to have a nurse a good deal of the time. Soon after that her family began to notice that she was acting queerly, and other strange maladies bothered her. She has recently been very sick and the doctor who has been treating her has been at his wits' end to know how to deal with her. Only recently he has discovered that she has been taking a very dangerous drug. She has taken it so often that she is not responsible for what she does, and the two children have had to be taken away from her. One day she tried to kill them. That nurse who started her on that drug is dismissed, but it is too late to undo what she did.

"The doctor has taken every precaution to keep the drug away from her, but somehow or other she has been getting it. It was to try to discover how it was coming into the house that I was there today and I planted the policeman on guard. You can imagine my amazement when I discovered that it was you who brought the stuff!"

Andy told the story dispassionately, without any undue emotion, but as he went on Jan's eyes grew wide with horror. He watched her steadily. Could it be that she was still playacting? Surely a girl could not acquire that clean clear look in her eye on occasion. She *must* have been tricked into this mess. He felt an infinite pity for her.

He watched one expression after another flit across Jan's troubled face. She was taking in the whole horrible situation. If she had denied her part in it, or cried, or showed anger Andy would have been suspicious of her. But she was simply reasoning it out, evidently aghast at all its implications.

At last she looked up at Andy in troubled wonder.

"And you shielded me from the law knowing that it might get you into trouble yourself!" she exclaimed in awe.

Andy was amazed. He had not expected her to grasp that angle of it. Most girls would have been so upset over their own entanglement that they would never have a thought for anyone else who might be involved. But he only raised his eyebrows and shrugged.

"I hadn't looked in the package then," he reminded her. "I

wasn't sure what it was. But—I would have done what I did anyhow," he added impersonally.

Jan looked up at him again, almost worshipfully.

"Why?" she asked in wonder.

He looked down at her with a gentle sadness. "Because I can't bear to see young people getting themselves into a peck of trouble when they don't know yet what it's all about. I sometimes wish I could get hold of some, even just a few, of the kids that are on the wrong track and straighten them out. It made me sick to think that here was another one, when I saw you on the doorstep."

That stern look settled over his fine face once more and Jan shrank before it. She felt humiliated again; to him she was just another scatterbrained kid. Her lips were pale and quivering and her big black woebegone eyes clung to his face.

He smiled sadly at her. "Don't worry too much about it now," he said. "Somehow I believe you are telling me the truth. Just be glad you escaped whole this time and don't carry any more packages again for people without knowing what they are. The Lord has been good to you in warning you and keeping you from getting into an awful mess."

"But you!" cried Jan. "You are going to be in trouble on account of me. I can't let you do that. I must tell them I did bring the stuff, and that I didn't know what it was."

"Tell who, young lady? Certainly not the police. They would never in a thousand years believe that you didn't know. The rascals who run this lowdown drug-smuggling business delight in getting innocent-looking young people to do their dirty work for them. And once they have done it the kids are never safe from the law. They don't dare back out and they all pretend innocence.

"Now don't you worry about me. I am the one responsible in this case, fortunately. What I say will go with the cops because I'm the one who stirred up the suspicion. I'll manage all right. But I want to be sure you are going to keep your skirts clear after this, little girl."

He spoke with such concern that Jan looked wonderingly up at him again. Why should he care whether she got into trouble or not? He scarcely knew her. It was remarkable that he even recognized her after all this time since Danny's accident. How marvelous that it had been he who was there on the watch! What if some strange doctor had caught her smuggling dope? A smothered sob escaped her.

But Andy had pushed the starter and the whirring covered her voice. She was glad he did not hear.

"I think we had better talk this over a little more," he said. "I have to run out home a few minutes and then back to the city tonight. Would your folks worry if you came with me and met my father and mother? We could phone them from my house."

"Oh!" cried Jan, in a flash of surprise and pleasure. "No, I don't think so. There's only Daddy, you know. I'm sure he won't mind, if I call him. But, oh," she breathed, *"what* will he say when I tell him what I've done? It's *terrible* to be a— *criminal!"*

She uttered the word in a low tone with a sob of horror. Suddenly Andy lost all doubt of her. He put his arm comfortingly about her shoulders. "Poor little kid!" he said tenderly. "I would like to choke the person who got you into this!" Then he was silent for some time, trying to reason out how she had been fooled. He recalled her loyalty to Danny at the accident, and Danny's defense of her when so much as a breath of criticism had been spoken of her. After a few minutes he said,

"Your friend Danny is a member of a gang now, isn't he?" and waited for her reaction.

Out of the tail of his eye he could see her gasp and glance at him sharply.

"I don't—know!" she flung at him. Then, "Don't get the idea that Danny knows anything about the—dope!"

He did not try to argue with her. He spoke quietly, in a matter of fact tone.

"Sometimes the kids who run for the smugglers don't

actually know what they carry, but that never can last long. Still, you don't need to worry. I have no desire to get Danny into trouble." Jan had never heard his tone more gentle.

"God knows I don't want to get kids into trouble. I want to help them. There may be a way to help Danny."

Jan was moved almost to tears, but she was afraid to open her mouth for fear anything she might say would confirm his suspicions of Danny. How had he guessed that it was Danny?

"I hope we may be able to save him before it's too late," Andy went on. "Let's see, how old is he?"

Jan opened her mouth and then closed it again. Even if she answered in a normal voice, it would sound as if she were acquiescing in the conversation about Danny and the dope. But if she didn't it would sound as if she was afraid to, and that would look just as bad. So she answered in a low mumble, which told Andy as well as any other way what he wanted to make sure of.

"I'm not going to squeal on Danny," Andy reassured her as if both of them had known that it was Danny all the time. "But of course this thing has got to be stopped. Suppose you keep out of it and let me handle it. Isn't there some way that you could get out of the neighborhood for a while? Because if you don't you are sure to be approached again. And what are you going to say? If you refuse you will be suspected and you won't be safe, perhaps. These people don't stop at anything. And if you *don't* refuse, well, you see what it leads to, now, don't you?"

"Yes," Jan's voice was a meek little murmur. She sighed, a long burdened sigh. He looked at her with that pity again in his glance. It was almost more than she could bear. He seemed so like a rescuing angel to her. The setting sun lit up the gold crown of his short crisp hair like a halo. She felt as if she would like to lie down and let him walk over her if only she could in some way repay him for saving her this afternoon.

Then all at once the car curved into a winding driveway through a gate of two rustic posts over which a beautifully carved rustic sign announced the name of the place as "Lookaway." Jan hadn't time to wonder at the strange name for her delight in the scene before her.

Elms rose gracefully overhead and a pleasant lawn stretched away to a small apple orchard beyond. An old stone house was set comfortably close to the ground, and its front and side doors stood open hospitably, on a level with the lawn. The grounds were cool and shady and inviting. They sloped away at the back to where a sparkle of water revealed a lazy little creek.

Involuntarily the girl clasped her hands with a cry of delight.

Andy noted her pleasure and smiled.

"I want you to meet my father and mother," he said in a friendly tone just as if nothing had happened that afternoon but a pleasant ride. "Come this way, I think they will still be out of doors."

Chapter 8

FATHER AND MOTHER Hightower saw them coming and Andy's mother caught her breath with a little gasp.

"Oh Father! Andy's bringing his girl!" She put her hands hastily up to smooth her hair. "But how very young she looks! Not a bit as I had imagined. Here, lover," she said, stepping over to his wheel chair, "brush those cookie crumbs off your vest, quick! I wish I had put on my voile dress this afternoon. I almost did. But it's too late now. Never mind, *you* always look nice, anyway."

Father Hightower smiled indulgently and put on his glasses and studied the two who came toward them.

Mother Hightower stuffed her darning into a voluminous bag. Andy must not be embarrassed by disarray, at least, before his wealthy friend.

She arose with a smile as they approached, putting out her hand. She was relieved to find Andy's girl so natural and wholesome looking, but she was somewhat taken aback at her plain garb. Why! She was fairly shabby!

"Lucile?" she said with a disarming smile before Andy could speak. "I have been wanting—"

But Andy broke in hastily.

"This is Janette Nielson, Mother," he explained. "She lives not far from the hospital, and I happened on her unexpectedly quite a distance from home and asked her to ride out here before I go back. I wanted her to meet you and Dad."

Mother Hightower's spirits rose suddenly. Could it be that her son was no longer interested in the rich Sommers girl?

Jan, too, felt relieved. She had had a fleeting dread lest her

doctor friend might tell all her crime right out before them all.
But he had introduced her as graciously as if she were a real
friend of his.

Mrs. Hightower quickly adjusted herself and welcomed the
new girl. She put her arm about Jan and drew her toward the
wheel chair.

"My father, Janette," Andy told her with a ring of pride in his
voice.

Jan gave an awkward little bow, thinking that this man
looked just as his son would look when he was older. She wondered how Andrew's face would seem with those deep lines in
it. Then she decided that Andrew's face was just right as it was.

But she liked the older man and felt a deep respect for him.
It surprised her when she glanced at him the second time to find
that he was quite a small man. She discovered now that the
impression of greatness and strength came from the look in
his face.

All of a sudden like a chill wind came the thought of who
she was and of the awful thing that she had done this afternoon. What would they think of her if they knew? Would
they believe as Andrew had that she had meant no wrong? She
felt she would never be able to show enough gratitude to Andrew for his faith in her. But she wondered again whether he
would bring out the whole story in front of his parents.

"I'm going in now," said Andy, "to call Janette's father and
ask permission for her to stay and have a bite with us and then
I will take her back to town when I go. Okay, Mother?"

His mother smiled warmly at Jan and said, "Of course, son,
we will love to have her. You know," she turned confidentially
to Jan, "I've always wished for a daughter. I wouldn't give up
my boy, of course," she nodded toward Andy's back, "but he
has always brought boys, boys, boys, home with him. I like them
all, but a girl is nice too, sometimes. Pretty soon you must come
in with me and help get supper."

Jan had no time then to wonder why a little feeling of gladness sprang up in her heart at the fact that her new friend never

brought girls home. She was too busy now getting acquainted and looking around at the beautiful restful surroundings. It seemed an enchanted place, and the very thought of going in with a lovely woman like this, a mother, to help with supper was a delightful prospect.

But then old Doctor Hightower spoke up.

"Leave our young guest here, Mother, for a little while at least, and let me get acquainted. Tell me about your school, Janette, and what you do with your spare time."

Jan forgot herself then and before she knew it she had eagerly given them a fairly good picture of her whole background, including Aunt Myra who wanted her to come and live with her.

The two pairs of loving eyes were watching her intently and they glowed with pleasure at the expression of her fine mind and her easy way of talking.

"I would like to meet your father sometime, Janette," said Andy's father. "I think he must be a pretty capable person to have done such a good job on you all alone," he laughed.

"Oh, he is!" agreed Jan eagerly. "He is wonderful. I wish he were here. He would love all this!" She swept her expressive little hand toward the wide lawn and the vista of apple trees and stream. "And he would like to know you, I'm sure," she added politely with a shy smile.

It was a new joy to Jan to be allowed to set the cosy table for four on the cool porch just outside the kitchen door. She handled the dainty linens and delicate china as if they were priceless treasures and exclaimed over each.

"I'm going to ask Daddy if I may buy some material at the store where I work and make some of these pretty little place mats. They shouldn't be hard to do. We never fuss much, but I like to. I guess Daddy being a man just didn't know about things like this. I'm sure he'd think it was nice."

Jan chattered on happily, little dreaming how much of her life and herself she was revealing. Mother Hightower came and showed her one or two points about the setting of the table, giving her a little loving pat as she did so, so that Jan had no idea that she was being corrected.

"Oh, that looks much prettier and neater," she exclaimed. "I never thought of doing it that way!"

Mrs. Hightower wondered where her son had found such a lovely fresh-looking clear-eyed girl. Probably she had been a patient of his—or maybe she was a relative of some crippled child in the hospital. She gave a little sigh as she found herself wondering whether Lucile Sommers had as wholesome an attitude of mind. Of course this girl was very young, and utterly unsophisticated. She looked like a child but perhaps that was because of the way she was dressed. There was a maturity about her speech and her carriage that belied her youthful attire.

They wheeled the dear invalid to the head of the table and then without any warning the three Hightowers bowed their heads and closed their eyes. Jan was nonplussed. She had never been anywhere where people prayed before they ate a meal. She had visited at very few houses during mealtimes, and those were only the homes of a few girls whom she knew in school. Most of the renters where the Nielsons lived did not have friends in to dinner. Their existence did not include neighborliness. They were having too hard a time, most of them, to get enough to eat themselves.

Jan's wonder grew as she listened to the loving words of her host. He spoke as if there was Another there in the room with them, a beloved One, to whose loving care they owed everything they had.

"—and give a special blessing to the dear girl here with us this evening," he prayed. "Draw her close to Thyself with Thine arms of love; guard her in all that she does, for the world is so full of evil. Let no harm come to her—"

Jan was startled. Had his son told him all that had happened that afternoon? A sudden fear shook her. Then she realized that there could certainly be nothing to fear from these loving people.

Jan's own home had always been full of her father's love but somehow there was a different atmosphere here. Perhaps it was because here there was a mother too. Dearly as she loved her father she felt that there was something in this house which she had never known. She had already begun to be subconsciously aware that her father felt uncertain, inadequate, in many situations. Here there was peace of mind, and a confidence that made the whole home glow as if a light were lit.

Jan's thoughts came back for the closing words of the prayer. ". . . and we shall always thank Thee for Thy faithfulness even as we know that we can always come to Thee for the supply of every need in our lives, when we come through the precious name of our Lord and Saviour, Jesus Christ. Amen."

Jan had never heard anyone speak to God as if He were an intimate friend. How did these people get that way? She decided she would like to know more about it.

The meal was simple, but everything tasted wonderful to the child who had been brought up on her father's simple cooking and her own crude attempts.

She listened enthralled as Andy told of an operation he had performed on a little crippled boy who would walk soon for the first time in his life. He was an only boy whose parents had not been able to afford to have his leg corrected when he was a baby. Andy's father and mother were all sympathy and interest when he spoke of his work. The patients he worked with might have been their own children, thought Jan.

The delightful time was over all too soon. Andy announced that he must get back to the hospital.

His mother took Jan in her arms and kissed her good-bye, saying she must come out again very soon. Jan thrilled to her soft arms and her roseleaf lips. As far as Jan could remember this was the first time she had been kissed by a woman since Mattie Puckett had died. She put her arms eagerly about Mrs. Hightower and gave her a girlish hug and a shy kiss with a feeling that she was leaving Heaven, for a long time perhaps.

As she climbed into Andy's car again she looked up at him with even more awe than before. To think that he had bothered with her, and with Danny. Why did he care?

She was aware that he would probably talk to her further about the events of the afternoon, but she broke the silence first.

"Do you always do that?" she asked. "Have that prayer before you eat dinner?" She looked up timidly to see if he would laugh. But he smiled a gentle serious smile.

"Why yes," he said in a matter of fact tone, "we always have. After all, it's no more than polite to thank a person for anything he gives you, isn't it?"

"Well, yes, I suppose so. I never thought of it that way. I never heard anybody do it before." Andy did not show the pity that he felt in his heart for this poor little girl who knew so little of the things of God.

"But why do you put it that way? Do you mean that God cares about people and has anything to do with whether they have food or not?"

"I certainly do," smiled Andy with assurance. "The Bible says that He cares to clothe the lilies of the field and feed the sparrows, and that human beings are of much more value to Him."

"Then why doesn't everybody have enough?" she countered.

"Not everybody is willing to accept it on God's terms," answered Andy.

"What are they? Being as good as you can and helping others and all that?"

"Not by a long shot! If that were the way, nobody would stand a chance, for nobody really does the best he can. No, the first thing to understand in the matter is that this world is now in the hands of God's enemy, the devil. It has been, ever since Adam forfeited it by obeying the devil rather than God."

Jan listened in amazement.

"That is why there is injustice in the world," explained Andy, "and it will continue until Christ returns to set things right. But even now, God has promised to look after His own family. They are sure to have trouble, yet He says He will supply all their need. The thing to do, then, for this life as well as the next, is to make sure you are a member of God's family by trusting His Son as your Saviour."

"Say, you know the Bible well, don't you!" she exclaimed.

"Not as well as I would like to. But my father is a minister, you know, or was, before he was taken sick, and he and mother taught me pretty thoroughly when I was young. I'm glad for that now."

Jan reflected.

"I wish my father could have taught me things like that," she said wistfully. "But I don't know whether I would like to have a minister for a father or not."

"Why not?" grinned Andy appreciatively.

"Oh," replied Jan in some embarrassment as she realized what her words implied, "I mean, wouldn't you have to go to church a lot? I've always hated to go to church. It's so dull."

"There are churches and churches," said Andy. "My father doesn't seem dull to me. Of course when I was a little kid I didn't like to sit still, and I suppose I didn't get as much out of his sermons as I might, but as soon as I could understand words at all I got something. I do recall a time when I was about your age when I thought I didn't like it either. But that was before I was born again." He flashed her a smile such as she had never seen him wear before. She wondered how she could have ever thought him stern.

"What in heck is that?" she asked him. "I'm not familiar with some of the new medical terms," she added apologetically.

He smiled again.

"It's not a new medical term," he said. "It's a very old one. Something else out of the Bible. It has to do with heavenly life, not earthly."

"Oh!" said Jan. "That's too deep for me, I guess."

"Not necessarily," he answered. "You know that everything in the physical creation was planned by God to picture something in the spiritual realm."

"No, I never heard that."

"Well, it does. You are your father's daughter because you

have his life in you, isn't that so?"

"Why, yes, I suppose so. Of course."

"All right. Translate that into heavenly terms. You are a child of God if you have His life in you."

"Why, everybody has that, don't they?" asked Jan puzzled. "Good, decent people, at least."

"Not by a long shot. Jesus called some men children of the devil, yet people considered them very good and they certainly had a high opinion of their own goodness."

They were coming into heavy traffic now and Andy had to give some attention to driving. A big truck honked loudly behind them. Jan was glad of the distraction. She wanted time to get her thoughts straightened out. She had never heard anybody talk like this in all her life.

They veered right and let the truck pass by so that there was a measure of quiet again.

"I don't think I know *anything* about what you are talking about," spoke up Jan in a meek little voice.

Andy smiled again, one of those gentle smiles.

"I'd like to tell you more about it, Janette, because I think it's the most important thing in the world. But I don't have any more time now. I must get right back to the hospital. Do you have a Bible?"

"No," said Jan feeling smaller than ever.

"Here!" He reached into his vest pocket and brought out a little leather book which he handed to Jan. "Read the third chapter of John," he said. "Read it over and over, asking God to show you what it means! I'll be praying for you, too!"

"Oh, but this is your own," breathed Jan in awe as she fingered reverently the worn covers which showed that the little book had seen much use.

"That's all right," Andy assured her gently. "It is mine but I'm glad for you to have it if it will help you to know Him." He smiled again on her, that winning smile and Jan felt as if she had been allowed a glimpse into Heaven.

"I'll take very good care of it," she promised holding it close.

He smiled again and said, "Will your father be home later this evening? I would like very much to stop around for a talk with him after I finish at the hospital."

He got out and started around the car to open the door for Jan but she was out and standing poised to say good-bye before he had got halfway around the car.

He wore his stern look again, but Jan was not quite so frightened of him now. Still she gave a little breathless gasp when he mentioned her father. She remembered that there was a reckoning yet to come with him.

"Don't be frightened," he comforted her. "You don't need to tell him anything until I come if you'd rather not."

The street lights were on now and Jan was standing so that the full light shone on her white tired face. He could see her set her little chin bravely and hold her head just a bit higher, and again he had the impulse to take her in his arms like a child and comfort her, as she said,

"I shall tell him myself *now*. But we will be glad to have you come later anyway," she added graciously.

Neither of them saw a shadowy boyish form slink around the corner of the building. Danny had been waiting for hours in a fever of anxiety lest he had brought some danger or disgrace to Jan by sending her on his errand. It was because he thought that he had been spotted the last time he went, that he had not wanted to go this time. He had reasoned that no one would ever think of suspecting a girl like Jan. But he had tormented himself ever since wondering what had become of her. He would never forgive himself if she had got into trouble. He recognized the doctor but he was too frightened of everyone now to make himself known.

So Jan went up to make confession to her father, and Andy went off to the hospital.

Mr. Nielson and Jan were waiting in anxious silence a couple of hours later when Andy came back.

There were traces of tears on Jan's face, and Mr. Nielson looked years older. His face was white and drawn. But he had shaved carefully and his sandy hair, partly gray now, was smoothly combed.

He rose and shook hands with the young doctor without smiling.

"We have you to thank again, sir," he greeted him sadly, "for helping out in a worse disaster than before."

His voice was near to breaking and Andy's heart went out to him. He looked so lonely and hopeless, as if he had met more than he could cope with.

"It's to try to keep it from being a disaster that I have come, Mr. Nielson," said Andy cheerfully. "It is not that yet, and it doesn't need to be."

Mr. Nielson's taut nerves relaxed somewhat at the confident ring of Andy's voice. The very atmosphere of the room seemed to be less tense.

"Well, I'm sure I am most grateful for all you have done already, Doctor. It evidently meant a great deal to my daughter to be in your lovely home today. It seems to me that she has learned much already through this terrible experience. Frankly, I am at a loss to know what to do. I have been thinking for some time that I ought to move from this neighborhood. But houses are hard to find anywhere, and I'm afraid that any place I could afford would have the same drawbacks. At least here I know something of what we are up against."

Andy listened sympathetically, and then looked at Jan.

"Didn't I hear you telling my father this afternoon about an aunt who would like you to visit her?" he asked abruptly.

A quick look passed between Jan and her father. They had hashed out the question of going to Aunt Myra's weeks ago and here it was coming up again. It seemed to John as if it had been lying in wait for him ever since Jan was born. Maybe he had done wrong in avoiding it this long. His face grayed.

Jan nodded assent, but somehow the thought of going to Aunt Myra's now, with this new trouble on her mind, did not seem alluring.

Andy looked from one to the other. Then he grinned.

"I can see that the prospect of going there is not one that pleases either of you," he said. "But let me put the situation to you plainly. Whoever it was that got Janette into this today is bound to try it again, since she apparently succeeded in her mission. If she is approached again and refuses, it will look as if she has discovered what it was she was delivering. That would not be safe for her because the dope dealers would be afraid she might report them. It is unthinkable that she would not refuse to do it again. Do you see why I think she should leave immediately? I mean right away, tomorrow." Andy appealed to John.

A dogged combination of hopelessness and courage came to John's face as he nodded assent. He set his chin just as his daughter had done downstairs under the street light. Andy's admiration for these two brave people increased. It was refreshing to find those who met difficult situations with courage and honesty.

"How far away is this aunt?" asked Andy.

"About a hundred miles."

"That is good. Could you phone her tonight and find out if it would be convenient for Jan to come?"

Then Jan spoke beseechingly.

"Daddy, if you phone now Aunt Myra will insist on knowing all that has happened to make you change your mind so suddenly. Wouldn't it do to wire, at least?"

"That's right, Jan. There is no need for her to know anything about it."

Jan breathed a little more freely.

A little later as Andy rose to go he went over to her and looked down at her earnestly, putting out both hands to take hers.

"I'm going to ask something that may be very hard for you, Janette," he said. "I want you to promise me not to see your friend Danny before you go."

Jan's face fell, but her eyes did not leave Andy's. She had been counting on letting her old pal know that she had been loyal to him to the end, but she owed this new friend her loyalty, too.

"I see that that will be disappointing to you," he said. "But it would be difficult for you to know just what to say about the whole affair, and it would be better if you did not have to say anything. You see, I am not entirely sure that the police will keep their hands off. That incident this afternoon must have looked a little shady to them. I would rather have you out of the picture entirely. Do you understand?"

He spoke so gently and looked so tired that Jan felt ashamed of herself again.

"Just whatever you say, I will do," she answered submissively.

Andy's face lit up in another one of those radiant smiles that had so surprised her on the ride back to town. Then he gave a last firm pressure to her hands as if to seal her promise. She had a strange sense of rest and peace. What a tower of strength he seemed!

It was going to be hard to have to go away and know that there would be no chance meetings with Andrew Hightower again. She wondered why it was that although she had spent so little time in his company, only a few hours altogether, that she felt the greatest confidence in him, as if she had known him all her life.

They followed Andy down the stairs and once more as he said good night, he took her hand and held it a moment warmly. His very touch seemed to give her strength. Her heart sank as she watched him drive away.

Jan and her father sat up late that night talking over plans. When at last they turned out the light and went to bed, Jan noticed a light in the Severys' kitchen. She had an impulse to run over and talk to Danny and then she remembered her promise to Andrew. It almost broke her heart not to let Danny know that she had been faithful to her trust even though it had been an evil one. Did Danny himself know what he was delivering in those little packages? How terrible that her dear old playmate should have been drawn into a life of crime. Was there no way to save him? Andrew had said he would like to look him up. She sincerely hoped he would. Perhaps there would be some strange power in what Andrew believed that could reach Danny. She slid her hand under her pillow and clung to the soft little Testament there. If Andrew's secret could be known, she determined she would find it out.

Chapter 9

JAN CLIMBED THE stone steps and faced the big polished oak door of Aunt Myra's house with terror clutching at her heart. Her impressions of Aunt Myra so far had never been very reassuring. Last night her father, for her sake, had made a good deal of the story of how he had come on Aunt Myra unawares that day in the hospital. He had tried bravely to give his daughter an unbiased attitude toward her. But as he had never built up any confidence in her aunt through Jan's childhood, he found it hard to eradicate old impressions.

But she stepped bravely into Aunt Myra's house and the new life.

Aunt Myra was on hand, taking everything in charge at once.

"Duncan, take Janette's bag up to the yellow room opposite mine," she commanded, as if she had not already used her husband to the utmost all day in preparing that very room for her niece.

Like a shadow Uncle Duncan glided up the carpeted stairs, bearing Jan's new suitcase which was pitifully light, even though it held all of Jan's wardrobe.

Jan had dreaded lest Aunt Myra would feel that she belonged to her now and would want to kiss her but she saw quickly that such fears were groundless. The woman stood stiffly aloof as if she were in full armor.

"You will want to wash up, Janette," instructed Aunt Myra. "There will not be time now for your bath before dinner, but you can take it this evening before you go to bed. I am not engaged to go out this evening, so I can be on hand to help you."

Janette gasped, and then laughed shakily.

"Oh! I don't need help, thank you, Aunt Myra."

But her aunt stared stonily back at her as if she had taken a great deal upon herself to answer.

"I shall be there to oversee what you do," she reiterated coldly. "You have never had a mother. You will need a great deal of training."

Jan's heart sank even lower. She did not answer but she raised her chin a little higher and determined in her heart that the supervision of her bath should not be. There were surely such things as locks; if there were none in this house, she would get one, or go without a bath until she did!

Jan followed Uncle Duncan up the soft padded stairs and into the loveliest room she had ever seen. She had visited some of her girl friends who went to the same high school with her, but none of them had rooms like this. Soft sunny yellow curtains moved forward gently as if to greet her. A yellow taffeta bedspread rustled in a ladylike way beneath its dainty organdy overdress, and the little vanity, dressed the same way, seemed to edge close to the pretty bed as if to say, "Look at us, aren't we pretty?"

Through a doorway Jan caught a glimpse of her own snowy white bathroom, with its yellow-flowered shower curtain and deep-piled luscious soft yellow towels. She gave a little cry of delight. Her first impulse was to rush down to Aunt Myra and give her a childish hug to thank her for preparing all this splendor for her. But even as she turned, she came face to face with Aunt Myra who had followed her. That stony countenance repulsed all the loving feelings she had. Instead of the hug which Aunt Myra would have given a thousand dollars for, had she known it, she simply said, "The room is beautiful, Aunt Myra," in a stiff polite little voice.

"It will do very well," responded her aunt. "But mercy, child, you mustn't lay your handbag down on the bed, it is soiled from travelling, you know. Be sure to put it away in a drawer every time you come in. The drawer linings can be changed. But, of course, you don't know. There will be many things, I'm sure, that I will have to be patient about before you learn them. Be down in ten minutes for dinner. Bertha does not like to be kept waiting. I would stay now and tell you more but there are things I have to see to, for Bertha has been with me for only a short time. And Janette, put on your best things. We always dress for dinner."

After her aunt had gone out, Jan had a desire to sink down on the floor and cry, but then she glanced at the fluffy rug of yellow and white and decided that she had better not sit on that; she might soil it. In fact, she really ought to step around it or those eagle eyes would notice some spot on it. She took a careful step on the bare floor, and then all at once the ridiculousness of her situation burst upon her and she held her hands over her mouth to keep her laughter from ringing out. Well, let Aunt Myra fuss about soil, and try to inspect her personal cleanliness! She could always laugh. And the room was beautiful. It satisfied the artistic longings that she had inherited from her mother. How did Aunt Myra know enough to pick out such beautiful things? She dressed very stylishly, but nothing about her could be called pretty.

Jan did not know that the minute the telegram came Aunt Myra had sallied forth to the finest shops in the city and, relying on the advice of their decorators, had returned with her car laden with the lovely coverlet and rugs and draperies.

Jan was almost afraid to step into the gleaming bathroom, but her aunt had commanded her to hurry down, and already she felt the compulsion of that strong will upon her. So she washed her face and hands with fierce thoroughness and put on the best dress she had, which was a simple white cotton with red collar and cuffs and a red belt. She combed her hair again, and as she was doing so, she caught sight of herself full length in the pier glass set into her door. Her father had never felt the need of a long mirror and Jan had never noticed its lack so far. But now as she glanced at herself, she realized that her dress was too short compared to the clothes she was used to seeing on other girls. She tried to smooth it down and make it look longer.

She decided that she would let out the hem before another day. Then she saw her hair as it hung loose about her face. It had never occurred to her to leave it that way. She had worn pigtails practically all her life. But it did look nice rippling out. The mirror at home had not been clear, and she had never spent much time looking in it anyway. Now she saw that she looked more like other girls with her hair unbraided. Her ten minutes were almost up, so she just left her hair fluffed out and ran downstairs.

Her aunt was on hand again at the foot of the staircase.

"A lady never runs, my dear, especially in the house," reproved Aunt Myra.

Jan gave another startled gasp and then sighed. There seemed to be so many things she was going to have to learn. How would she remember them all?

"Your hair looks better that way than in braids," Aunt Myra remarked, still in her cold tone, as if she were making more of the fact that it had not looked well before than that it did look well now.

Somewhat encouraged, Jan followed her aunt to the dining room.

It was a rather silent meal, punctuated by instructions only, from Aunt Myra. Uncle Duncan did not speak.

Jan was told how to hold her fork. Corrected in her use of a knife, taught how to serve her plate from the dish that Bertha brought around, and rebuked for crossing her legs under the table, though how Aunt Myra discovered that they were crossed Jan could not imagine. And when Jan in her nervousness upset her glass of water and ran in dismay from the room, she was allowed to stay up there without comfort until Aunt Myra finally came up to superintend her bath. She found Jan already in bed and apparently asleep. After a minute of standing beside her bed gloatingly, during which minute Jan scarcely breathed, she went away and left her, concluding that the child must be tired from her trip.

But Jan cried herself to sleep, keeping her tears safely in bounds with the paper handkerchiefs she found in the bathroom. She was afraid they might not dry on the pillow over night and Aunt Myra would discover them.

It was only the comforting feel of the little book under her pillow that finally quieted her. It was like the strong firm pressure of Doctor Hightower's hand as he took hers the night before. She recalled again the wonderful smile he had given her and took courage. She was here at his command, and she would show him that she was not a quitter. Let Aunt Myra scold as she would, it was something to know that all people were not like Aunt Myra. There was a family in the world who loved each other, and even loved outsiders like herself. Sometime, perhaps, she would get to know those Hightowers better.

It was nearly a week later that John received the first real letter from his daughter. A wire had come to let him know she had arrived, and then a post card, but there was little or no news on that.

Age had seemed to fall about him like a cloak after she had gone. Day after day he would come home to his silent apartment and after restlessly going about from one thing to another that reminded him of her, he would generally betake himself to the river tramping and tramping, on and on, until he was tired enough to go to sleep when he came home. Even at the riverside everything he saw made him want to tell Jan about it. And always at the back of his mind was the recollection of what Myra must have done to her mother to make her forget him.

He grew almost frantic until at last Jan's letter arrived.

"Dear Daddy, extra special and super duper:
"Only since I have been imprisoned in this ogre's castle have I realized what a wonderful parent I have had all these years! I simply can't describe to you the forbidding aspect of the ogress herself nor the formidable chill of the castle. It is unbelievable! But I am sure you will be interested to know that it is true, as you long ago suspected, that Uncle Duncan *does* have to take

his shoes off before he comes into the house! And he still wears gray woolen socks, just like you described to me once! I really feel sorry for him because he doesn't dare to breathe if Aunt Myra looks at him cross-eyed.

"But oh! the dog, Daddy! She's seventeen, and nothing but a shapeless mass, so fat now that she can scarcely waddle. In fact, she has never had enough chance to walk. And her name is—guess what? *Dimples!* Aunt Myra actually blushed when I asked if she named it! And she looked as if she could chop my head off. There must be a weak point in the poor soul somewhere, but she sure does hide it. Brother! can she tell you where to get off!

"She has me stand up and sit down over and over again in the 'drawing room,' on that slippery scratchy haircloth thing she calls a sofa. She has told me the story of it at least six times already, of how her own great-grandfather made it and how he was found dead on it the morning after it was finished. After I finish my 'posture training' I sometimes think I will fall dead on that sofa. I have to walk across the room in front of her about eighty times a day until she thinks I do it correctly. She says all young ladies have to learn those things. Well, at least it gives me exercise! But not enough. I go up to my room afterward and stand on my head to relax.

"But I must say she is generous. You should see your enchanted princess. I look like Astor's pet horse now, with new suits, new dresses, new hats, new *gloves* (I detest them!) and new shoes galore.

"But Daddy! What makes up for all the prancing in the drawing room, and all the criticism of my table manners, etc., etc., is a marvelous violin! Oh, Daddy, I can't wait to play it for you. It sounds simply heavenly! And I am to start lessons with a wonderful teacher next week. I am so thrilled I can't wait.

"Another horrid thing, though, is that I'm going to have to go to church every Sunday. I'll never be able to sit still through it. And if I move, Brother! Will I get called down! Well, I'll tell you about that later if I live through it.

"School starts in another week and I'm a little nervous about that, too. I'm going to feel like an alley rat, I think, among all the high hat girls I hear about. I've been absorbing their family trees. Aunt Myra climbs at least one a day and feeds me the fruit—but it tastes sour to me! Golly, what I would give to be back home with you and walking down by the river or even gazing out at my dear old Mississippi River crack in the wall. I miss you frightfully, Daddy. I hope you will come to see me, though I really can't wish that too hard for I don't think the female dreadnought who owns this castle would put herself out to give you a good time.

"I will write often for I have to let off steam. If only these solemn old birds knew how to laugh! They don't like it if I laugh either. I have to run up to my room sometimes and bury my head in a pillow. I guess the wrong things seem funny to me. I may break out in all my varicolored language to you some day, because I sure have to keep it corked up here. I called something 'lousy' the other day and Brother! was I called down! Well, so what? I can take it. Maybe I'll even learn something, who knows?

"All my love, dear Daddy, and please take care of yourself for
                                    "Your Tomboy, Jan.
"P.S. Do you suppose you can do anything to help Danny get straightened out? I would give anything to see him. I wish that nice Doctor Hightower could get hold of him. He gave me a little Bible and I'm reading it a lot. There's good stuff in it. I have an idea it might be a help to Danny.
                                                "J. N."

John Nielson read and reread that letter. He tried to read between the lines to tell whether his daughter was too unhappy. There was one sentence that seemed to bear with it an ugly aura. That was the one in which Jan said she wanted him to visit her and then checked herself. Quite evidently he was not going to be invited to come. Not that he wanted to visit Myra Fetter, but it was a long ghastly time that he had to look forward to, until Jan should come home at Christmas. He sighed deeply. He was sitting in the big old platform rocker where he had sat and hushed Jan's crying at night when she was a baby. The same rocker where he had sat and sighed the day he first came home to it from Cuba. He wondered whether his efforts at training his daughter had been such a failure that the God who he supposed must order things on earth had had to take her away from him. Then the danger of her illicit trip to that big brick house rushed over him again. Yes, it was good that Jan was away from here. Certainly there would be no danger of drug smuggling in the vicinity of Myra's uprightness.

So John tucked the letter away in his pocket to be brought out and read over and over until the next one should come. It arrived on Tuesday.

"Oh Daddy!! I simply *must* boil over to you or I shall perish with boredom and disgust. If every Sunday is like this I can't take it. Guess what I've had to do today?

"First, this morning I was herded off to *Sunday School*. Can you picture me? Dressed up like a circus pony first, and inspected within an inch of my life and instructed as to each word to say. 'Remember you will be meeting *my* friends, my dear!' Oh, how could I forget the privilege! But what a lot of drips they turned out to be! And honestly, Daddy, it seemed to me that not one of them cared a bit for Aunt Myra herself. I'll bet if she didn't have money and strut around showing off not one of them would look at her. (I know you will be thinking by now that you must tell me not to be critical, but honest, Daddy, I'm not. It is the truth. Anyway, this is only to *you*. I am politeness itself to Aunt Myra *so far!* I don't know how long I can keep it up.)

"I feel like a heel for being so insincere, yet if I don't behave I'd be fired right home and that would be letting you and that nice Doctor Hightower down.

"Well, at Sunday School I was taken on a silver platter and dished out to a half dozen dolls who sat in a circle and looked

me over. Maybe I didn't look them back, too! Snooty things!
But really I don't blame them, come to think of it. I was introduced as Mrs. Fetter's niece, and they had every reason to believe
I would be just like her. But I didn't warm up to any of them
anyway. They seemed like a lot of fine clothes and nothing else.
All they did was whisper and giggle and although I'm supposed
to be a poor relation brought up in the slums, at least you taught
me to be courteous enough to listen to a speaker or else get out.
But the teacher didn't know what she was talking about. She
kept her long wet pink nose in a little magazine they called a
'quarterly' and asked us questions in a kind of worried whiny
voice. Only one girl knew the answers and she sat up straight
and answered them all with a self-righteous smirk on her face.
She was an awful drip. She needed a good shampoo and a
bath. If you have to look like that to know all the Sunday School
answers, preserve me! The teacher asked me a lot of the questions because I was almost the only one who was quiet enough
to hear her. But of course I didn't know any of them. There
was just one thing that did sound as if it might be going to be
interesting. That was what she called a memory verse. It was
about being born again, and that was something Doctor Hightower started once to tell me about. I wanted to ask him some
more. If you see him find out about it. I was going to ask the
teacher but the bell rang then, and I doubt if she knew anything about it anyway. Anyway the teacher sure looked as if
she needed to be born all over again!

"Brother! If I have to go there again I'll have to have a headache every Sunday morning!

"Well, then church was the same old stuff. A tired old man
droned on and I didn't even listen. I was out with you walking
by the river. Because I do miss you something awful, Daddy
darling. It's great to be able to talk to somebody like this, so
please forgive me for being caustic. I will truly begin to try
to find somebody or something to admire after this. They
announced that a new minister, a *young, handsome* one is to
come next week. The tired one is retiring. The girls talked

about it in Sunday School. They are all a twitter. I hope he is as nice as he sounds. His name is Stancel Egbert. This afternoon we are supposed to be napping. You can picture me! And church again tonight. Wow!

"Write to me often. Your letters are a break in my prison life. Your disgraceful daughter, Jan."

After he read that letter John looked up Doctor Hightower's name in the telephone book. But after trying two Hightowers, neither of which was their Hightower, he gave it up with the groundless feeling that the young man didn't care to be bothered.

He had already tried to find Danny and talk to him, but the boy shied away with a hostile look as if he suspected him.

Jan's next letter was taken up with her school.

"It's a boarding school, you know, Daddy, but I'm allowed to go as a day student because I live so near and because (I gather from Aunt Myra's talk) my 'awnt has done so much for the school.' I don't know what she has done except to present them with one of my mother's paintings, with a plaque under it saying she had been a student here. That is nice, though, one of the nicest things I've met with. It is a lovely painting, of a river and ships, something like the one on the screen in our living room. I love to look at it, and I have a feeling that my mother knows I'm here.

"I say hello to it every time I come in, for it hangs right opposite the entrance of the reception hall. It has given me a sort of feeling that I'm not so alone here. I'm glad you married such a sweet person, Daddy, and gave me such a grand mother. That's the nicest thing about Aunt Myra. She never tires of telling me how wonderful my mother was. I can forgive her everything else when she does that!

"And I really believe she cares for me in her own strange way. She softens up a little when she looks at me sometimes, and then she says in that stiff voice of hers, 'You look just like your mother, child!' as if she were scolding me for it. I'm beginning to believe she is really very soft-hearted—in places—and she's afraid or else ashamed to show it. I doubt if I could ever get to love her, or even like her, but I am sorry for her.

"Well, I've met a good many of the girls at school by now. I wonder what you would think of them. There's Audrey Clawson. She's the belle. Everybody has to copy her clothes, her ways, her cosmetics, and even her test papers! Fortunately for them and for the school, she's smart, because the rest would copy her anyway. She has what it takes to be popular. She is a beautiful blonde asset. I don't know yet how she chooses her special friends, nor do I care. She took one look at me and decided against me. So what? I did the same. A couple of dozen other girls are not worth describing because they are all poor imitations of her.

"Among the rest there are a few also-rans each of whom has a small following; a few grinds; and yours truly. I don't seem to fit in anywhere. Maybe I'm the school clown. Anyway, a lot of things seem terribly funny to me. I haven't found anybody to laugh with me yet, but I surely hope I will. They all take their clothes and their makeup and their boy friends so seriously. Their rooms are lined with boys' photographs. I don't like the faces of most of them. They look conceited, like smart alecks. Perhaps I should have asked Danny for a picture. I still can't give up hope for Danny, Daddy. Have you had a chance to tell him I didn't let him down? Sometimes I wish I could see him but the girls here would only make fun of him. Of course I *might* give them some real fun and have you send me a picture of Mrs. O'Leary's youngest. Tell him not to bother to wash behind his ears, that part won't show.

"Oh Daddy, life seems such a huge joke to me! Why am I so different? What ails me? I can't be satisfied with what other girls seem to live on. I always did feel sick after too much cotton candy! And I find I'm more and more hungry for solid food, but I don't know where to look for it, 'if you know what I mean!' And you do, Daddy dear, you always did. You used to feed me stories of foreign ports, and boats, and sunsets, and fun. But since I've been off here alone, I can see that even they aren't going to answer a lot of my questions. Do you know if there is an answer? If anybody does, I think those Hightowers know it. They had something I never saw before. Music comes nearer to making me feel well fed inside than anything so far. Daddy, my music teacher seems to think I will really go to town with my violin. And I love it best of all. It *almost* makes me love Aunt Myra for giving it to me, but not quite!

"I'm an ungrateful wretch, but I love you, Daddy dear.

"Jan.

"P.S. I'd give anything for a good catch with you or Danny in the alley. These girls are flat tires when it comes to sports."

It would have taken a far less loving and understanding parent than John Nielson to have missed the note of unhappiness in that letter.

As he worked away in the factory, John found himself following Jan through her days. He found he resented these wealthy, sophisticated girls who had not the perception to see that his daughter was exceptionally desirable. He told himself that surely they would discover her value before long. Then he would begin to dread that if they did they would spoil her wholesomeness in some way. He couldn't stand it if his daughter should turn into one of those artificial dolls he and Jan had often laughed over as they walked down the main streets of Chester. Jan had mimicked their self-conscious preening then and she had been disgusted with their swaggering boldness when she had seen it through his eyes, but when she was with that sort of thing every day, would her standard of values hold?

He watched keenly in each letter for any subtle change in her. But her next letter did not mention school.

"Oh, Daddy! I have done it now! I blew up at Aunt Myra. I've known it was coming for a long time.

"As you may have gathered, she does not hold the highest opinion of you. Since she has always spoken so wonderfully of my mother, I have tried to swallow her disparagement of you in silence. It was not that she said anything horrid about you, but her very lack of response when I mentioned you was damning. Yet there was nothing I could pick on to blow up about. The poor old thing just doesn't know how wonderful you are, that's all. And her outlook is so narrow that she can't see beyond her social blinders.

"Well, she had some callers here, two stiff old dames that were 'of fine old families'—that's all she cares about—I think their family trees are so old and dead that the branches may crack off at any minute and leave them out on a limb, because they would certainly have nothing left without their background. They are not smart, either as to clothes or brains, and if either of them ever loved anybody except themselves, whoever it was is dead now. They panned everybody in their silly women's club, and everybody in their church, which by the way, seems to me to be nothing but another club. People go to see what the rest have on, or to meet the rest and tell some juicy bit of scandal—now truly, Daddy, I'm *not* too critical, they *do*.

"Well, anyway, I came in from school and found them there and of course Aunt Myra hauled me in as she always does, to show me off. 'My dear sister's only child' is what I am. That would be all right if she didn't imply in her tone that it was somebody's fault, meaning yours, that my mother died and didn't have any more children.

"They began asking all about me, and about you, and Aunt Myra told them her idea of us as if I wasn't even in the room, or as if I was about a year old and couldn't understand.

" 'The poor child was being allowed to grow up like a weed,' she said, 'until I took her. I couldn't bear to think of poor Janette's only daughter being positively vulgar and unmannerly. And just think, she had *never* even been sent to Sunday School! That man had brought her up just like a heathen! I doubt if he has ever been inside a church in his life! And her language! Well, you can imagine what she had picked up in such a life. I had feared her environment might be pretty bad, but I was hardly prepared for what I found when I finally rescued her. It was providential that I went when I did. If she had been any older it would have been almost impossible to train her at all. Well, what could you expect of a man who would entice a lovely innocent young girl like my sister? But fortunately there is something of her mother in Janette. Her inheritance is not all bad.'

"At that point I blew up.

"I told her right in front of those old hags that you were the finest father anybody ever had, that you lived a lot better life than she did, and certainly had a lot more loving kindness, and if she was going to talk like that I would not stay here another minute. And Daddy, I swore at her! I know you will not like that, but I told her it was hell to live here in her house and that I hated her.

"Well, she looked as if I had exploded an atom bomb and it practically was. The two so-called ladies excused themselves to let her 'deal with me.' But then, *what* do you think happened?

"Aunt Myra, yes, grim stiff old Aunt Myra burst into tears! She sobbed and sobbed. I stood there awhile and hated her. And then believe it or not, I got to feeling sorry for her. She blubbered out, 'Oh-h! I thought *you* were going to love me! *Nobody* loves me. Nobody but my poor sister *ever* loved me, not even my own mother. She was as hard as nails and I guess I'm just like her. Oh-h-h! I've lost you, too, just when I thought things were going to be happy at last. Oh-h-h!'

"Well, Daddy, what could I do? That poor old soul, with nothing but an empty shadow for a husband, and a sofa pillow for a dog, and yours truly stabbing her in the face with my hate, to think that *she* was desolate and unhappy. Well, I might have known it. And of course it's her own fault in a way, yet I suppose she's like this because her mother was and she can hardly help it, it's her nature. Daddy, isn't there *any* way to get rid of your 'nature'? Anyway, I just had to put my arms around the poor soul and tell her I was sorry. I tried to hug her up like you used to do me when I was little and got hurt or scared but it was like embracing a poker. And I didn't have too much desire to do it anyway. However, I do think it helped. And the atmosphere is somewhat clearer now. She still runs Uncle Duncan in the same old way, but she seems—not more gentle, she'll never be that—but at least less harsh with me. So take heart, Daddy mine, the first atom bomb has exploded and we lived through it. Now let's hope there are no radioactive waves to eat our eyes and hearts out.

"That's all tonight, Daddy. That's enough, isn't it?

"Your own Jan.

"P.S. Next Sunday the Reverend Stancel Egbert will preach for the first time at church. Maybe he will improve me! Your heathen."

Just a hasty note came next.

"Oh Daddy! I've seen the new minister and is he a knock-out!! Tall, blond and handsome, and quite a dresser. All the girls are simply gaga about him, but he's to come *here* first to dinner. I'll have first shot at him. Fortunately, Aunt Myra realizes the importance of the moment and has got my hair done especially and I have another new dress for the occasion. Wish me luck. Maybe I'll be a minister's wife some day! Laugh that one off!

"Don't worry, Daddy, I haven't lost my mind. But it *is* quite a thrill! Especially as I think I'm not such an eyesore as I used to be. In fact I'm pretty sharp. Several boys from the boys' school here in town have wanted to date me already. I sort of liked them, all but one who wanted to kiss all the time. Pretty risqué? Anyway it's fun.

"Lots of love,

"Jan."

John Nielson really worried over that one. Not that he took too seriously Jan's remarks about the new minister. He was familiar with her bubbling way of expressing herself. But he could see a subtle change in her outlook. It had never mattered to her before whether she had pretty clothes and boy friends or not. If she had someone who could play ball with her and climb trees that was all she had ever asked. He sighed deeply. Of course she had to grow up. But he wished he could be on hand to look over some of those boys. He did not trust Aunt Myra's judgment of what was good for his daughter any more than she had trusted his. Well, poor Jan was in the middle and she had always had good sense. He would just have to trust that it would not desert her now.

Chapter 10

THE REVEREND STANCEL EGBERT drove up and parked in front of Mrs. Fetter's big gray stone house with satisfaction. It was gratifying to think that he had been only two days in his new charge and he was already invited to dinner at one of the handsomest residences in town. He hoped he would make a good impression, for he had been informed that Mrs. Fetter was quite influential in church affairs and it would be wise to consider her views in general before taking any departure from the old customs. He had been warned of her austerity. But he had small fear of that. He had always had a way with old ladies and he had not found one yet that he could not melt.

He was a personable young man fresh from seminary. He was tall, with rather light hair and a clean smooth complexion. He wore his excellently tailored clothes well, and his bearing was dignified. So dignified, in fact, that people were always somewhat surprised and pleased when he broke into his smile. That smile of his was a great asset. It showed beautiful teeth and emphasized a cleft in his chin. He hoped that his smile would help a good deal in breaking the Fetter ice.

He rang the bell and then straightened the handsome blue tie that matched his eyes. He could catch the glitter of the one tiny diamond in his heavily embossed fraternity ring as he did so.

Then he could not repress an inward grin as the door opened and he beheld the woman whom his richest deacon had described. There was no doubt that this grim female was Mrs. Fetter.

He put on his smile and was a little crestfallen not to receive

one in return. He did not know that the expression on **Myra**
Fetter's face was the most cordial one she owned. Nor was he
aware that this was a moment to which she had looked forward, not only because a new, younger man would be more
pliable, more easily managed than the old minister but also
because she had a beautiful niece. Janette was still young, of
course, but in a vague future which Myra hoped was far distant, she would be of marriageable age, and Myra's soul cherished the thought of marriage to the successful minister of a
big city church as the highest fate a kind providence could
bestow upon a young girl.

Her thin nose quivered slightly as she put out her hand and
said, "Reverend Egbert? We are delighted to have you in our
midst."

For an instant the guest thought that it was an elderly butler
who glided up behind him at that point and divested him of
the lightweight topcoat he wore. But Mrs. Fetter paused to say
to the man, "Be sure to hang it carefully, without any wrinkles."
Then she commented apologetically, "Mr. Fetter is *so* heed-
less about hanging garments!"

Reverend Egbert cast a pitying glance toward the thin gray
figure of his hostess' husband, wondering if she were not going
to introduce him, then he forgot all about him as a beautiful,
dainty, black-haired young girl entered the living room.

Jan's pigtails were gone now and her soft black hair waved
naturally about her face. Myra's hairdresser had given it a
fashionable upswing when she set it, and it made Jan look
exceedingly smart. Her new gown was the last word in Junior
teen-age styles. Even though Myra did not know how to make
herself attractive, she knew style, and the saleslady at Myra's exclusive shop had done her best, too. Combined with Jan's naturally simple taste they had achieved a most charming effect.

Involuntarily Reverend Egbert gave an exclamation of surprise and pleasure.

"Ah, Mrs. Fetter, I was not told that you had a daughter!"

he displayed his most winning smile and went forward to take her hand.

"This is my niece, Reverend Egbert," corrected Myra, not without pride. "Janette, say how do you do to the new minister."

Jan blushed. Would Aunt Myra never realize that she was old enough to know how to greet a stranger, and didn't have to be told like a child to say how do you do? She held herself straight in order to look her seventeen years. She wanted to erase the little-girl look she knew she had always had.

The newcomer noted the little tinge of annoyance and endeavored to smooth over the incident by his own cordiality. He succeeded so well that Jan immediately forgot Aunt Myra. She enjoyed watching the man's face light up in answer to Aunt Myra's questions as he spoke of his own home, a beautiful country place in Massachusetts. Jan was fascinated with his slight accent. She had not happened to know personally anyone with a Bostonian accent and it sounded just a little foreign and altogether entrancing to her. He was handsome, there was no doubt about that. Wouldn't the other girls be filled with envy when they knew that she had met him first! She giggled to herself. She had not yet taken young men very seriously, but as Reverend Egbert talked he kept casting complimentary glances at her, as if he was aware that she was made of different stuff from her aunt, and that they two were in sympathy. Jan had had little of understanding and sympathy since she left her father's home and it seemed good to think that perhaps this man was going to be a real friend.

Anyway it was fun to be receiving his admiration. It was not that Jan had not had admiration from boys before, but she had always considered them just boys, and herself just a little girl and a tomboy at that. She had no illusions about herself. But this was not just one of the boys she had always known, or even a pupil from the exclusive boys' school nearby. This was a young *man*. There was a big difference. He was a stranger, and handsome, and his background as he sketched it sounded very romantic.

At dinner Aunt Myra manipulated the conversation as skillfully as she carved the chicken. She wisely allowed Jan and the guest to do a good deal of the talking.

Jan felt more like herself than she had since she came to Aunt Myra's. It was the first time there had been another young person at the table to talk to. Up to this time she had had to struggle with the heavy load of conversation with Aunt Myra alone, since Uncle Duncan scarcely ever opened his mouth. He was seated now like a shadow in his big arm chair, receiving what was passed to him, hardly raising his eyes from his plate. The rest seemed to forget that he was even there.

But Jan fairly sparkled. Aunt Myra listened to her brilliant repartee with the stranger and grew stiff with pride in her.

"My niece is exceptionally talented, Reverend Egbert," she said. "She expects to go on the concert stage with her violin."

Jan gasped. But the guest exclaimed, "Oh, how delightful! We shall have to make use of you in the services. I hope that we shall be able to have the pleasure of hearing you play after dinner?"

And that week Jane wrote her father:

"I am at last released from that tasteless Sunday School class, Daddy. I play along with the organ every week, through the service, and a solo for the prelude and often for the offertory (I never heard of that one before). We are supposed to practice just before church time, so that lets me out of Sunday School. Brother, am I glad! Reverend Egbert (we all call him Stan now) hangs around and really seems to enjoy the music. Besides, it's good practice. I'm beginning to love some of the church music. I never realized that a few of the old church hymns are really fine music, Daddy. Did you know that? Maybe if we had found a church that had good music I wouldn't have hated it so.

"But I still don't get too much out of the sermons. I'm beginning to wonder whether Stan knows the Bible as well as Doctor

Hightower and *he* isn't even a minister, although his father was. Because this man doesn't often refer to the Bible. I was hoping that I would learn something about it at last. He gives very flowery talks on how nice it will be when nations love each other instead of fighting, and how nice it is to have peace of mind, and how we ought to be better than we are, but I keep waiting for him to tell how these things can happen and he never seems to get to that. I suppose there just isn't any answer, is there? Those nice Hightowers acted as if they had peace of mind, though. I wonder if they do or if I just happened in on a good day? Sometime I'm going to ask Stan about my little book. He seems to have taken quite a liking to your only daughter and I'm having a lot of fun—sometimes."

John Nielson heaved another sigh after that letter and frowned. What did he know about this young minister? He sounded very attractive but it wouldn't be pleasant to have even a minister turn up as a son-in-law sight unseen. There were times when John almost wished for the old days back again when Jan was a little girl and played all day long with Danny Severy. It was a responsibility to have a daughter. Then after all, he would decide that he must let Jan work things out for herself.

But Danny Severy had no idea of leaving Jan to the uncertainties of fate. He had puzzled and trembled over her failure to see him or report on that dangerous afternoon trip she took. He had decided that the truth must certainly have leaked out, and that he might momently expect to be apprehended. One day he would find himself cursing Jan in his heart for being a punk and a squealer. Then the next he would recall her unfailing loyalty in every situation they had ever faced together and he would decide that it was that Doctor fellow who had somehow queered her. But surely, he reasoned, if Doctor Hightower had found out what was going on he would have told the cops, and Danny would have heard from them before this. Then his suspicions would turn toward Jan's father. It must be he who had discovered the undercover business and spirited Jan away. Or could it be that Jan had been put in jail? Danny clenched his skinny fists and vowed he'd get revenge if that had happened, yet a tearing conviction made him writhe for he knew if she were in jail that it would have been because of him. He knew he had had no business to send her on that errand. But Danny caught sight of John Nielson several times and while the man looked sad and lonely he did not look as if he had been disgraced by having a daughter in jail. Danny was bewildered. He tried every way he could think of to trace her without going directly to her father. He was afraid to face him without more knowledge of how things stood.

At last he hit upon a plan. The post office had refused to tell Danny Jan's address but they had assured him that a letter to her would be forwarded. So he decided to write to Jan and see what happened.

It was an undertaking for Danny to write a letter. His schooling had not carried him very far. In high school he had slipped and stumbled and floundered through a day now and then, and the little learning he had gained had not taken effect.

But Jan, in the midst of her unhappiness and homesickness, fairly wept when she opened the soiled pencilled envelope and saw Danny's name signed crookedly to it. All she could see was Danny's dear dirty face before her and his big eyes looking wistfully up at her as she read:

"Dear Jan, What I want to no is are you a punk or not? If you ran away from me and the gang dont answer this. I can do without you. But if you are in trubbel let me no wear you are and I will come and get you.

                              "Your old frend Dan."

Jan hugged the smeary letter to her and the dear old yellow brick building that meant home seemed to rise up before her and the tears came in great sobs.

When she grew calmer she began to wonder what she ought

to say to Danny in reply. That wonderful young doctor had asked her not to see Danny before she left, but surely the whole affair had blown over by now and there would be no harm in writing him a friendly little note just to let him know that she was still loyal to their old friendship. She had a worried feeling that in doing so perhaps she was being disloyal to the man who had helped her, but she must not break her friendship with Danny, her first friend, by letting him think she had turned against him. So after much thought she wrote:

"Dear Danny:

"It surely was good to hear from you. I told you I would always be your friend and you ought to know I meant it. I never did let you down and never will. My aunt has always wanted me to come to live with her, and she came one day and offered to send me to a good school and Daddy persuaded me I ought to go. So here I am. I don't like it here. I am awfully lonely and it seems rather like prison sometimes because she is very strict, but I guess it's all right and good for me. I sure would love to see you and have a good game of ball. I hope you are okay.

"As ever your pal,
"Jan."

Jan read that over and over before she sent it. Surely not even Doctor Hightower could find anything in that to object to. She had made no direct reference to that unfortunate afternoon's experience. It was only a friendly reassurance of her loyalty. So at last with many a misgiving she mailed it.

She had written on plain stationery and had given no street address for she had a fleeting dread lest sometime Danny might turn up at her aunt's and she could guess what a furore that would create.

She was not prepared for the answer that came.

"Dear Jan: I am comming over to Oak Hill to see you. I will

meet you in front of the post offis after skool next Thursday. I will get you out of there if you want.

"Your pal,
"Dan."

It was like Danny to give her no choice of dates. Gang standards demanded loyalty to the uttermost.

Jan was torn between dread lest her aunt should find out what she was doing, and delight at the thought of seeing Danny again. But not for the world would she let Danny down, even though it meant that she would have to change her beloved music lesson. She was reasonably sure that that could be managed without lying to Aunt Myra. John Nielson had taught Jan to hate a lie.

Very early on a Thursday morning Danny boarded a train. He took it instead of a bus to boost his morale.

He had plenty of money in his pocket. He had bought a new green suit for the occasion and a bright tan topcoat with the new style cut that some of the leaders of his gang affected. He had even acquired a new hat with a red and green feather, and he wore it with a swagger.

He had had to climb on a rickety kitchen chair to survey himself by sections in the cracked and clouded Severy mirror, but he was pleased with the effect. Jan had not mentioned the financial and social status of her aunt but he recalled hearing her or her father say once that she had money. If it turned out that he should be invited to visit in the aunt's home, he must not shame Jan by looking shabby.

His heart was beating fast when he reached Oak Hill and took up a sauntering watch on the main street near the post office. He was a little taken aback at the fashionable aspect of the suburb.

A girl came skipping down the street a block away and Danny's heart missed a beat. The girl had short dark pigtails like Jan's and wore a red plaid dress that looked like one Jan used to wear. But she turned in at a doorway next to the drug store and did not come out again. It couldn't have been Jan anyway for this girl was not tall enough.

Danny watched a group of fashionably dressed girls come gaily down the street arm in arm and go into the drug store. He walked past the store and stared in the window. The girls were seated at the counter throwing back and forth bright bubbles of chatter with the handsome young soda clerk as they sipped their drinks. But none of these girls looked like Jan.

Just then he heard a familiar voice behind him.

"Hi, Danny!"

Startled, he turned and stared at the girl who spoke to him. For a moment he thought that it was one of those stylish girls he had seen in the drug store. Then he recognized Jan's big black laughing eyes and Jan's good old smile. The girl put out her lean strong hand to shake hands with Danny, unconscious of the fact that in the old days they had never thought to shake hands. It was a part of her newly acquired manners that she did so now without thinking.

Embarrassed and not without resentment, Danny stared at her. Then seeing her hand out he suddenly realized that he should put out his. He thrust it forth with a jerk and missed hers entirely, sliding right by it. More mortified than ever he turned red and wanted to run away. He had a feeling that those girls in the drug store were watching him and laughing.

This was a Jan he did not know. The old playmate was gone. This was a strikingly beautiful, handsomely dressed, well-poised young lady with unquestionable swank. He couldn't open his mouth.

But Jan laughed easily, and falling into step with him she took his arm and drew him along with her, saying in a warm comradely voice,

"I'll bet you didn't know me without my pigtails, Danny, did you now?" And she chattered on to help Danny over his first awkwardness. She swallowed down her first shock at Danny's looks. In her lack of sophistication before she came to

Aunt Myra's she had not been aware of how cheap and tough he appeared.

Across the street from a car parked at the curb, the Reverend Stancel Egbert stared in horrified amazement to see the young lady he had admired at dinner a few nights before, picking up the tough-looking fellow whom he had noticed hanging about the drug store and post office for some time. He gave a shrug as he noted the start of surprise that fellow gave when Jan spoke to him. These teen-agers! They were not bad, though, just looking for a thrill. It would be a thrill to him to try to mold that lovely girl. He was sure he could win her to better things.

Half a block behind Jan and Danny marched the English teacher from the Oak Hill School for Girls. She had witnessed the scene with horrified pink-rimmed eyes. Her delicate nostrils spread indignantly and she wet her pale lips as she began rehearsing in her mind the phrases that would appropriately convey the scandalous news of what she had seen to the dean at the school who was one of her best friends.

But Jan and Danny walked arm in arm on down the public square and over to the park.

A gray shadow of a man led by a gray dog passed near them and paused to stare furtively but Jan did not notice him.

The next evening Jan was summoned to the dean's office.

Chapter 11

As JAN WALKED across the beautiful grounds of her school the next evening in response to the dean's summons, she tried to steady herself by taking deep breaths.

Whatever it was that she was to be called in question for, there was nothing on her conscience. Perhaps they had discovered that she had had a visit from Danny, but what if they had? Surely she had a right to see her own friends. And she had been careful not to take him on the campus.

Could it be that they knew something about what Danny was doing? Surely not! Jan had heard no more about the matter of the dope running. She had not mentioned it to Danny and Danny had not brought up the subject either. Perhaps he hoped she still did not know what had been in that package and he wanted to leave her in ignorance. Most of their talk on their long walk had been reminiscing. Then she had told him some of the funny things about her aunt and the school, mimicking for him some of the teachers. They had established their old friendly basis again; that was all she had expected to do.

Jan had firmly declined his invitation for the evening, saying that she simply had to get back and study. So Danny had taken his train back to Chester, disturbed at the great gulf now fixed between them, but at peace about her safety at least. Jan's new clothes and new manners left him speechless. Still, her jokes and her laugh were the same. She would never change inside, he told himself, and he would always love her, that was sure.

Jan had said nothing to Aunt Myra about his visit, of course. She was completely at a loss to account for her summons to the office.

When she reached there she was confronted by Miss Persons the dean, Miss Athol the English teacher, and last but not least, Aunt Myra.

Jan wanted to burst out laughing, they looked so severe. Perhaps they were going to expel her for some reason. Well, there was always home. But the violin lessons! If they went out of her life, that would hurt!

For support and comfort Jan's hand sought the little book she had slipped into her pocket. More and more lately, as one trial after another had confronted her, she had been turning to it. And as she read it she would recall the warm tender smile of the wonderful young man who had given it to her. Now it seemed to comfort her as his strong handclasp had comforted her that other time she was in trouble. Then the dean spoke.

"You have been summoned here," she said severely, "to answer for us some questions as to your conduct on the street yesterday afternoon. Even though you are a day student, and you are not under our jurisdiction off the school grounds your aunt has requested that we take your case under consideration as it reflects upon the standing of the whole school. Your aunt has made plain to us that because of your background," she said the word in a tone which implied unspeakable things, "there may be some ground for leniency since this is your first offense.

"Now you will answer yes or no to our questions. And understand that we *require the truth,* Miss Nielson."

During this speech Jan had flushed red and then turned perfectly white but she did not answer. She held herself rigidly under control.

Then the inquisition began.

"Did you or did you not speak to a boy in a public place yesterday afternoon?"

Miss Persons pronounced the word "boy" as if it indicated some sort of reptile. Her neat lips gave a kind of smack every few words.

Jan froze. "I did," she said calmly.

The three pairs of eyes sought each other, shocked at Jan's lack of shame.

"Are you aware that it is unseemly and unladylike, not to say actually *dangerous* for a young girl to speak to a strange boy on the street?"

"I suppose it would be," replied Jan scornfully. She was too indignant to try to defend herself now. The truth would be bound to come out sooner or later and she was too proud to try to straighten things out.

"We are not interested in what you suppose. You are to answer yes or no!" blazed the dean, snapping off her words.

"Did you or did you not walk down the public street arm in arm with this—*boy?*" went on the relentless voice.

Jan gave a contemptuous little smile.

"I did." If they wouldn't let her say enough to explain then let them have a good long time trying to find out.

"Perhaps this boy appeared to you to be a gentleman?"

Jan hesitated. According to the standards of these women her answer would have to be definitely no. And according to her own new standards, or, even according to her old ones she could scarcely find it in her honest heart to rate Danny as a gentleman. He was poor and neglected and illiterate; a criminal, actually, whether he was aware of it or not. Yet go back on her old friend she would not.

She opened her mouth and then closed it and grew red.

"Ne-ver mind, young lady! Your confusion is answer enough! Do you realize that you have brought shame upon your beloved aunt who has befriended you?"

"That's a dirty rotten lie!" Jan burst out in rage.

"Janette!" shrilled Aunt Myra. "You for-*get* yourself!" Miss Athol put her thin hands over her ears, and Miss Persons' eyes blazed righteously.

Aunt Myra actually wiped away an indignant tear. "I beg you," she addressed Miss Persons, "to make some allowance for my niece's background."

Angry and humiliated, Jan turned on her aunt. A torrent of

bitter words rushed to her lips, when all of a sudden her hand found the little book again in her pocket. She clung to it, seeing before her, as it were, the reassuring smile of Andrew Hightower. She had a feeling that he was telling her to keep calm, that her answer was to be found in the little book. The words she had been about to say died on her tongue and instead she found herself calling silently to Andrew's God for help.

The dean had arisen and stalked toward Jan as if she were about to take her into custody when suddenly there set up such a screeching and howling outside the window that the ladylike gasps of Miss Athol were completely drowned out. Then there came a long agonized wail, unearthly in its anguish.

Miss Persons forgot her little culprit and ran out of the room crying shrilly,

"It's Cleopatra! Oh, my poor little Cleo! Some awful dog has killed her!"

Jan wondered how a cat could howl like that if it were dead.

Doors opened down the halls and girls and teachers rushed out after the distraught woman. The tottering old janitor could be seen standing under a tall tree wringing his hands and pointing upward.

Miss Persons ran out of the building with Miss Athol after her, right through a light fall of snow.

"She's up there, mum," pointed the old janitor. "Thet ole yaller dog whut was hyar this mornin' got 'er. They-all fit fer sure. An' Cleo is purty bad hurt, I'se 'fraid."

"Oh! Oh!" moaned Miss Persons wringing her pale weak hands. "My poor little darling. Cleo!" she called desperately. "Oh, Cleopatra, little kitty, are you hurt? Won't you come down to me? Here, Cleo, come Cleo."

"I'll go get a ladder, Miss Persons, an' see can I git 'er."

He trundled off and was gone several minutes while the girls giggled, coughing to cover the giggles, then each suggested a different plan to try to show their interest in the dean's distressed cat, with an eye to better marks than usual.

But the awful howling went on and the gleaming eyes of the

big white wounded cat could be seen through the darkness where she was stretched far out on a high limb.

Meanwhile Aunt Myra, disdaining to follow the hullabaloo, remained in the dean's office, holding Jan with her fierce black eyes.

For a long moment they stood there glaring at each other without speaking. Then Aunt Myra broke the strained silence.

"While the others have taken leave of their senses, I will take this opportunity to inquire of you, Janette, why it is that you have chosen to disgrace me in front of these your teachers and the school and this whole town?" She drew herself up to her stiffest.

Jan struggled to speak courteously but her voice held suppressed indignation.

"It all seems like much ado about nothing, to me, Aunt Myra." She paused. "I only—" But Aunt Myra broke in.

"You mean it is *nothing* that you would be so common as to brazenly pick up a strange loafer on the street?"

"I didn't do that, Aunt Myra," Jan retorted fiercely. "A friend of mine whom I have known and played with all my life wrote that he was coming to see me and I happened on him first. I suppose it did look as though I had picked him up, if anyone was watching. But I didn't, and we just had a nice walk in the park and I enjoyed his visit. I've—I've been pretty homesick, if you want to know!"

Aunt Myra opened her astonished mouth but no words came.

Jan stood looking at her with pity a moment and then she turned and walked out of the room.

Outside the hubbub was still going on. Various girls were trying with sticks and brooms to reach high enough to scare the poor hurt cat down from its limb but they only succeeded in making her climb higher.

As she scrambled up to another limb crying piteously, Miss Persons who was standing directly beneath her gave another shriek and held out her arm.

"Oh!" she screamed. "Blood! It dropped on my arm! She's

bleeding to death. Will no one rescue my poor, poor little Cleo before she di-i-es?"

There was a loud snicker, quickly smothered. Then before anyone realized what was happening, a lithe little form in dainty plaid shorts was ascending the tree as adroitly as the cat herself had done, and a billowing plaid skirt was settling slowly on the ground, beside Jan's handsome tweed coat.

A few girls gasped with delight at the shock such undress would cause in Miss Persons' modest bosom. Shorts were taboo at the school except for indoor gymnastics.

But Miss Persons seemed oblivious of the costume of her cat's rescuer. Her hands were clasped in an ecstasy of relief that somebody was at last taking measures to aid her Cleo.

With easy grace Jan climbed up as far as the limb on which the cat clung meowing horribly. Then slowly she inched herself out onto the limb, which bent downward with her weight.

The whole length of her body she crawled, until she could just touch the cat. But Cleo resented that and tried to edge farther out. Holding firmly with her knees Jan freed one hand and began to stroke the frightened animal, talking softly to it. But Cleo did not welcome her advances.

"She's torn pretty badly," she called down, "and she's afraid."

Aunt Myra had left the office to follow Jan and now she joined the group about the tree. When she discovered who it was risking her life for the dean's precious cat she cast one look at the dean, and then breathing fast stood perfectly still a moment.

Suddenly she grabbed a girl near her.

"Get a blanket!" she ordered.

Some one threw one from an upper window. Then she requisitioned four girls to hold the blanket tightly beneath the cat.

"Janette, drop the cat down!" she commanded.

Miss Persons gave another shriek, but Jan for once sided with her aunt. She was really grateful for her help. She tore the cat from its perch and dropped her into the blanket.

With a compassionate cry Miss Persons swooped down upon the cat and gathered her close in her arms, blood and all, soothing her with endearments.

"Get on your clothes, Janette," said Aunt Myra when Jan had alighted on the ground, "and come with me now. We will take Miss Persons and the cat to the veterinary." She stalked out to her car with Jan behind her. The dean with her howling cat wrapped in the blanket, brought up the rear of the distressed procession.

The doddering old janitor appeared just then with his unnecessary ladder and stood looking in bewildered amazement at the ways of some women.

The girls stared after them, suppressing their snickers until the car door closed upon the strange group, and then they turned back to their rooms to get warm and laugh it all over again and mimic Miss Persons' discomfort to their heart's content.

But Jan rode calmly along in the front seat with her silent Uncle Duncan. She realized that the atmosphere had been cleared in a remarkable way. She wanted to cry with relief, although she thought she would never respect those evil-minded cruel women again.

As she thought it all over suddenly she remembered the quick prayer she had flung up to God. She raised her eyes to the dark sky and spoke in her heart, "Well, You *did* it, God! You helped me. I didn't really think You would. I'm sorry for not trusting You better. Thank You. Now I'd like to ask You something else. Won't You please save Danny somehow from what he's been doing? And God, if it isn't too much, please bless that nice man that told me about You. Good night, God."

The next morning Jan was sent for again to come to the dean's office.

Stiffly, with some embarrassment, Miss Persons said "Good morning, Miss Nielson." But she did not ask her to sit down.

"I have called you in," she said, "to express my thanks for your timely help last evening." But she spoke in a tone that fairly reprimanded Jan for having done something worthy of thanks.

Jan merely nodded coldly, murmuring something about being glad she could help the cat.

"Now as for the matter we were discussing last night," she went on, as if it were after all a small thing compared to the cat's dilemma, "your aunt and I have discussed it again and we all feel that in view of your lack of early training, you should be given another chance."

Jan flushed crimson and interrupted.

"Miss Persons," she said with a dignity that became her, "I have tried to be as courteous as possible all the time when you have spoken evil of me, but when you begin to insult my wonderful father, I will not be silent! I can't help thinking that if some of the other girls here who pretend to be so very cultured had been brought up by my father they would show a great deal more respect to *you,* for instance, than they do!"

Miss Persons froze. But all she replied was,

"That will do, Miss Nielson. You may go now." And then she pretended to turn back to her desk work.

Jan marched out of the office with her pretty head held high. She was immediately joined in the hall by several girls who had discussed the events of the night before until the wee small hours, and had decided that in view of everything, they would transfer their allegiance from Audrey Clawson to Janette Nielson. After all, Janette was far more interesting, and she was bound to be more popular after her daring feat last night. Besides, she wore simply enchanting clothes. Her aunt must be immensely rich. It would be worthwhile to get in on the ground floor with Janette and possibly be invited to the fine big stone house for festivities some time. Not only that, but all of them had learned that the handsome young minister at the First Church where most of the nicest girls attended, was quite intimate at the Fetters', having been there twice within the first week he was in town.

Jan had a strong desire to throw up the whole thing and go

back home to her father and her old life. Yet she had a deep contempt for a quitter. She had given her word to her father the night they had decided that she must go, and she meant to stick it out if it was humanly possible, no matter how unpleasant it might be. So in the days which followed she read her little Book still more, and plodded on, deciding that it might be well to try praying again, since it had worked so well that evening.

Chapter 12

DOCTOR ENDICOTT WAS tired. He had performed six major operations that day. He felt as if he deserved some pleasant relaxation. So he drove a mile out of his way to stop at his friend George Sommers' house. No doubt he would be asked to stay to dinner and perhaps George's charming daughter would be there. Doctor Endicott was in his sixties, but he had not lost his lifelong interest in pretty girls. Each of his two wives had disappointed him. One had gone off with another woman's husband, and the second one had nagged him and then disgraced his name by bringing out in court her ridiculous accusation against him of mental cruelty. All of his friends, of course, knew better than to take her seriously. He had not heard of her for some years now. He did not miss her. In fact, he liked the freedom of being without a wife. There was nobody to accuse him of philandering with the pretty nurses now. That had always been so annoying.

He was a short man, rather plump, with white hair and a shiny tight pink skin and small very bright eyes. He was known far and wide as one of the best surgeons in the east. His fees were enormous. He enjoyed his work but he felt that it was time to begin to slow down and feast on some of the fruit of his labors. So he had selected Andrew Hightower as the most promising young doctor in view and he meant to train him and attach him if possible.

When he arrived at the Sommers' front door, he was told by the butler that nobody was at home except Miss Sommers. Doctor Endicott smiled and said he would be glad to have a few moments with Miss Sommers if she were so inclined.

Just then Lucile herself came flitting across the hallway and caught sight of him.

"Oh, Doctor Endicott! How delightful," she smiled charmingly putting out both hands to him. "You have come to take dinner with me, haven't you! I'm all alone tonight and I was just getting desperate. I can't stand to be alone. Do come in. Henry, take Doctor Endicott's coat and tell Essie to set another place for him."

Lucile was nearly as tall as the doctor and her rosy mouth was almost on a level with his as she smiled into his face and said,

"Let's go into the library. It's so much more cosy there." She flung open the door and showed a warm bright fire on the hearth and a large comfortable divan in front of it.

She took the doctor's arm and drew him into the room.

A gleam came into his eyes and he reached for her soft bare arm.

"Come here, you little darling," he cried laughingly. "You're just as beautiful as ever, aren't you? More so, I believe. Give your old 'Uncle Doctor' a kiss, child. Do you remember how you used to call me that?"

She accepted his caress with a little laugh and gave him a pat on his shiny pink cheek.

"You don't look old enough to be my uncle now that I'm grown up," she told him flatteringly.

He straightened himself and looked pleased.

"What! With this white hair of mine?" he laughed. "I declare, though, I still don't feel my age. If it weren't for the color of my hair, I believe I would make a try at getting a certain promising doctor's young lady away from him, how about it?" He laughed again and patted her arm.

"Well," said Lucile, cocking her pretty head on one side as she stood before him where he sat on the couch, "how would it be to dye it?" She gave a coquettish little wink as if she might be willing to consider him in the same class as Andrew Hightower.

"Oh, you little minx," he cried. "Come, sit here on my knee the way you used to do when you were a little girl!" He drew her down to his knee and kissed her again.

She put both her dainty hands on his shoulders and held him off after the kiss, making a remark about her childhood when he used to have some sweet in his pocket for her.

Henry came in a few moments later and announced dinner, and the doctor took her arm in an intimate clasp and escorted her out to the dining room.

They had a gay time of it, bantering back and forth. After dinner at which plenty of drink had been served, Doctor Endicott sat close to Lucile on the couch again before the fire. They talked of Andrew Hightower.

"I really am very anxious to have that young man of yours, my dear," said the Doctor seriously. "That is one reason why I stopped in here tonight. I thought I might possibly find him here. I would like to solicit the interest of one of your family to intercede in my behalf. You see, there are two others of my colleagues who wish to have a young fellow to turn over some of their work to, and both have expressed an interest in him."

Lucile's big blue eyes were wide open with an innocent pleased look but they narrowed slightly as he talked on.

"Now this is just between you and me, darling," he said, turning to face her. One arm was across the back of the couch behind her. Now and then he stroked her hand as it lay near him.

She let him hold her hand as he liked, for she was anxious to hear what he was saying. This sort of talk was just what interested her. It had a great deal to do with her own future. So she turned her blue gaze flatteringly upon the old man.

He crossed one short leg over the other and that brought him still nearer to her. He leaned toward her as he talked and Lucile shrank from his heavy breath, but what he had to say was too important to let a thing like that hinder.

"Now what I have in mind, my dear, is to secure your assistance in persuading Andrew to give up his ultra-philanthropic ideas. I don't believe anyone but you can do it, for you must know that he fairly worships the ground that you walk on."

Lucile blushed, smiled and raised her eyelashes at him side-wise.

"I don't blame him a bit, you understand!" he assured her giving another squeeze to her hand. "But as I said, he is difficult, once he gets his mind set. Of course that makes him all the more valuable. I don't have any use for a vacillating character. If a man isn't headstrong he's weak, I always say. But a woman has ways," he winked slyly at her and gave a coarse chuckle, "influence, we'll call it, to get a man to see things a little differently. As you probably know, Andy is hipped on the idea of helping poor young teen-agers to better things." Doctor Endicott let the tinge of a sneer creep into his tone. "Of course that is all very praiseworthy in him, makes a more sympathetic bedside manner, if you know what I mean," he laughed. "But it can obsess a man so much that it spoils his own chances, and then, I say, of what use can he be to his teen-agers? He'll have no money or influence to help them any more. Do you see my point?"

Lucile nodded and they talked on for some time before he finally gave her another affectionate pat and departed.

Lucile laughingly blew him a kiss as he drove off but she went in again and sat by the fire thinking for a long time. Then with a little confident smile she started upstairs to get a good night's rest in order to be looking her best for the next evening when she expected Andrew Hightower to call.

But Andy had been busy that evening probing for a bullet in Danny Severy's shoulder, and setting the bone in Danny Severy's leg.

"Lord, it seems strange," he said in his heart, "that this boy should come under my care again. I believe You really want me to do something for him. I started to try to find him before, but I didn't do it. I got too busy with my own interests. I'm sorry now, Lord. Maybe he wouldn't have gotten into all this trouble if I had. Forgive me, Lord, and give me a chance with him again." A gentle humble look was on his face, the kind of look that made all the nurses adore him.

Then to the attendant nurse he said, "We'll put the patient in a private room tonight. I'll see to that. I'll be in in the morning."

On the way home, Andy felt heavily the guilt of his failure to hunt up Danny as he had intended to do that summer when he had found out what the boy was doing. He knew that it was dangerous business for a man to meddle with those gangs of youngsters in the city. They were well organized and utterly lawless. And it was still more dangerous to meddle with the drug-smuggling business. There were more vicious, more clever, older minds behind that than any youngsters'; men who might be far more influential with the courts than a mere young medico. But it was not the danger that had hindered him. He realized that he had allowed Lucile to take up all his spare time. He had persuaded himself that he had been too busy to look up Danny.

As he drove along through the cold night he began to pray aloud. "Lord, You know I don't want to choose the easy way. I told You that a long time ago. I want You to take my life and use it any way You want to. Maybe I've been sort of taking it back again lately. If I have, forgive me, Lord. I don't want to do that. I want You to make my will Yours. And, Lord, if You want me to talk about You to that beautiful, wonderful girl, show me what to say. Don't let my love for her get in the way of anything You want me to do. I *mean* that, Lord."

The old question which he had started to bring up to Lucile several times pushed its way into his consciousness now as if it were a personality seated there in the car beside him. He knew that that question must be settled soon, one way or another. But his mind flew back to poor Danny's problem now. He was not quite ready for that other one. It hit too close to his heart and he was tired tonight, too tired to be able to consider it squarely. He must wait until he could think more clearly. So the question sat still in the car there and waited for him.

Still he prayed on: "And help Danny, Lord. Make him well

again, and let me introduce him to his Saviour. *Please* give me another chance, Lord."

But it was the next afternoon before he found time to see Danny. And the boy was in no condition to be talked to. He had a high fever, and he moaned in his stupor. He called out for Jan over and over again. Andy felt even more conscience-stricken than he had the night before. What if the boy did not pull through? As far as he knew, Danny had never even heard of salvation from sin through a Saviour. Maybe he himself was the only person Danny had ever met who knew that Saviour well. And he had failed!

Andy sat a long time that afternoon watching his patient and as he watched he was reviewing his own life as he had lived it the last few months. When he finally got into his car and went home to dress for his evening with Lucile, he found that same old question sitting there beside him, patiently waiting to be considered. He knew that he could not keep it waiting much longer.

As he left the house he paused and looked back at his father and mother sitting there before the fire. He would like to ask them to be praying for him and Lucile. He had a feeling that tonight was to be a difficult time. But he was shy about mentioning his problem. He could not bear even to breathe a hint that perhaps his beautiful girl did not see eye to eye with him in everything. So instead he asked prayer for Danny:

"That young fellow I picked up on the street two or three years ago, the one who fell off a plank riding a bicycle, remember? He is in the hospital again. He got into trouble with the law. I'm afraid he's going to have a pretty bad time of it. I wish you two would be praying for him. I'm sure he doesn't know the Lord and he's too sick yet to talk to. Thanks, folks." He smiled, a little solemnly his mother thought, as he closed the door behind him.

"There's something else on his mind besides a sick boy," his mother said after he had gone. "Didn't you notice how serious he was at the table, Eric? Oh, I do hope he won't get in too deep with that scheming hussy before he comes to his senses!"

"Why, Mother," rebuked her husband gently, with a teasing smile, "what makes you think the girl is a scheming hussy?"

"Oh, I don't have any reason to think so, but I just know she is. You know our Andrew never cared much to go with girls."

"But Mother, Andrew is grown up now, it is reasonable to suppose that at his age he will begin to think of marrying. Why, you would be distressed if you thought that he was to go alone through life. Think how lonely it would be for him after we are gone."

"Yes I know, Father, but it's not like Andrew to pick out a high society girl on his own account. She has gone after him and no mistake. You mark my words. And if she has a grain of sense in her pretty blond head she won't easily let him go, either."

The father made no answer and both of them fell into a thoughtful silence, which turned into earnest prayer for the boy who meant so much to them both; and then they prayed for Danny.

But Andrew, on his way to Lucile, groaned as he entered into battle with his soul.

Chapter 13

LUCILE WAS LOOKING especially charming as she opened the door to her lover.

She was wearing a gown of soft blue that matched her eyes. It was of sheerest chiffon, made with little girlish looking ruffles of blue and white about the low round neck and encircling the pink smooth tops of her plump shoulders. It was the dress that she had worn the night that Andy had told her he loved her and sealed his words with their first kiss. He had often spoken of how sweet she had looked in the dress that night and had asked her to wear it again for him sometime.

So she had put it on although normally she would have discarded it weeks ago as "an old rag." She knew that Andrew liked it because it made her look sweet and innocent and that was what she intended to be tonight.

She smiled and put up her lips to be kissed as he came in, as if she were eager for his caress. She had toned down her lipstick, for she knew that Andy did not care for "greasy-looking red-mouthed hussies."

"We will have the whole evening to ourselves tonight, dearest," she told him with the light in her eyes that told him she was just for him.

The same old thrill took hold of Andy as it always did when he came into her presence, the wonder that God could have made anything so exquisite, and made it for him!

But tonight it was as if another Presence entered the mansion with him. At first he thought that the Presence was only that same old question that had waited beside him in the car and he felt a little irritation. He wished he could have at least his first few minutes with Lucile alone to himself without any other presence, seen or unseen, to mar the ecstatic joy of holding her once more in his arms.

But he could not shake off the sense of Someone else at his side, the feeling that he had not come to that house alone this night. It gave a seriousness to his smile and a quietness to his greeting, so that after a few minutes Lucile noticed it and began to chide him. She drew him down on the couch and laid her bright head on his shoulder. Then she began to stroke his face with her soft fragrant little hand. It stirred him tumultuously.

"Why so solemn tonight, darling?" she asked him. "Did something go wrong today?" She spoke gently, trying to prove to him that she was sympathetic with his work and understood the great responsibilities of a doctor's life. Ordinarily she might have made some flippant quip to rally him on taking his mistakes too seriously. But tonight she was trying to fall in with his mood.

Rather startled that she might have read his thoughts, he took a deep breath and tried to shake off the concern he felt.

"Oh, not wrong exactly," he smiled down at her. "A young fellow who was brought in last night to have his leg mended and a bullet taken out of him isn't doing so well as I had hoped."

"Oh my word! How did he come to be in such bad shape?"

Andy sighed and looked troubled again, even as he thrilled to her nearness.

"He had been tangled up with one of those teen-age gangs I told you about, and got himself into trouble with the law this time. Even if he gets well I don't know how he is going to escape jail or at least reform school."

"Well, why should he?" retorted Lucile. "I should think jail was the place for him! Or better still, why shouldn't such people just be allowed to die? The world would be better off and he certainly couldn't prefer to live, I should think, if he knew that he might have to spend his life in jail!"

Her small rosy lips drew taut in a prim line that took away from her soft charm and Andrew frowned a little and turned his eyes away. He could not bear to see any fault in her. He must try to explain. She would understand. It was just that she had been so sheltered. She had no idea of what odds a boy like Danny had to fight against.

With a gentleness born of pity Andy drew her closer and tried to make her see.

"Lucile," he began, "you have always had everything you wanted or needed all your life. I know it is hard for you to see from the standpoint of a poor child who has never had anything. Just imagine how you would feel if you had never had a warm bright home to come to at night. Suppose your parents were practically never home all your young life. You got some scraps to eat when and where you could find them. Your father, when he did come, was drunk and beat you. Perhaps your mother was drunk half the time too. With a background like that, don't you suppose that if somebody offered you something to do that would bring in quite a bit of money, and painted a picture of ease and wealth to you, that you would be inclined to take the chance of a run-in with the law and try it? Remember these kids have never had any teaching at home about right or wrong."

As he talked on Lucile clasped his arm close, clinging to him like a child, and her big blue eyes filled with tears. Charming tears they were, and Andy had to take out his big fine linen handkerchief and wipe them away, planting a kiss where they had been.

"I knew you would feel that way if you could understand about those poor kids," he said, tingling with the ecstasy of being so near to her. It was a great relief to find that she really had the sympathy he had hoped she had. Suddenly he determined to bring up the question then and there. She was in a softened mood, and was really seeing things as he saw them.

He looked long into her eyes, with the sweet serious look that sometimes frightened her, but she dropped her lashes and then smiled up at him again.

"Lucile, darling," he began in a low intimate tone, "there's something I have wanted to ask you for a long time."

Her blue eyes fluttered up to his again and then dropped shyly. It was coming, then, his actual proposal of marriage. She had been waiting for it, for so far he had only told her he loved her; he had not actually asked her to set a wedding date. Perhaps he was going to find out what she thought about Doctor Endicott's proposal. If he accepted it they could be married right away. She began to breathe a little excitedly as she waited, gazing up adoringly.

But still Andy hesitated, looking down and away from her.

"It's about something that means more to me than anything else in life," he said slowly.

Oh, she was right, then! Their marriage!

He took one of her hands in his gently and held it like a treasure.

"Of course I know you go to church and all that, dear," he said apologetically, "but I have often wondered whether you really know the Lord Jesus Christ as your own personal Saviour, and love Him as I have learned to do."

With a disappointed impatient jerk Lucile snatched her hand away and pouted her rosy lips.

"Oh, Andrew Hightower!" she exclaimed angrily. "What a dull subject to bring up on our one evening together for maybe weeks. If you are going to turn our nice time into a holy-roller revival service I think we might better have gone to a show. For heaven's sake cut it out. You're too religious already. Let's be human for tonight, at least."

There was a contemptuous sneer on her pretty face that cut Andy to the heart. It was as if his question was standing there in cold triumph saying "I told you so!"

"Oh, darling!" he cried, putting his arm about her and drawing her near again from the corner of the couch where she had shrunk from him. "You don't realize how wonderful the Lord can be to you or you wouldn't call Him a dull subject. Just tell me, sweetheart, that you do really trust Him as your Saviour. I want to hear you say it." He looked her clearly in the eyes, a great longing in his own.

Somewhat mollified and remembering her intention to live up tonight to what Andy seemed to want of her, Lucile answered, a little pettishly.

"Of course, I do, Andy. You know we have always gone to church. But it doesn't seem to me that religion is a subject to talk about with your best girl in front of the firelight!" She made an attempt at a laugh. "That is, if I am your best girl." She glanced at him slyly, with her dimple in evidence.

For answer he held her close again and kissed her full on her lips. He was almost swept off his feet by the wild thrill of holding her and every little move she made seemed to electrify him anew. Yet in his mind he was more confused than ever. His question seemed to keep prodding him insistently, as if to say, "I am not settled yet." And then he was aware again of that Other, that Presence who had entered the house with him, who was standing aside now, waiting as if in long-suffering understanding sorrow, until Andy should come to himself once more.

It was almost a fierce kiss he gave to Lucile as he let her go at last, and he was displeased with himself for so nearly losing control of his own emotions. It was her little caresses, so light and yet so intimate and alluring, suggesting such a world of pleasures yet to be tasted, that had thrown him off his usual balance.

"Now," smiled Lucile, her own sweet dimpling self again, "now that you have settled your religious old conscience, let's talk about us." She snuggled down beside him again, and clung to his arm with that little childish gesture that made him feel he would like to hide her within his heart and protect her from every harm. But he was still stirred up and could not seem to find the way to peace in his mind.

"Tell me," she coaxed, "what Doctor Endicott was talking to you about yesterday morning when I passed you both in the hospital."

"Oh, just an idea he has."

"What idea?" she urged. "About you?"

"Well, yes," Andy reluctantly admitted. "He has suggested it before, but I have never felt I was ready for it myself. He seems to think he wants me to go in with him, and take over his practice when he retires." Andy spoke casually, as if his thoughts were somewhere else.

But Lucile gave a little cry of delight, and squeezed Andy's arm.

"Oh, *Andy!* How perfectly wonderful!" she cried, as if she had not had a hint of such a thing. "Why, that would start you off without all the long waiting to build up a practice that most young doctors have to go through."

"I suppose it would," agreed Andy still without interest. He looked down in Lucile's happy face and thought what a sweet child she was. It would be wonderful, he thought, to be the one to lead her along in the precious things of God, through all of life's deep experiences!

But Lucile had no thought of being led along, and all the experiences she wanted from life were gay ones, like the frosting on a cake.

"Oh, when are you to begin?" she asked eagerly, starting already to plan how soon they might set the wedding date.

Andy looked at her as if he had only just put his mind on the subject.

"Begin? Oh, I don't know that I shall begin. In fact, I don't have much intention of going in with Doctor Endicott."

"Oh, *Andy!* How perfectly insane! How *could* you pass up a chance like that? Or—" she thought an instant, her canny mind jumping even higher in the scale of honors for the man she had chosen, "do you have an offer that is still better?" she queried giving him a keen look. "Because, you know," she flattered, "*I* don't think *any* honor is too great for my Andrew!"

He smiled deprecatingly, then he thought a moment.

"Yes," he said at last, "I do have a better offer." She gasped with delight. "From One," he went on, "infinitely greater than Doctor Endicott, much as I respect his professional skill."

He smiled again at her and a deep steady fire seemed to glow in his eyes. To the girl who admired him he seemed like a god, with that look in his eyes and the firelight blazing across the waves of his cleanly cut gold hair.

"Oh-h-h!" she breathed. "Tell me about it." Her promise to Doctor Endicott went by the boards as one not to be considered if something greater offered itself.

Andy turned and studied the girl beside him a long moment, trying to read what depth lay behind those blue childlike eyes. At last he said,

"I'd like to, sometime. I wonder whether you would see it as I do."

"Of course I would, dearest," she assured him. "You know I want the best for you."

"Well, I will, then," he decided impulsively, releasing her and clasping his hands about his crossed knees as if he were about to give himself to something more serious than love-making.

He gazed into the fire intently and the girl beside him waited in tense eagerness. She saw that it was no time to hasten him. She was content to wait for him to tell her his great news. Her eyes shone in anticipation of the plans they would make. She could picture herself the wife of the famous Doctor Andrew Hightower, "the young doctor who has lately" so and so. There was no limit to her imagination of the honors that might come to him and to herself as his wife.

Thoughtfully he began, unaware of the reason for his reluctance to state at last in words the vision that had been taking more and more possession of him lately. He searched for words and phrases that would touch the responsive chord that he thought he had seen in Lucile a few moments ago.

"Can you imagine that boy I told you about," he said slowly, "multiplied by scores? Since I have been at this hospital I have tended many of them. Sometimes at night their faces seem to be massed together before me, their hungry wistful eyes looking for somebody, somewhere, to care about them. And then I seem to see their eyes grow slowly defiant as, searching and searching for a meaning to their lives, they find none. And I am amazed as I realize that no man cares for their souls, or their bodies either. So they have to look after themselves, and they band together in gangs, to fight their way through life, desperately trying this and that to find something to satisfy them, something to fill that empty place which has never been filled by parents' love, or by childish fun."

Andy was speaking out of his heart now and Lucile recognized that. She grew angry and resentful but she was too canny to let him see it. He must be won some other way than by a blaze of scorn. She forced herself to control her distaste of the subject and wait for him to finish. Perhaps someone actually had offered some grand plan that would solve the civic problem of uncared-for children and make famous the one who worked it out. Her lips were tight and hard, but she was quiet.

Fortunately Andy was still staring into the fire, seeing those hungry faces before him. It was as if he had forgotten she was there. He had never opened his heart to her in this way before. Why, she thought, he was positively eloquent! Of course it was wonderful of him to care so much for such outcasts, but she must see to it that he did not carry it too far.

"Of course," Andy went on, "you and I know there is only one solution for such youngsters and that is the Lord Jesus Christ Himself. It might take one man all his lifetime to win even a few, but I feel more and more that the chance to do just that is being offered to me. It would be a great task. It would take all a man's strength and courage and patience to do it, but—" he suddenly turned to her and smiled his radiant smile. "I'd *love* to do it!"

He searched deep into her eyes then to see if he could find an answering longing there to share in the tremendous work of reclamation that was beckoning him.

He saw only rosy lips pursed in an attempt at a smile, and blue eyes coolly estimating in terms of fur coats and diamonds the value of what he was saying.

He sighed with disappointment. She had not caught his vision. She did not see what he had tried to make her see. Well, of course he must be patient with her. She had not come to grips with poverty and sin and neglect as he had. Her light tasks at a receptionist's desk in the hospital did not show her the seamy side of the cases that came in.

He tried again as she obviously waited for him to explain further.

"Can't you see," he urged gently, "what it would mean at the end of our lives if we could look back and realize that even a few of those kids were on their way to Heaven instead of hell because we were willing to *love* them enough to win them and make them listen to the good news that their sins have been accounted for on the Cross? I have lots of plans in mind. They come clearer the more I think of it. But do you see how God Himself seems to be offering me the chance to take on a work like this that nobody else is bothering with in this city? It would have to be more than mere occupational therapy, you know. Games and fun, or even fascinating constructive work will not change a boy's heart, but those things may interest him and give us a chance to tell him of the One who can come into his heart and give him a new nature."

He turned again eagerly to her, sure that she could not have failed to catch at least a gleam of his own vision.

But her blue eyes were hard as she spoke in a tone that cut like a steel blade.

"That is certainly a praiseworthy and philanthropic plan, Doctor Hightower," she said mockingly. "There is only one thing the matter with it as I see it. I am wondering just where you would expect to go to draw your salary for a magnanimous work of that sort! And do you think the salary would be commensurate with the self-sacrifice involved?"

Andy felt suddenly deflated. All at once he saw himself as he would be if he did this thing, simply a poor struggling doctor with frayed shirt cuffs and too little sleep.

"Oh," he grinned awkwardly, "I know it wouldn't amount

to much financially. I would have to be just a good old-fashioned 'family doctor,' you know, in order to win my way with the kids and their families, for of course getting the kids started off on the right track would mean in most cases getting the families saved and living right too. Otherwise the kids would just have to be taken out of the community entirely, until they were established. But I have a little left me by my uncle, you know," he added humbly, "enough to live on comfortably. Enough for two, in fact, with care."

The boyish humble, wistful look he gave her then would have melted any but a very hard heart. Lucile merely laughed; a little light, contemptuous laugh, saying,

"Don't look at *me* when you say 'we' in a proposition like that. If that's the kind of life you are planning you had better find a long-faced welfare woman to share your lot. But seriously, Andy," she laid her hand caressingly on his arm again and stroked him as he always loved to have her do, "let's skip this idealizing and get down to brass tacks. You know as well as I do that a man can't get anywhere in this world if he is going to sacrifice everything to sentiment. It's all very well to give to charity and probably Father would like to hear about your project and help too. But don't you realize that you would have far more means to do what you want to and support a work such as you dream of if you took Doctor Endicott's offer and made enough so that you wouldn't have to be cramped in your plans? Think what good a man like you could do with a lot of money!"

Lucile paused to let her logic sink in, feeling that she had scored a high point in her last remark.

Andy looked questioningly at her, sighed and turned again to the fire as he said, "Oh, yes, I know it would take money to do some of the things I have in mind, but surely there would be some interested party who would help."

"*Andy!* You are certainly more independent than that! I never thought to hear *you planning* to take charity!"

"Why, that wouldn't be charity for *me!*" he laughed. "It would be for the boys."

"Oh, but don't you see? You wouldn't want to go begging. Why not make your own money and plenty of it, then you could do as you like and there would be no strings to it."

"Well, that would be nice," he admitted, suddenly feeling weary. "But I don't think one could do both. Each job would take a man's whole life."

"But you could make the money and hire someone else to do the work with the boys. That's what I meant. And you know you are fitted for great things in the medical world. You are not cut out to be a reformer except as you dream up the ideas. Let someone else who can't do the work you can, do the 'dirty work' with the youngsters."

Andy shook his head.

"But that isn't what I want," he objected. "And I think it is not someone else but me whom God is calling to the work."

"Oh, Andy darling!" cried Lucile, taking his face between her perfumed hands and giving his head a little shake. "You are so incurably religious! Do keep your balance, dear, or you will lose all you have gained by all your hard work so far."

There was a smile on her face but it was not a pretty smile nor a sweet one. There was hardness in it and grim determination in the set of her head. Never would she let her Andy get himself involved in such a silly notion as he had set forth just now. It was shocking to think that he had allowed himself to get so unbalanced as even to consider it. He would take careful handling, but Lucile felt that she was the one to handle him. She probably would have to handle him carefully all her life, but it would be worth it, for Doctor Andrew Hightower was going to be a name that would carry great weight in high circles, if Lucile Sommers had anything to do with his future.

Andy only sighed in a tired way and kissed her tenderly.

Just then the butler appeared and called Andy to the telephone. When he returned it was with a troubled face.

"The youngster I told you about is worse," he said. "I'll have to go right away."

Lucile pouted.

"I'm sorry," said Andy as nearly annoyed with her as he ever had been. Then he drew on his gloves and kissed her good night once more, adding: "You be thinking over the plan I told you about, won't you? And, pray about it, dear! I'm sure you will see it then."

He went out into the cold and dark, leaving Lucile standing in the warm hall looking after him defiantly, a grim confident smile on her red lips.

Chapter 14

JAN WAS COUNTING the days until Christmas. She was planning
to leave Oak Hill on the very first train that she could get as
soon as school was out, and get home to her father and the
river, and Danny, and all the dear home scenes that had made
up her life until this fall. She found it hard to keep her excitement to herself for Aunt Myra noted every sign of it and made
some cutting remark calculated to embarrass her. Mealtimes
were most difficult. It seemed there was no topic of conversation
that would not stir up trouble.

Shortly before she left for the train her Aunt Myra came up
to her room with a triumphant air to tell her that she was
wanted on the telephone.

"It's Professor Morelli, my dear," she said, with a sort of
triumph in her tone. Jan hastened down stairs with a vague foreboding. She was familiar with Aunt Myra's slight changes in
tone of voice.

But she was more than a little thrilled at the message. The
Van Ordens, who owned an enormous estate on the river, were
giving a big Christmas party on the Wednesday evening after
Christmas, and the violinist they had engaged had been taken
sick. Would Jan be willing to take his place? Professor Morelli,
her teacher, had recommended her highly. It would be a wonderful experience and splendid publicity for her. The honorar-
ium offered was to be fifty dollars.

Jan gasped. With that amount promised she could actually
go ahead and get the overcoat she had wanted for her father
for Christmas.

Swallowing down a stab of disappointment realizing that if

she promised to take this engagement it would cut short her long anticipated week with her father, Jan consented.

But all the way home on the train she argued with herself as to whether it had been worth it. It never occurred to her that perhaps her father, too, would have preferred her company for the three or four extra days to the new overcoat. He never took much space in his letters telling her how desolate he was without her. There was always the simple statement, "I miss you," but that was all.

She reached home at last, and after the first excitement was over and John had begun to get used to his young lady daughter, she explained to her father about the playing and how important it was that she go back for it. He hid the pain of his chagrin from her, for he would not hinder her musical success for any sentiment of his own. But the shadow of the early parting was over them both all the short time they had together, and John could not help the feeling that Myra had begun her deadly work already. Especially when a long distance call came through Monday night from Aunt Myra, commanding Jan's presence back at Oak Hill on Tuesday instead of Wednesday morning.

"The dressmaker says she cannot possibly have your new evening gown ready for Wednesday night unless you are home Tuesday," stated Myra as if that settled it.

"Oh, Aunt Myra!" cried Jan in dismay. "It seems as if I had only just got here. Let the dress go then, I'll wear my old one."

"Impossible!" cut in Aunt Myra's icy voice. "I would be ashamed to have you appear at the Van Ordens' in that old dress. You will have to come on the early train Tuesday. I have told your uncle to meet you." And Aunt Myra hung up without giving Jan a chance to argue any more.

With distress in her face Jan turned to her father and burst into tears. But he soon soothed her and assured her that now he had seen her and they had had Christmas Day together, it was only right that she should go back and do as her aunt wished. After all, it was Aunt Myra who was buying the dress and Jan must show her at least the courtesy due her generosity.

But John never let his daughter know how disconsolate the shortness of her visit left him, or how desperate he felt at the thought that Aunt Myra could command her as if she were no longer his. Bravely he finished the last precious day with her and saw her off in the morning with many signs and protestations of her love for him ringing in his ears.

Jan had wanted to look up Danny while she was there, especially because she had not heard from him since that dire day when he had been to see her. But she had been down three times to the Severys' kitchen door and knocked and knocked but there was no answer. Someone said that Danny had not been around for two or three weeks. It was rumored that he was either in jail or in the hospital. Nobody seemed to know which. So Jan's heart was very heavy as she settled down in her seat on the train.

The truth was that Danny had been so impressed by the change in Jan when he had seen her at Oak Hill that it had frightened him at first, and then he had made up his mind that if he was not to lose her entirely he must acquire sufficient funds to dress as stylishly as she did and learn how to walk with as much poise and assurance. So he had plunged into his late activities with more fervor than ever, until he had made a misstep and landed in the hospital where Andy was again ministering to him.

He had been there nearly a week and Christmas Day had come and gone without his consciousness of it when he awoke one morning with a clear mind. Perhaps the absence of the strong narcotics he had been indulging in recently had helped to bring him back to himself. Or perhaps the prayers of Doctor Andy and his devoted parents, who took every one of their son's patients to the Throne of God daily and sometimes hourly, had carried him through the really serious fever and brought him out on what seemed a clear level plain of understanding such as he had not known for months.

When Doctor Andy came in that morning he found Danny looking anxiously for him. The boy made a pathetic sight.

His thick brown waves of hair were tossed and his pale, thin face looked white enough to be more dead than alive. But his big brown eyes were alert and they held a great anxiety.

Still he did not speak first, although Andy had a feeling that there were questions he was longing to ask.

Andy sat down gently by the bed and told the nurse he would not be needing anything just yet. He wanted a chance to talk to the boy alone. He had kept him in the private room at his own expense all these days just so that he might have an opportunity to talk quietly with him when the time came.

"You've had some tough going, Danny boy," he said tenderly. If the lad had been his own brother his tone could not have been more loving. Danny gave him a surprised, suspicious look.

"I'm glad you're better, son," Andy went on with a smile.

Danny gave a weak grunt, but did not smile.

"I almost thought for a while there that you were not going to be here with us any more." Andy spoke as if he cared, and the boy glanced at him in amazement.

Andy kept his finger unostentatiously on the boy's pulse, surprised to find it so strong and steady. He must be a tough little fellow to stand all that he had gone through, besides the mental strain that had troubled him through his delirium.

"Woulda been a lot better if I had corked off!" growled Danny scowling.

"No, don't look at it that way, son," said Andy. "You wouldn't want to go just yet. Why, you wouldn't get any crown yet, would you?"

Danny looked at his doctor with a puzzled frown.

"Wadd'r ya handin' me?" He questioned insolently.

Andy smiled his most winning smile, praying silently for guidance in what to say to this forlorn waif.

"I wondered if you knew about the crowns," he laughed mischievously.

"Naw!" responded Danny grouchily.

"You never heard that the Lord Jesus Christ offers rewards He calls "crowns" for our service to Him?"

Danny turned his head away and made an ugly noise.

"Of course you don't get to try for them unless you belong to Him," Andy added, paying no attention to Danny's rudeness. "But, boy oh boy! It's great enough just to know Him and know your sins are all gone, without looking for anything more. That's the way I figure things. Do you know Him?"

Danny was listening but he had not taken the scowl off his face.

"I don't know what yer talkin' about!" he mumbled. "I wish I had a stick!" he burst out.

Andy had not been in contact with the scores of young boys in the neighborhood without learning some of their lingo. He knew what they called their marihuanas.

"Not on the doctor's list," he laughed. Then he rose. He decided that Danny had had enough talk for a while. Let him rest and ponder if he would. Perhaps tomorrow he would soften up enough to ask a question or two.

"Time you had a fresh dressing on this shoulder," he said with a professional air, as he stepped to the door and called the nurse. "Another time we'll have to go into the subject of those crowns. God has brought you back, son, and not for nothing. Maybe you'll have a chance to win one yet." He smiled again and Danny gave another discontented grunt.

But Danny was not ungrateful for the young doctor's interest in him. He did a good deal of thinking that day, between begging the nurse to get him cigarettes, and cursing his weakness and the heavy cast on his leg, the pain in his shoulder and the awful headache that hammered at him.

When Andy came the next day Danny half hoped he would begin to talk again. There was something intriguing about the thought that he might yet amount to something. If only to show Jan that he could be somebody, too. The change in her had hit him hard. Andy's remarks had brought the first ray of hope to his heart since he had begun to grow up.

Andy entered his room with a prayer in his heart and a secret thankfulness that he had a father and mother who he was sure were praying at that moment for him and for the boy who had probably never had a prayer offered for him by anyone else in all his life.

Danny's eyes quickly veiled their eagerness as he came in. It was the way of a gang member to hide all possible sign of emotion or interest in life.

Andy sat down and put his hand on the pulse again.

"You're doing all right, pal," he smiled.

"When can I get outa here?" snapped Danny.

Andy laughed.

"Take it easy now, son! Just keep your shirt on. Not tomorrow or next day, anyway. You'll be a lot better off staying here until you're strong enough to use your two good legs."

Although Andy had had no thought of suggesting that Danny try to run away as soon as he got out, Danny was so constantly aware of his precarious standing with the law that he suspected a reference to his crime in every remark. He wondered how much Doctor Andy knew about what brought him here, but his pride would not allow him to ask.

So Danny shot a startled glance at his doctor when he mentioned two good legs. All legs were for, in Danny's estimation, was escape.

Andy did not miss the alarm in the boy's face and realized instantly what he had said. But he made nothing of it. He simply went on with his routine examination.

"Yes, there are better things in store for you, son, than you have any idea of. Just be patient a little while." That was all he said that day.

But the following day Danny broke the ice himself. He had puzzled and puzzled over what the doctor could have meant about better things. Either the man didn't know that it was the cops who had shot him, or by some marvelous chance the law had missed fire in his case. He felt he had to know.

"What'd you mean, better things ahead?" he asked almost humbly.

"Just what I said," replied Andy, apparently busy with his dressings.

Danny waited as long as he could. If there was good news, he had to have it. He had writhed and twisted in his mind, worrying about the clutches of the law these last weeks until he was fairly desperate to know his fate.

"I don't see how that could be!" he said. He had tried to think of a way to ask more without giving himself away, just in case the doctor really didn't know why he had been shot. He felt that he had stated his thought satisfactorily.

Andy looked up and spoke seriously.

"It couldn't if Somebody hadn't taken your sentence for you!"

Oh! Then Doctor Andy did know! That was a relief. And the reason he was still nice to him instead of being cold and stern was because he was not "wanted" by the law. But why not? And who, *who,* of all the fellows he knew, would care to take his jail term for him? There must be some mistake. It couldn't be as good as that sounded.

"Whaddaya *mean?*" he burst out after he had waited in vain for Andy to explain himself.

Andy smiled one of his special smiles, looking straight into Danny's big eyes that were so wistful and incredulous.

"Why, God didn't send His Son into the world to condemn the world, but that the world through Him might be saved. He died in your place, you know."

All Danny took in was the last sentence.

He started up from his bed in alarm.

"Died! Were they goin' to kick me off?" His voice was hoarse with horror. "All I did was tote the stuff, honest! I wasn't even gointa get much of the moolah. They told me if I didn't punk out on this deal they'd see about giving me more gold next time. I didn't handle no rod. Honest I didn't!" He spoke fast and excitedly and his big eyes were wide with fright. Andy gazed back with sorrowful sympathy.

In an effort to get the doctor to speak again, Danny explained further.

"Pad wasn't gointa use the gun, either. Honest, Doc. If he did use it on that rich guy it was only cause he got in a jam. An' *I* didn't even touch it, I swear ta God I didn't. I don't see why they would have *me* up fer that!"

The boy's frenzied hands were clutching the covers and Andy feared his fever might come up again if he were not quieted.

"Calm down, son," said Andy gently. It was pathetic to hear the boy tell so much of the sordid case without even being questioned. "There's nothing for you to fear. I told you, Somebody else took your place, you know, but I wasn't talking about the police courts here. I meant that you have been saved from the sentence of a higher court than that, where God is the judge. Did you ever think about how not just you but *all* the people in the world have sinned against God, pal?" As Andy talked he took Danny's weak skinny clammy hand in his strong warm one and tried to give it a comforting pressure.

The boy's agonized eyes still held fear, but he listened.

"And God said once that the soul that sins *it* must die. That means die forever, in hell, son." Andy's voice was low and calm, with a sorrowful gentleness in it.

"But God didn't want that to happen to the people He had made, so He made a way for them to escape the death sentence. He sent His own Son down here to become a human being so that He could take the punishment in our place. See? Jesus Christ died on the cross for you and me. He hadn't done anything wrong Himself, so He didn't have to die for His own sin the way any ordinary man would. It was all for us. Then because He was sinless He didn't have to stay dead. He rose again, and now He's alive forever. That means our sins—yours and mine and everybody's—are *gone,* pal, all dealt with and put away! I don't know how you feel about it, son, but I have a feeling that I want to give my whole life to serving a God who would do that for me. I've sinned, too, you know."

Danny looked keenly at him, as if to ask, "Did the law get you once? For what?"

Andy smiled and said, "There's a lot of ways of sinning that this world's courts don't call sin, you know."

Danny had nothing to say. He stared and stared at this man who told him things he had never heard of before.

"Of course," went on Andy, "if a fellow prefers to take his own punishment instead of accepting what Jesus Christ did, that's his business. He'll have to go ahead and take it. But I think a guy like that would be a fool, don't you?"

Danny nodded almost unconsciously as he continued to try to puzzle out the meaning of all that Andy had said.

"Now I think you have talked enough for today, pal," said Andy, "and I want you to rest a lot until I come tomorrow and then you can ask any questions you like, about this and your own special trouble, too. But you don't need to be afraid of anything, son. You have friends who are going to stand by you. We'll see you through. Let's just talk to God about it all a minute."

Andy closed his eyes but he spoke in the same conversational tone he had been using, as if he had simply turned to another person in the room.

"Lord," he said, "I'm going to leave this dear boy in your hands to look after tonight. I know how You love him. Speak peace to his heart and teach him to trust You because of what Your Son did for him. Amen."

Danny's eyes were on Andy in solemn amazement. Never in all his life had he been called a dear boy, or told that anyone loved him. There were no words to say. He didn't know whether this kind doctor was out of his head, or what, but it sure did make a warm feeling around his heart to think that maybe somebody cared a little.

After Andy left, he lay a long time thinking with his eyes

closed. The nurse thought he was asleep and let him alone.

And five miles away a gray-haired couple were speeding the recovery of his soul and body by their faithful prayers. But Andy was driving through the dusk toward Lucile Sommers' house.

Chapter 15

JAN HAD TO force back the tears as her train left the station and she caught the last dear glimpse of her father waving so bravely and disconsolately after her. She had a strong desire to rush out to the platform and jump off the train, but she held herself under firm control. She wished she had never promised to play at that Christmas party. She had bought the overcoat for her father on the strength of it but she could see that her being there with him would have meant far more to him than any overcoat.

She was disappointed, too, not to have stayed long enough to hunt up Danny. It troubled her that he had dropped out of the picture. Who would there be, if not herself and her father, to care where he was or what he was doing? She must write and ask Daddy to take pains to hunt him up and let her know his present address.

But even though she had that much settled in her mind, and though the exciting prospect of playing at that important place tomorrow night began to loom enchantingly before her, she still felt an undercurrent of nameless disappointment. Her visit home had not been what she had thought it would be. She had had two good long walks with her father down by the river and out to the park, and she had enjoyed seeing the various changes here and there: new buildings, a new street cut through two blocks from home, a new bridge started over the river; and she had greeted her Mississippi River crack with joy, as well as the dear old ship's lights and her mother's precious screen. Her old room looked good to her still, although she had to admit that it was sadly shabby and bare compared to the dainty splendor of her room at Aunt Myra's. Of course, Daddy didn't have money to spend on things like that, and he wouldn't know how to fix up a girl's room if he had. But dear Daddy, it was good to be with him again. How wonderful it had been to have his arms about her. And how surprised he had been at her looks and her fine clothes! She laughed as she remembered how he had blinked and stared at her at first.

But no, there was something else that lay like a dark shadow of emptiness on her heart. At last, as she went over the things she had planned to do at home and all the people she had meant to see, she realized with a little shock of surprise that that big empty space in her vacation should have been filled by a young doctor with gold hair and a warm smile. All of a sudden she realized that one of the main things she had looked forward to was asking him some questions about what she had been reading in the little Book. She had longed, too, just to see him, and watch for that gentle understanding look in his eyes, maybe have him clasp her hand again with that warm pressure that she had never forgotten.

She sighed. She was surprised to find how very much she had counted on seeing Andrew Hightower. And she had let a mere fifty dollars and a glamorous concert stand in her way! How could she have been so foolish and careless? Why, a few minutes with him seemed now of more value to her than ten thousand dollars or a hundred playing engagements.

Tears of remorse and chagrin welled up and she had to turn her head toward the window to hide them from the fat curious woman who shared her seat.

Now it would be six months, perhaps, before she would have another chance to talk to him! It seemed an eternity.

She told herself she was getting positively silly, longing to see a man who had probably never given her another thought. Very likely he would not even have recognized or remembered her if she had seen him. She was as bad as some of those drippy girls at school who were always gushing over some new man they had met, acting as if they thought he was about to fall head over heels in love with them. But then Jan assured herself that this feeling was nothing of that kind. She did not imagine the man in love with her. But he was like a nice big brother, and she would have liked to ask him those questions. Also, he had spoken once of trying to help Danny in some way. She wondered what he had meant to do, and whether he had ever hunted him up. She thought how fine it would be to be able to give one's life to helping boys and girls like Danny who had never had any love or care at home. Perhaps when she grew up she would be able to help in some such work.

But as the miles flew by, and the next evening's doings began to claim her thoughts more and more, Jan found herself living in the Oak Hill world more than in her old world, and there was a certain spice in the new life that intrigued and enchanted her. She wondered with a little self-conscious smile whether the Reverend Stancel Egbert would be at that Christmas party. The new dress that she was going back to have fitted and finished was going to be most becoming, she knew. It was white with a crimson sash and it set off her white skin and black hair wonderfully. She felt sure and confident about the playing she was to do. Professor Morelli had suggested what she should play and the pieces were all ones that she had learned thoroughly. Nothing very difficult yet: a few soft and tender ones, and one or two gypsy dances which sounded a great deal more technical than they really were. She played with pleasing accuracy and a verve that always attracted her listeners. She had no real fear of the public appearance, only a little excited flutter in the region of her throat as she thought that this particular event might mean that she would soon be well started on a concert career, if these influential people liked her.

And then when the train drew into the station in the city, even before she had stepped off the bottom step, an eager hand reached for her suitcase and she felt someone take her arm. It was not Uncle Duncan, but Stancel Egbert. Her face lighted up with surprise and pleasure. It was nice to have someone care enough to come all the way to the city to meet her!

"Welcome home," he greeted her, taking her arm companionably and steering her over to his car parked in a line with some taxis.

He gave a confident smile to the taxi dispenser as if he were sure that *his* car would not be considered a nuisance, parked where no private car was supposed to be. And sure enough, the man subserviently waved him on with an admiring glance for the handsome young couple.

Jan noticed it and was flattered. It was quite a new thing to her to have a handsome escort who treated her like a princess. He was no callow boy from the alleys of Chester. He was a man perhaps older than Andrew Hightower, yet he found her interesting. She bloomed into smiles as he told her how dead the town had been over Christmas with her away.

"You don't know how I have missed you," he said looking straight into her sparkling black eyes, and she blushed just as he had hoped she would do. It was delightful to awaken into bloom a young bud such as she.

They chattered gaily on the seven miles to Oak Hill. Jan enjoyed the ride. She had expected to have to take the local to Oak Hill and be met by Uncle Duncan. So far she had never been able to get more than a few words at a time out of him. If Aunt Myra was around he always stole a look at her before he said either yes or no to anything. He was not exactly an inspiring companion.

But this man not only flattered her; he was interesting. He liked books, just as Jan did. He had read most of the modern ones, as well as many old classics. He had had the advantage of attending concerts given by the best artists in the world and he talked intelligently of music. Jan drank it in. She was receiving an excellent all-round musical education at her music school, and she was learning to recognize great names in music. Aunt Myra had been taking her to the city once a month for fine orchestra concerts, but next month Aunt Myra had said she had another engagement and she had asked Stan if he would mind escorting her. Oh, Oak Hill life did seem good! Compared to her old life it was like rich frosted cake beside plain brown bread. Sometimes Jan had to admit a longing for the bread, and wondered whether she wouldn't feel better nourished, especially if that bread could be eaten in the company of Andrew Hightower and his dear parents. But being here, Jan enjoyed every bit of the frosting that came her way.

"Am I to have the honor of taking you to the Van Ordens' tomorrow night?" asked Stancel courteously with a complacent smile.

Jan glanced up with a quick look, and dropped her eyes again as she met his admiration.

"That would be very nice," she said demurely. "I didn't know whether there would be anyone there I knew or not. I thought I might feel rather lost among all those strangers."

"I'll see that you don't feel lost," he assured her, patting her hand. "There are some very worth-while people who will be there and it will be my pleasure to introduce you to them. One of the most influential families are members of my church." He spoke with pride. All at once it came to Jan to wonder whether old Doctor Hightower had mentioned the people in his church in that way. Would he have cared whether they were influential in the world or not? It seemed to her as if he might be more interested in how much influence his people had at the Throne of God. But the thought slipped away again as Stan went on telling her about some of the guests who were to grace the Christmas party.

"I'm glad I will be there to steer you around," he said, "for sometimes these parties get a little rough!" He laughed deprecatingly. "But I've made it my business in the short time I've been here to find out a little about who is who. There will be a few newly rich there who are inclined to get a little 'high'; I'm warning you because I don't want you to be shocked. But there are plenty of nice ones, so don't be alarmed."

"Oh!" Jan cried. "Will they *drink* there?"

"I suppose there will be drinks," Stan answered casually. "Most parties do have them. But of course if you don't care to drink you don't have to. If they drink anyone's health you can just raise your glass to your lips with the rest and no one will notice whether you drink or not. But this may be such a large affair that there won't be any toasts. I'll look after you all right."

But Jan looked troubled.

"I didn't realize that *nice* people would drink!" she said. "I've seen it make so much trouble in poor homes, I should think good, rich people wouldn't have anything to do with it."

Stancel Egbert gave a condescending laugh.

"You precious little innocent," he said. "It would certainly be very fine if all people had that much common sense. But I guess we'll have to take the world as we find it and make the best of it. Never mind, no one will notice that you don't drink, I'm sure. And I admire you all the more for sticking to your temperance principles. It's a rare thing to find a girl nowadays who has any. But of course we mustn't carry things like that too far, nor make an issue of them," he added, wondering apprehensively whether this lovely niece of the rich Mrs. Fetter was really as unsophisticated as she sounded, and whether perhaps she might embarrass him before the Van Ordens and others. He must give her a few pointers. But, Gad! she was a stunning child.

They arrived at Aunt Myra's then and Stancel helped Jan out of the car as if she had been a queen. Jan took a deep breath of luxury and liked it as she stepped once more into the spotless cold glamor of Aunt Myra's mansion.

Meanwhile back in the hospital in Chester, Danny was twisting and turning restlessly wondering how long before Doctor Andy would come back.

He had been thinking a great deal, between his spells of desperation over the fact that he wasn't given any cigarettes and couldn't get up to get them himself.

He had at last made up his mind to come out straight and ask Doctor Andy some questions. Doctor Andy was a right sort of guy, he might have known it from that other time. And he had certainly tried to do everything he could for a poor fellow who had got himself into trouble. Danny called him "Doctor Andy" now chummily, just as he had heard the nurses speak of him.

That last talk Doctor Andy had had with him had made a deep impression on Danny. Never in all his life had he heard all that about Somebody who had died for him. It didn't make sense, and yet Doctor Andy seemed to take it seriously. He wondered whether it was that which made Doctor Andy so different from the other doctors around there, different, in fact from anybody else he had ever met, unless perhaps it was the Nielsons. Yes, different even from them. For there was a warmth about this man that drew Danny in spite of himself even though he recognized that he was just a no-account strange boy whom Doctor Andy had picked up on the street. The Nielsons were old friends and sort of pals. Doctor Andy was a perfect stranger on whom Danny had no claim whatever. So he lay and wondered about it all.

It was two weeks after Christmas and the rush of extra sickness that often comes after the holidays had kept Andy so busy that he had had little time to visit with Danny. But he had not forgotten the boy, and his parents had been asking about him, and continued to pray for the poor friendless child. Just that morning Andy's thoughts had been centered on him as his father spoke of him in their family prayers.

"Save that poor boy Danny, Lord, and use him as a means of winning many more such as he."

More than ever the strong desire had taken hold of Andy to throw himself heart and soul into working with young people who had nothing in the way of a home, and no advantages at all; the kind of boys who left school as soon as they could and loafed around in gangs pilfering and playing, wasting their lives, without aim or purpose or reason to exist. In fact Andy had doctored more than one who had tried to take his own life.

He made up his mind to see Danny again that very day. If he could win one boy to begin with, perhaps he could enlist his help in starting some kind of place where the boys could meet and have good wholesome fun, and with it all, hear the good news that their sins were already forgiven by One who died for them. No heathen in the heart of Africa could be more ignorant of the Bible than most of those youngsters.

So when Andy reached Danny's room his face was alight, and Danny looked wistfully at him, thinking he would give his soul if he could be like that doctor.

Andy noticed the new look in the boy's eyes, as if a fresh purpose had sprung up.

"Sit down, Doc," said Danny unceremoniously, motioning with his scrawny hand to the chair beside the bed.

"I want to ask you something. What was all that stuff you was handin' me th' other day? Was there anything in it, or was you jes' kiddin' me, tryin' to get me well or somethin' by gettin' my mind off what's comin' when I get outa here?"

Andy smiled and laid his warm hand over Danny's. Danny always loved to have him do that, although he wouldn't have admitted it if his life had depended on it. It seemed to make up for the loving he had never received in all his starved young life.

"It's the truest thing in this sad old world," Andy declared. "Listen pal, it's just this true: if I didn't believe it and know by experience that it is so, I might have been tempted more than once to get out of this rotten old world by my own hand as I've known so many to do."

Danny looked sharply at him. How did Doctor Andy know that he had thought of doing just that many a time, especially since he had got into this recent trouble?

Andy caught the look and it confirmed what he had suspected before, when he had seen desperation staring out of those big brown eyes. He had warned the nurses to be careful what instruments they left around Danny's bed.

Danny thought awhile. He was determined to get the gist of this.

"You said somebody died for me once because I had sinned? I don't get that. How long ago?"

"About two thousand years ago, son."

"Phooey! I wasn't alive then, so how could he know there would be me or that I would sin?"

"Remember we're talking about God, pal. You have to realize that He knows the end from the beginning. He knows everything that's going to happen. He knows what you are going to say next."

"Gee!" breathed Danny, then hardened again with unbelief. "Then if it's all laid out what I'm goin' to say what diffrunce does it make what I do say?"

"It does, though," replied Andy. "Even though God knows what you're going to say, He doesn't make you say it. That's your business. He has given you a free will, you know. I admit you can't reason all this out, but He's told us it's true, and I'm telling you you'll never find the answer to any problem until you find it in Jesus Christ and His Word. Did you ever read the Bible?"

"Nope. Never even saw one, I guess. My mom usedta go to meetin's now and then, but I couldn't see it made no diffrunce in her. Jes' a lot o' whoopin' and howlin' over nuttin'."

"Going to meetings won't change anybody, that's true," agreed Andy. "But listen, pal, meeting the Lord Jesus Christ and finding Him as your Saviour will. Because then He gives you His own life, and you get to be more and more like Him as you let Him have His way with you. It's something like having a wonderful Friend to walk right with you all the time and tell you what to do and give you the power to do it."

"Gee! Can He get ya out of trouble?"

"He not only can but has, out of the worst trouble anybody could be in. It's bad to fall into the hands of the law, here on earth, Dan, but it's a terrible thing to fall into the hands of a

God who can put you in an awful jail not just for a few years or a lifetime, but forever."

"Gee!" Danny thought over that and nodded unconsciously. Then he gazed at Andy again and studied the loving smile on the doctor's face as he looked straight back at Danny.

"That must be it, then," Danny decided at last.

"Must be what, kid?"

"That must be why you're so different from everybody else. You said a guy gets to be more and more like—Him! You are, I guess. 'Cause I believe you'd die for a fellow if he needed that!"

Andy's eyes grew moist and a look that Danny thought was the sweetest he had ever seen on a human face, stole round Andy's mouth. It was an utterly humble look. Then he said, "I wish it was that way more with me, Danny. I wish I were more like Him. When you get to know Him and love Him, you will wish so too."

Danny was silent for a moment. Then, "I'd like to now," he said in a voice so low that Andy could scarcely hear him.

The glad light sprang into Andy's eyes, and he said quietly, "Okay, pal, let's tell Him so. Lord Jesus, here's a boy who wants to get to know You. He needs a Saviour, and I think he sees that You are the only one who can save. Come and be with him here in his room, all the time now, and make him understand what You will be to him, and what You want him to be. Amen."

Danny's eyes were closed as Andy looked up and the doctor saw a slow tear steal down the white cheek. Danny quickly turned his head away, brushing at it with the sleeve of his hospital gown. Then as Andy looked at his watch and rose to go, Danny gave a weak grip to Andy's hand, muttering hoarsely,

"Thanks, Doc. Come *soon* again, won't you? Bye."

Chapter 16

JAN SCORED A TREMENDOUS success at the Van Ordens', and her handsome escort took her around proudly and introduced her to those whom he considered the best people in Oak Hill. Everyone admired the beautiful girl who played so well and laughed so gaily, flashing her black sparkling eyes in delight at everything. Jan had a wide mouth, and even white teeth. Her laugh was guileless and most attractive. It was not often that society discovered a young bit of talent so unspoiled and charming. What a fine couple she and that handsome young preacher would make!

Aunt Myra swelled with pride, saved all the newspaper clippings, and went on scheming and planning. At last she was enjoying her heart's desire that had been denied her these many years.

Jan cut out a clipping, too, and sent it to her father.

When he received it he sat down and wrote her happy congratulations on her success, and then added a word of warning.

"Don't let all this go to your head, child. Try to see through the glamor and take only what is real. All the admiration and applause can turn to ashes if the tide turns the other way for some reason. Don't imagine that these rich people have all become faithful friends of yours simply because they are making much of you now. I want you to enjoy life, but don't get to living on frosting."

Jan read the letter in a few breathless moments between a violin lesson and a date with Stancel Egbert.

Dates with Stan were getting to be more and more frequent. Even Aunt Myra had begun to wonder whether it was a good thing for Jan to be in one man's company so exclusively. She had no thought of giving up her new prize yet to any young man, no matter how desirable.

Jan had no time to reread her father's note as she usually did; even the first reading had been done cursorily as she undid the pins in her hair. When she came to the last part she smiled a little condescendingly.

"Dear Daddy, he thinks I'm going to lose my head." She laughed as she tossed up her pretty waves and edged a comb carefully through them. "But I think I know my way around by now! I'll be eighteen this summer. Goodness knows I ought to be able to manage my life if I am ever going to!"

Slipping a strapless gown over her head she zipped it up, gave another cautious swirl with the comb, and taking the mirror, surveyed herself on all sides. She still did not feel quite at ease in those bare-top dresses. Except for her play suits Daddy had always been careful to keep her quite covered. But, of course Daddy was older than most of the other girls' fathers, and he just didn't know about the modern ways. The rest all wore these dresses, and Aunt Myra had assured her that this was just the thing for her date tonight. So she gave a prideful conscious glance again at her smooth bare shoulders, thought of the admiring glances that would be sure to be cast her way, and went gaily to the closet to get her evening wrap.

As she preened before her mirror she wondered what her old pal Danny would say if he saw her in her grandeur now. How very far she had come from that old life, and how much she had learned! She was glad now that Aunt Myra had schooled her so carefully in walking into a room, and taught her just what to say and do in certain circumstances. She did not need to feel ill at ease as she had at first in her school.

Just as she turned out her light to leave the room her glance fell on the worn little Testament lying on the table beside her bed. She had made a habit of reading it every day last fall, but lately she had been so rushed that she had let it go. The thought stabbed her. What would Andrew Hightower think of her now? Would he be pleased that she had learned the ways of the world? Or would he look at her with that stern puzzled expression as he had that day at the brick house? On a sudden impulse she picked up the Book and slipped it into her white beaded evening bag before she went down to meet Stan. Then she forgot all about Andrew Hightower, and Danny too.

But it so happened that Danny was thinking about Jan.

He was still lying in his hospital bed, although he was well enough to have it raised up now so that he could see glimpses of the city. He watched the lights come on in the tall buildings round about the hospital. They looked like stars in the blackness of the winter night. Somehow they reminded him of Jan's eyes one time when they had gone on a picnic with her father and he and she had confided to each other that they were afraid of the dark. He wondered whether Jan still felt that way. He took a deep peaceful breath. The last few days were the happiest he had ever spent in all his life, even sweeter than the times he had had with Jan and her father. Fear seemed to be gone. He could lie and watch the dusk steal on and simply trust. The joy of knowing that there was Somebody caring and loving and watching him, holding his hand when the way looked dark, smoothing his bed when the pain was worst, made life a different thing for Danny.

For Danny had come to the end of his old ways when he woke from his fever and realized that he had ruined his life. He had been ready to grasp at the simple truths that Doctor Andy taught him. In those few days he had already begun to know the peace that passeth understanding. Not only that, but Doctor Andy assured him that the Lord had already begun to work out Danny's earthly problems, too; Andy had been having some dealings with the powers that be and he thought he would be able to gain permission to take Danny under his own wing on probation, after he was out of the hospital. His bullet wound was healed, and his leg was better. It had been badly broken by his fall from a roof when he had tried to escape from the pursuing police.

Doctor Andy came in almost every evening and sat quite a while with him, answering his questions. He had brought a lightweight, large print Bible, and just last night he had explained to Danny the part that prophesied the return of the Lord Jesus Christ to the earth. Danny listened in amazement and delight. He had thought of nothing else ever since. Now he lay and wondered whether Jan knew all this. When he was able, he intended to write to her, or better still, go and see her again, and tell her all about what he had learned and how wonderful God had been to him. If Jesus was coming back soon, not knowing *how* soon, it was certainly up to Danny to make sure that the beloved friend of his childhood was born again and ready.

As Danny lay with his eyes on the stars, Doctor Andy put his head in the room with a bright smile for the boy he had begun to love like a brother. He had only time for a brief word tonight, for he had been spending his precious minutes at the city hall in Danny's behalf, although he did not tell Danny yet how things were coming out.

So Andy hurried home and after supper that night, instead of going out to Lucile's as he had had half a mind to do, he sat down with his father and mother in front of the fire.

He had a medical journal in his hands, but after they were all settled comfortably he looked up. So did his mother. She was alert to his moods and she could tell that he had something very special on his mind tonight.

She trembled lest it might be an announcement of his engagement to "that hussy."

"Dad," began Andy, "aren't you feeling a little better than you did last summer?"

"Why, yes, son, I believe I am a little stronger. I was thinking the other day that if it were only summer time now, I would feel like trying to take a walk in the garden." He laughed as if his illness were a small thing. "Remember, Mother, I told you how well I felt yesterday?"

Mrs. Hightower nodded happily. She was anxious to hear what Andy had to say.

"Well, I have been wondering whether you two would feel up to doing a little welfare work," said Andy rather hesitantly. He had thought long about this thing and he was not even yet sure that it was right to put any more burden on his family. Still he could see no other way.

Both the older people dropped their reading then, and looked up with interest.

"You know I'm always wanting to help," answered his father readily. "I only wish I could do something worth while for the Lord nowadays," he added sadly.

"Now, Father, there's no use your talking that way," rebuked his wife. "You know He uses the books you write and you have always said yourself that when a servant of God is laid aside for a time from active work it may be that it is so that he can spend the time in prayer. There's many a saint, I guess you'll find, who has come through a trial bravely because you have been praying!"

The invalid shook his head. "It seems like very little I accomplish," he said. "But what's on your mind, son?"

"It's Danny Severy, Dad. He'll soon be out of the hospital. It wouldn't be safe for him to go back to his old haunts even if the court would let him. I've about fixed things so that I can take him myself on probation. I don't know why I did it, for goodness knows I'm too busy now, except that there's nobody else to look after him, and I can't see that boy, now that he's really saved, going into one of those reform schools where like as not he'd learn more evil than he knows now, if there is any more to know. I just wondered whether you two would think I'm crazy if I bring him out here for the rest of the winter, and let him soak up good food and love and some sound Bible teaching from you, as well as a little English and any other education you see fit to give him. Now does that sound like an awful imposition? What about you, too, Mother? I know it'll make more work for you, at least until he is strong enough to help, and I don't even know that he would know how to do anything around the place. He might have to be taught everything."

"Oh, my boy, you know I'd love to do it. It would be almost like having one of my own back again as a boy! As for loving him, I've learned to do that already from what you have told us, without seeing him. The rest Father would have to look after. How about it, Father?"

They both looked at the quiet man in the wheel chair and saw that his eyes were shining.

"Son, you've helped to answer my prayer! I've been asking the Lord if there wasn't something more that I could do, even an old broken-down preacher like me. It would be the greatest joy to me to teach a new-born child of God to 'walk.' Bring on your Danny, and any other boys you want to. Mother here'll feed them up and maybe we can make them into preachers to go out and take my place!"

The room seemed fairly to glow with the joy of the three as they sat and planned.

Andy had had several vague schemes in his mind for some time, and as they talked these began to take definite shape.

"I've always thought, you know, that there ought to be a good-sized room right down in that area where there would be a couple of saws and a workbench and maybe a machine shop where the fellows could tinker. Then we'd want a piano, and a ping-pong table, with booths, perhaps, for checkers and chess, and maybe a snack bar. There ought to be a vacant lot for baseball, too, and a good coach. Of course, I don't suppose all that would be possible right away; I'd have to find out which particular things interested the boys most. I know a swell fellow who is studying in Bible School and he could give them down-to-earth Bible lessons in their own language, just casually, you know. Nothing formal until they asked for it. Between us he and I ought to be able to bring enough into the conversation now and then to get the gospel across plainly. After that he could go on farther, with any who were interested, or maybe one of the Bible Institute teachers would turn out to be helpful."

Andy was so fascinated with his subject that he did not realize that his parents were fairly weeping with joy over his plan.

"Of course I'd have to go slow at first and wait to see how the Lord leads in this. It may not be what He wants me to do at all, but I haven't been able to get it out of my mind. I think I'd like to have my office in the same building and be just a plain family doctor. Don't you think I could reach them better that way?" As Andy looked up he met the benediction in his father's eyes, a light so bright that it almost embarrassed him.

"Father, I told you," quavered his mother struggling with happy tears, "that our Andy wouldn't forget what he had in mind when he started on the doctoring. Remember how, even when he was a little boy, he always said he was going to be a medical missionary? Oh Andy, boy, don't you know we'll give the rest of our lives gladly to helping you?"

"Well, I might have known you'd both fall in line," said Andy with a pleased grin. "But I want you to take care of each other, too. You are not to overdo in this business."

"Just let us manage that, won't you?" retorted his mother. "Didn't your father and I bring up two of the wildest scamps that ever lived, and teach them to do a good deal of the work around the house for us? We'll have your youngsters doing so much around here that all we'll have to do is sit around and enjoy them."

"Oh, yeah?" snorted Andy. "I can just picture that! Wait till you see some of them. You think Dave and I were tough! These kids know enough evil to make your hair curl. But I'll try to make pretty sure of any boy before I ship him out here. We can't have any stealing—or worse. I'd be in the soup if I had to appeal to the police about them."

"We will have to lean hard on the Lord for that end of things, son," advised his father quietly. "There will be snags, no doubt.

It won't be an easy work. But we'll hold you up in prayer."

"Thanks, Dad, I know you will. You can start by asking the Lord to find me the right room. I'm going to begin looking tomorrow. Maybe I'll have one ready by the time Danny is well and able to be back there to help. You see I'm counting on his being worth while when you finish with him."

They fell to planning once more about the whole scheme and bedtime came before they knew it.

There was only one catch in it all for Andy. He couldn't seem to see Lucile's place in it all. But he had had it out with the Lord about it and he felt that in His eyes he was committed to the plan.

As he lay down he got to thinking about Danny again. How strange that God should have made their paths cross once again; and the boy had taken a strong hold on him. Now that he was on the right track, Danny couldn't seem to get enough of the Bible. Each time Andy went to visit him it seemed that he had grown by leaps and bounds spiritually. The Word of God was even cleansing his lips, and oaths that had been common in his speech began to disappear. Andy's heart was full of praise.

He fell to wondering about the black-eyed daredevil girl whom Danny admired so much. She had a lot of personality. And courage, certainly. If only a girl like that could be found who would surrender her life to the Lord, what a marvelous help she could be. He sighed, and longed again that some miracle might happen to his beautiful lady that would change her attitude toward this cherished plan of his. He had said very little about it since that first night, and she had never brought up the subject again. Maybe she thought he had given up the idea, but now he knew that would be impossible. He had given himself to the Lord's will and in that will he would stay, at any cost.

So at last he fell asleep.

But Jan was still out, riding through the night in Stancel Egbert's car. When she had tucked that Book into her purse she had had some thought of asking Stan about what she had read, but no chance had come during the evening's entertainment.

Now on the way home she thought of it again. Stan ought to know the answers as well as Andrew Hightower. Had he not graduated from a school for ministers? He never talked the way the other young man did, but no doubt he knew those things. She patted the Book in her handbag and had a comfortable sense that Andrew was with her tonight. It gave a sweet dignity to her bearing. She had always felt that those hours she had spent with the Hightowers were the nearest to Heaven that a mortal might attain on this earth. For a long time after that she had walked more softly and been more conscious of a watching God.

"Why so pensive tonight, little one?" asked Stancel Egbert as he stole a hand over hers in the dimness of his car. Jan had never been used to allowing any intimacies at all with boys, but of late she had eased up in what the girls at school called her primness. Stan seemed so like a big brother in his friendliness that she thought surely there could be no harm in relaxing her standard.

"Oh, I was just thinking," she responded gaily as if there was nothing more serious than the evening's party on her mind.

"About what, if I may ask?"

"Would you really like to know?" she asked mischievously.

"I would really like to know—anything about *you*," replied Stancel in a low rich meaningful voice, which Jan chose to ignore.

"Well, I'll tell you. I was thinking about what I have in my bag," she told him impishly.

"And what do you have in your bag, my lady?" went on Stan, catching her mood playfully.

"Just a book, kind sir," she laughed.

"A book? What book, my lady?"

Jan hesitated. She had not meant to fall into such a silly way of talking. Somehow she often found herself doing that when she was with Stancel. Either that or she merely listened while he told her of music or art or of his travels. Now it seemed somewhat irreverent to refer to the Bible in such a foolish way, so she hedged.

"A book that was given to me," she said more soberly.

"Given you? By whom? Isn't that the next question?"

Suddenly Jan found herself irritated that she couldn't get the conversation back on serious lines. Then she realized that her irritation really came because she didn't want to tell this man about Andrew Hightower. She had a feeling that he wouldn't understand about him. And Andrew was too fine, almost too holy, in Jan's estimation, to be joked about.

"I don't know that it is," she parried.

"Oh, come now, don't back out. You started this."

"No, I don't think I did," said Jan annoyed.

"Well, what is the matter with the person who gave it to you that you don't want to tell?"

"Nothing at all," said Jan now thoroughly serious. "He is as fine as they come. I really didn't mean to joke at all. It is a Testament in my bag, and I thought maybe I'd ask you some questions I've wanted to know about."

"Why, that's very praiseworthy, I'm sure," responded Stancel instantly dropping his banter and speaking in what Jan sometimes called his ministerial tone. "There are some really wonderful passages in the New Testament. The Sermon on the Mount, for instance. It has nothing in literature to equal it, I believe."

"What's the sermon on the mount?" asked Jan innocently.

Stancel smiled gently in the darkness.

"It is the loftiest pattern for human conduct ever pronounced," stated Stancel. "Was it about that you wished to ask me?"

"I—I don't know," she said in a small voice. "I don't know exactly which part that is. But I have been wondering just what it means to be born again?"

"Ha!" cried the young man. "You have been reading the

gospel according to John. Rather stiff stuff for a beginner, if I may presume to call you that. But you have a good mind, and, I've always thought, rather a head for philosophy, if you had a bit of coaching. I'll do my best to explain, though what you ask is really beyond the finest minds to understand. The expression is an esoteric abstract euphemism for a psychological experience that certain idealistic people take very seriously."

The minister paused and Jan wondered whether he had finished.

"Oh?" she said politely, utterly mystified.

"Yes," he went on rather pompously. "With some it takes the form of a reformation of life. Drunkards, for instance, have reformed and claimed to be born again. To tell you the truth, my dear, I think you have been reading quite beyond your depth, if you will permit me to suggest it. Nobody really knows exactly what Jesus meant when he talked about being born again. He may have had some thought of reformation in his mind, although it seems hardly possible, since Nicodemus, the man to whom he made the statement, scarcely needed reforming. My opinion is that many of the statements Jesus made must have been given out in a moment of spiritual rapture when he was in a sense not his usual sane self, for when He was asked to explain them afterward, it seems as if He did not understand them very well himself; his explanations are sometimes very lame. It is much better, my dear, to confine your reading to simpler portions of Scripture, if you want to read the Bible. The lovely book of Ruth, for instance, the wisdom of the book of Proverbs, or the charming brochure on the Life of Jesus by John Mark. There is not so much of difficulty in those as in the idealistic book of John. Though, of course, I wouldn't want to discourage you. I really believe that the reading of the Bible is valuable for anyone. It broadens the mind, since there is so much in it that is worthy. And of course, its pure English is beyond reproach."

"Oh," said Jan again, feeling as if the thing that she had

thought a treasure had turned out to be dust.

They reached Aunt Myra's just then and no more was said about the Bible.

But the next Sunday Stancel preached an eloquent sermon on the value of the Bible as literature, proving beyond question that there was a great deal of good education in its pages.

Still Jan was not satisfied. Andrew Hightower had spoken as if the Bible were the very book of God. Who was right? More than ever she longed for another talk with the young doctor.

Chapter 17

THE WINTER AND spring rushed on. Jan was excited a good deal of the time, and the rest of the time she was pitifully bored. The dinner table at Aunt Myra's was the worst. Her aunt questioned her as to every detail of the day, and pried into Jan's very heart, it seemed to her, although it was done under the guise of love and interest in her. Aunt Myra had softened up to the extent of calling Jan "my darling girl" once or twice, and then she froze afterward as if she were ashamed of so much emotion. Uncle Duncan continued to be a blank, and Jan after several efforts to draw out the poor man when his wife was not around, finally gave up, deciding there was nothing there to draw. Perhaps his wife had ground out of him anything that ever had been there.

Jan found learning easy, and she worked hard at her studies, especially her music. But as spring came on, her long hours of practice with the excitement of the dates and concerts she had, were making dark purple shadows under her eyes which were becoming but not desirable.

She had begun to notice them herself and wished for summer to come that she might get away from the strain of such a full life. A quiet walk by the dear old river would seem like paradise, she thought. And then the old longing to see Danny would return, and a great desire to have a talk with Andrew Hightower. He had begun to seem like some mystical hero, unreal, but wonderful to dream about.

It was late in May before she received the letter from Danny which he had planned to write when he lay in the hospital. He had kept hoping he would be able to go to see her but he soon found that would not be allowed. He might not leave the pleasant Hightower grounds unless accompanied by Andrew Hightower himself, and he was required to present himself to the court with Doctor Andy every week and give account.

After a few days at the Hightowers' he had no more desire to leave there than an angel would have to leave Heaven. Never before had he been tucked into bed and caressed.

"Do try to bring the boy before he is well enough to go to bed by himself," Andy's mother had begged that first night when Andy brought up the subject. "Then he won't feel too ashamed if I tuck him in. I'm just longing to mother him a little."

"All right, Mother," laughed Andy, "but remember the boy is nearly seventeen, though he looks no more than fourteen if you judge by his size."

"I'll remember, son, but you know you don't mind your mother giving *you* a little tuck and a kiss now and then, even at your advanced age, now, do you?"

Andy laughed again sheepishly, and took his mother in his arms for a hug.

"But you're my own mother, of course, for which I thank God!" he said in her ear.

But it did not take Danny long to learn to submit to loving ministrations, and with the start he had gotten in the hospital on a strengthening diet Andy had prescribed, and then the good food that Mrs. Hightower gave him, he soon began to grow more solid and sturdy looking.

It was his spiritual growth that astonished them all, however. He was so eager to learn that he fairly wore out his teacher. Doctor Hightower found himself indignant at the school teachers who had failed to notice the fine mind of the boy and do everything in their power to encourage it and hold his interest.

Danny struggled manfully with the grammar he should have learned when he was eleven, and took the corrections they gave so lovingly in good part.

Andy took pains to see that Danny's clothes fitted him nicely and that his hair was kept cut, on their routine trips into the city. Andy had kept the boy in the hospital without drugs long enough he hoped, to break him of his old habits, and that, with the boy's willingness to make a fresh start, was most encouraging.

Not that there were not many faults to correct and many times when the faithful couple at "Lookaway" felt as if their efforts were in vain. Danny had slovenly habits that went terribly against the grain of those cultured people, and they dared not try to set everything right at once lest he should become discouraged. But he was humble and willing, and gradually a great change could be seen in him.

He was not apt at the work about the place but he tried hard and in time there were certain chores that were handed over to him, for he told them plainly he wanted to earn his way.

He had thought much about Jan, but never had got around to writing to her all winter. For one thing, as he began to grow in understanding he began to realize how far short he had fallen from what he might have been, and from what Jan must be now. He felt as if his penmanship and his spelling, for instance, must be considerably improved before he would want to set himself down on paper to her again. No doubt she had been ashamed of him last fall. Mortification stung him now. So he waited and worked and at last he felt that the time had come when he could write Jan.

The day his letter arrived Jan had dragged home from school tired out and with the hopeless feeling that summer would never come. She had a wild thought of calling up her father long distance and having a talk with him. But she knew Aunt Myra would never hear to that.

Listlessly Jan opened the big oak door which she had begun to hate; she cast a glance on the polished hall table where the mail was always placed. Yes, there was a letter for her postmarked Chester. Probably it was from one of the girls or boys she had known in high school there. A few had written once or twice, or sent cards at Christmas time. Any word from home was welcome, so she ran eagerly up to her room. She always had a feeling that she might be spied on and questioned if she read her letters downstairs where her aunt might come upon her; although once she had come upon her aunt with a packet of letters in her lap, and Aunt Myra had given such a start and scolded her so that she always had a feeling that Aunt Myra had been trying to hide something herself.

So Jan closed her door and snuggled up in her big arm chair.

"Dear Jan:—

"At last I am writing the letter to you that I have wanted to write for months."

Jan puckered her brows and looked at the end of the letter. Danny! Her heart gave a leap of amazement. Had he written this himself? It was certainly a great improvement on his former penmanship and style.

"The greatest thing that ever could happen to me happened around Christmas time and I have wanted to tell you about it ever since.

"You may think I'm crazy when you hear it, but I'm not. I know it's all true and it gets more wonderful all the time.

"Remember Dr. Hightower, that swell guy that picked me up the time I fell? Well, he had to fix me up again in the hospital, as I had been doing a lot of things I shouldn't and got myself into trouble. I'm ashamed of all that and won't write it but I'll tell you some time.

"Anyway, I was pretty well down. I wanted to get done with life, and I didn't see any way out. Dr. Andy started to tell me about what Jesus Christ did for me on the cross and somehow it began to seem real to me. I knew I needed *somebody's* help, and the worst thing about me was all my sin. So I took Jesus as my Saviour and boy, oh boy, things are a lot different now! I had never heard of such a thing before as God giving a person His own life just for believing on His Son, but it's true. He does. He has done it for me. I'm all different inside.

"I'm living out at Dr. Andy's home—it's a beautiful place and his folks are wonderful to me. His father is teaching me, and I will never be able to pay them back for all they have done.

I'm planning to get a real job and go to some night classes at the Bible School when I get done here, and then maybe the Lord will have some place for me to work for Him. That's all I want to do with my life now, because it's all that seems worthwhile, since we are here on earth such a short time, anyway, and have such a very long time up there with Him.

"I don't know whether you have thrown down this letter by now but if you haven't I just want to ask you if you won't accept the Lord Jesus Christ as your Saviour too. Doctor Andy calls that 'being born again.' And it sure feels like it!

"Maybe you will think I have no business writing you like this because I've never amounted to anything. I've always wanted to apologize to you for the way I got you into a mess. I've had all that out with God and He has forgiven me. I sure hope you will, too. I know I'm no good, but I've found Somebody who is, and Dr. Andy and his folks are like Him. I mean to be, too.

"Well, I just wanted to tell you, and let you know I'm praying that you will find Jesus this way too.

"As ever, only different,
"Your pal, Danny."

Jan's eyes were misty before she had finished that letter. It sounded so like the dear old Danny at his best, before he had started going with the gang. Only there was something, as he said, very different about it. It was not only that he wrote well and used good English; there was a peace and confidence that breathed through it which Jan longed to know for herself. Oh, to be free to go back and have a talk with Danny now. And with Doctor Andy, and his father and mother too. Jan seemed to see the wide quiet lawn and the old stone house nestling among the shade trees. How lovely it must be there in the spring! And to think that *Danny* was *living* there! It all seemed incredible. What a man that Doctor Andy must be!

And here in Danny's letter seemed to be at least a part of the answer to her wondering about being born again. In Danny's letter! Of all people! All the time that she had been wishing something could be done for Danny, Danny was far and away beyond her, spiritually. *He* was *praying* for *her!* And she hadn't even learned yet how to pray for herself.

It occurred to her to wonder why Stancel Egbert had not been able to tell her this. Could it be that he did not know the reality of it himself?

A long time she sat and thought. Then she got up and reached for her little Testament and read over once more the chapter in John that had now become familiar to her.

At last, almost shyly, she slid down on her knees.

"Oh, God," she said softly, "I don't understand all about this yet, but I want to. Please take me for Yours and show me. And thank you for helping Danny. Amen."

Then as she started up from her knees, she sank down again adding,

"Oh, and please bless that wonderful man, Doctor Andy, and his family. I would love to see them again. Please let me."

Jan had a feeling that she had been drawn into a strange bond again with those friends at home, and that her life here in Oak Hill was something outside of herself now. All the more she longed to go home but there was nothing of the quitter in Jan, and she knew she would stick it out until school was over. She would graduate early in June and then she would be free.

But a sharp rap came just then and Jan jumped up in a flurry of embarrassment that she had been caught on her knees. For Aunt Myra, while she never failed to knock before entering a room, always opened the door instantly after the knock.

She looked at Jan now with suspicious eyes, noting her little flush and her manner of being ill at ease.

But fortunately Aunt Myra had an important message for her and did not wait to question her.

"Reverend Egbert is downstairs to see you," she told her.

Jan was glad of something to take her away from Aunt Myra's prying just now and she raced down gaily with a happy feeling that wonderful things had opened up for her.

Stancel wore his most beaming look as he greeted her, although he never did quite relax from a certain dignity that he felt he must assume on account of his position.

"I have some splendid news for you, my dear," he told her when Aunt Myra had seated them properly where she wanted them.

"A college friend of mine is managing a summer hotel this year and he has written to me, knowing of the famous music school here, to know whether I could find him a good violinist for the summer season. He would like a young lady, 'attractive, if possible,' he said." Stancel laughed. "Of course I thought of you right away, as the most attractive young lady violinist I knew." Stancel beamed down indulgently at Jan so as not to miss the pretty color that came up in her cheeks. "So I'm here to tell you to apply at once. I have no doubt you can get the position, with the recommendation I shall give you. You see, this young man knows that I am something of a music critic myself, and my judgment can be relied upon." Stancel looked complacently from Jan to Aunt Myra who sat stiffly by, exuding satisfaction.

"Oh-h-h!" cried Jan, pleased and astonished, yet her spirits sank as she realized what it would mean if she took the job. Her face fell with her voice.

Instantly Aunt Myra spoke up.

"My niece will be delighted to take the position, providing it pays well," she answered for Jan.

Jan looked wildly at her, trying to get her bearings. Of course she would be glad to begin to earn something regularly, but would it mean that she wouldn't get home *at all?*

"When—would it start?" she asked timidly, aware that Aunt Myra wished her to do it, and there would be a scene if she demurred.

"I'm not sure," answered Stancel, "but I believe it would be about the last week in June."

Jan saw her cherished summer at home fading into the distance.

Rather reluctantly she listened to the eager plans Stancel and her aunt discussed.

"You don't seem to be thrilled, young prima donna," teased Stancel. "Is your professional standing already so assured?"

Jan flushed. More than once she had noticed a little sting in Stan's remarks.

"I was just counting how many days I would have at home," she said guilelessly.

Aunt Myra sniffed. Jan had learned to interpret her sniffs. They spoke volumes. Jan flushed again with indignation but she kept her mouth closed.

That evening Aunt Myra dictated a letter for her to write applying for the position.

But Jan was not the only one who was giving thought to the summer. Andrew Hightower had been watching his father pretty closely. The summer heat even at "Lookaway" would be more than his father ought to stand. He was turning over in his mind various plans.

John Nielson, too, was looking forward to the summer. His beloved daughter would be home and he would have her all to himself. They would take their walks again down by the river. They would fish together, and picnic. They would go to the band concerts, and perhaps an orchestra concert or two. He had been saving up for those. Now and then a little tremor of dread would run through him lest perhaps Jan would be so sophisticated that she would no longer care for walks by the river and the simple joys of fishing or picnicking. Then John would sigh and gird his loins with patience to wait for the closing of school.

Danny, too, was thinking, rather apprehensively, of the coming summer. Doctor Andy had let him in on some of his plans. A couple of large rooms not far from the hospital had been rented and Andy was arranging to fix them up for a boys' club. He was going to let Danny do some of the painting and the little carpentry work needed, and then Danny was to help in inviting boys there. So far Andy had kept Danny strictly away from his old haunts, and Danny had been relieved that he had had no necessity for meeting up with any of the gang. Now he was torn between a longing to tell some of them the new wonder that had come into his life, and a real terror of the tougher members of the old gang. For he knew them well enough to be aware that he would be considered a quitter and that they would have less than no use for anything he had to tell them about his spiritual experience. They could get very rough on occasion. But he kept his fears to himself, bound and determined to ʳtick by his beloved friend the doctor in whatever task he chose to set him.

As for Lucile Sommers, she was biding her time. Andy had confided to her what he was doing, eagerly at first, then a little shamefacedly. She had carried the news to Doctor Endicott without delay. That gentleman frowned, then shrugged off his worry with a careless laugh.

"Let the boy work out his philanthropy," he advised. "I've seen more than one who broke out with it at his age. The best cure is to let him go ahead and see what headaches he'll have. Before long those roughnecks will tire of it. They'll drop off and he'll be done with his slum work. Then he is ours. Don't worry."

So Lucile did not worry, but it was hard for her even to pretend to an interest in Andy's project, and she was constantly teasing him about it, so that he gradually told her less and less. As his eagerness over the plan grew, at the same time a sadness increased in his eyes. His mother, ever-watchful, noticed it and it sent her to her knees, whether for rejoicing or for sorrow she could not tell as yet.

Aunt Myra was looking forward to the summer with great complacency. She had worked hard and efficiently to bring about the events which had transpired so smoothly. Her fierce pride in her niece and in her accomplishments, made her take great satisfaction in having her to show off on every possible occasion. She had taken pains to tell several wealthy and eligible young men where Jan would be, and she was certain that the summer would be a success.

At last school with all the commencement doings was over.

John had not gone up to Oak Hill to see his daughter graduate, chiefly because he had not been invited. Jan had not urged him to come because she was afraid that her aunt would insult him somehow and Jan could not bear the thought of it. John plodded to work as usual on his daughter's graduation day, although he would have liked to be with her. He realized, however, that her schooling this past year had been at Aunt Myra's expense and that Aunt Myra should enjoy the fruit of it without the un-desired presence of a brother-in-law.

It was Stancel Egbert who put Jan on the train for home, and looked deep into her eyes as he said good-bye.

"It shall not be for long, I promise you that," he told her. "I have planned to take my vacation at your mountain hotel, too." He held her hand with both of his in the seclusion of the train seat's high back.

"Look for me, darling, will you?"

He pursed up his mouth and taking a swift glance up and down the car, he kissed her passionately full on her lips. Then he left her and went outside where he stood waving gaily to her until the train pulled out. He did not notice that her eyes were wide with shock and bewilderment. She managed a polite smile and waved to him, but her heart was disturbed. Why was it that she felt disappointed in him? Most girls she knew would have given much to have received his kiss. But now she had a revul-sion toward him. She wished he had not come to see her off.

Chapter 18

JAN HAD BEEN home nearly a week before she saw Doctor Andy.

It was early on her first Sunday morning that the telephone rang.

"Andrew Hightower speaking. Remember me?"

Jan's heart did a quick somersault of delight.

"Oh-h!" she cried. "How could I forget you! You will never *know* all you did for me!"

"Well! I'm glad of that!" he responded heartily, "especially because I'm going to ask something of you now! Please be frank and tell me if you don't care to do it."

"If I can do anything at all for you it will be a great pleasure," answered Jan with a happy lilt in her voice.

"It's this way," he explained. "A friend of mine who runs a little mission in a foreign settlement just outside of town, has called me saying his mother is very sick and he wants me to take over this afternoon. I was wondering whether you would come along and bring your violin. Is that asking too much?"

"No, indeed, I'd love to do it." An eagerness welled up in Jan's heart that fairly overwhelmed her.

"All right, fine. I'll stop for you about two o'clock, okay?"

"I'll be ready," promised Jan, happily.

She turned away from the phone and began wondering how Andy Hightower had discovered that she was home, and how he knew that she played the violin. It must be that she had mentioned it in a letter to Danny, for she had answered Danny's letter immediately and they had corresponded several times.

Jan surprised and pleased her father by asking to go to church instead of taking their river walk, and when she came home she hurried through dinner and started eagerly to get ready for the afternoon. She told her father where she was going but she did not invite him to go along. She wanted the time with Doctor Andy all to herself.

But when he arrived promptly at two, there was another girl in the front seat with him; and a slight pale young man with dark wavy hair and big brown eyes, dressed in a well fitting brown summer suit, climbed out of the back seat of the car and stood waiting to shake hands with her. He looked strangely familiar but he walked with a limp.

"I believe you know this young gentleman, Janette," Andy smiled.

"Danny!" she exclaimed and put out both hands to him.

Danny grinned and returned her handclasp a moment with a strong sure grip, quite different from his old limp manner.

Andy shook hands with a warm smile. Then he turned to the beautiful blond girl in the front seat. Jan noticed that she was gowned and groomed in the very latest style and wore an exquisite frock which Jan considered far too dressy for a little country mission meeting. Jan herself had on a simple yellow organdy, with a Peter Pan collar and short puffed sleeves. It made her look like a little girl again. Jan found time to cast a grateful thought Aunt Myra-ward that she had provided her with garments every bit as tasteful and fitting as the lovely lady's in the car. She would not have wanted to shame Andy Hightower by looking like the gauche, crude little girl that she had been when last he took her for a ride.

She could not help noticing the slight start of surprise and admiration that Doctor Andy gave when he first saw her. It brought the pink up in her cheeks and a confident little sparkle to her eyes when she acknowledged the introduction to the other girl.

Lucile Sommers gave a sharp look at the strikingly lovely girl who was dressed so tastefully, then she gave another suspicious look at Andy and turned back to Jan with only a haughty nod. She was puzzled. She had not expected this type of girl to emerge from that shabby apartment house. From what Andy had told her she had expected an uncouth, rather foreign-looking child. This was a turn of affairs not to her liking.

"Come on, Andy," she said to him impatiently. "Let's get on and get this beastly meeting or whatever it is over with."

Jan caught the sound of a stifled indignant gasp from Danny in the back seat beside her, and she glanced at Andy's profile and saw the lines of sorrow deepen. Something gripped her heart. This was not going to be the pleasant little ride alone with Doctor Andy that she had thought it would be. She almost wished she had not come. Yet she would never say no to anything he asked if she could help it. She wondered who the Sommers girl was. Had he asked her to sing at the meeting, perhaps? No, she had a more possessive attitude toward him than mere singing would warrant. As the conviction took hold of her that Andy and this girl must have some special relationship to each other, her heart sank. She chided herself. Why should she care? He was nothing to her but a kind friend. But she did feel crushed. She argued that her distress was caused only by the attitude this girl seemed to have toward what interested Andy. But she could not shake off her depression.

She turned to Danny and began to question him about their old friends and reminisce about the good times they used to have. Once Lucile turned around and stared at them both and then curled her lip in an unpleasant way.

But Andy half turned with a smile and said, "I have a feeling that I am very presumptuous in asking you to come this afternoon, Janette. I wouldn't be surprised if you had soared to heights of fame since I saw you last. This little gathering is far beneath your talents, I'm sure. It's a sordid little settlement, you know. I've been out once or twice before with the friend who has charge of it. Don't be surprised if untoward proceedings take place. The people are informal, to say the least!" He laughed.

Jan laughed too, with a little trill in her voice. Doctor Andy sounded so cordial and friendly. At least he did not look down on her, even though his girl friend did.

"It takes a lot to shock me, I'm afraid," she giggled. "Anyway, I'm glad to help."

There was a warmth of loyalty in her voice, although she tried to make it impersonal. Andy felt it and turned a fleeting smile on her again at which Lucile stiffened and Jan quickly changed the subject.

"Tell me what I'm supposed to do, please. I've had some little experience playing in church."

Andy laughed. "The service is far from conventional. It won't be like any church service you ever attended, I'm sure."

"I'm glad of that," returned Jan. "I must admit that I think most meetings are terribly stuffy."

Lucile turned full around again and stared disapprovingly at her.

"I'm afraid I agree with you," remarked Andy seriously. "Well, at least you won't find this dull, I think."

They were winding through a country lane bordered by big old beech trees, and the pungent odor of slippery elm pervaded the air. Jan took great deep breaths of it.

"It's lovely out here, isn't it?" she said. "I don't know why anyone would choose to live in the city if they didn't have to. See all those little paths winding through the woods! I'd like to get out and try them." Lucile gave a withering glance toward the woods. But Andy nodded his head.

"Yes, I love this ride. I think the poor strays who live out here have something, perhaps. But of course you won't find their homes beautiful! Here we are."

They rounded a curve and saw huddled a dozen unpainted shanties, where half-naked children, dirty chickens and a nosing snorting pig mingled in the littered yards. Above the houses towered the waving green of beech trees and big old oaks; the sky beyond was blue and smiling. Jan caught her breath at the sight of the pitiful houses set in so much natural beauty and then gave a merry little laugh as the swarm of dirty children rushed over to Andy's car and surrounded him.

Danny had been utterly silent since Lucile's last cutting remarks. Now he climbed out with relief, helping Jan out courteously. All the while he kept his eyes glued on Andy for directions.

Andy turned over to him the keys of the ramshackle building beside which the car was drawn up, saying,

"You open up and let the ladies in, Dan. I want to go up and speak to those men up there on the porch. They may be drunk, but I might interest one or two to come over. Sometimes they do."

He was holding the car door open for Lucile as he spoke, but when she sighted the filthy ragged children and saw one of them come up to Jan and thrust a droopy bunch of wildflowers into her hand and grasp at Jan's dainty dress, she drew back.

"No thank you, Andy," she said icily. "I shall wait here in the car for you—if you think it's *safe*. I declare I don't know why you thought you could bring me out to a horrible hole like this! I'd like you to know that I'm perfectly furious at you, Andy Hightower!"

She spoke in smothered wrath and her blue eyes flashed. Andy flushed and looked troubled. Jan saw his embarrassment and turned away, giving a friendly greeting to the grubby child who had grabbed her hand. But neither she nor Danny could help hearing the conversation between Andy and Lucile.

"Maybe you remember, Lucile," Andy said gently, "that I did not ask you to come. I didn't think you would like it."

"Well, it was a case of either come with you or miss our date entirely," Lucile blazed. "You are so stubborn in this ridiculous idea of yours to try to do people good!" She said the last words in a disagreeable tone of voice and Andy turned away sadly.

"You do as you like then, Lucile. I think you would be safe out here, yes, but I still think you might find it a little more interesting inside."

He left them and went up the cluttered yard to one of the houses where a group of men in their dirty undershirts were gathered, resting from their labors of the week.

Jan followed Danny into the building where a rickety piano and straggling rows of benches were the only furnishings. She sat down at the piano and played one or two chords and snatches of church music. The piano was minus most of its ivories and many of its notes did not sound at all. So Jan took out her violin and, tuning it, began to play softly. She had seen at once that the children who crowded in were boisterous and might become unruly before Andy got back unless there was something to take their attention.

They stopped their rowdy play and listened open-mouthed to the music, watching Jan's graceful fingers in delight.

Lucile sat still in the car but she could see dimly through the broken-paned window which Danny had raised and propped open with a stick. She glared with hatred and frustration at the beautiful girl who played so exquisitely. Who was she, and where had Andy picked her up? She couldn't be anything but some common foreign gutter girl living in that awful house. But how had she learned to dress and walk with that poise and dignity?

As she played Jan glanced through the scrap of a window and saw Doctor Andy coming across the road followed by one or two tired-looking, hard-muscled laborers, and a couple of their women. Others were stirring on the little porch, discussing whether they would go along or not. The violin's tones had reached them and their Latin love of music was stirred.

On the other side of the room Danny opened another dirty window and showed more beautiful trees arching over a mill-race. A stone quarry yawned between it and the building they were in. And on a ridge beyond, there crouched another squalid dwelling. It seemed to cling precariously above the quarry. Jan wondered idly how one reached there. But surely nobody lived in that hovel!

Jan continued her playing until Andy came in and took charge. He thanked her with a grateful smile for her help in keeping the young hoodlums quiet.

There were dozens of children there now, some filthy, a few

scrupulously scrubbed, all scantily clad; here and there a baby in its mother's arms.

When the sound of their singing floated out the open window a few men came sheepishly in, shuffling noisily to the benches at the rear. One, a little older and more worn-looking than the rest, came to the front and sat down, eagerly reaching for the hymnbook that Andy held out to him.

"Leaning, leaning, leaning on the everlasting arms," they sang as Jan's rare-toned Cremona led them. A light of peace shone in the eyes of the tired old man on the front row.

"Poor soul," thought Jan, noting the deep seams in his weather-beaten face. "He looks as if he needed some strong arms to lean on."

After the songs Andy brought instant quiet by bowing his head and speaking very simply and briefly to the Lord for them all.

Then he looked up and smiled at the row of wiggling youngsters down in front.

"Who can give me a verse in the Bible that tells how we must be saved?" he asked briskly.

Several dirty hands went up. Andy pointed to one boy of about ten.

"Ax tixteen tirty-one," he piped up. "Believe on the Lord Jesus Christ an' thou shalt be saved."

"Right. Another?"

The little tousled-haired mite next to Jan stood up, swished her dirty skirts, and recited in a singsong cadence:

"John tree tixteen: Fer God s'loved the world 'at He gave 's only fergotten Son, twosoever b'lieveth in 'im sh'd not per'sh b'tave 'verlasting life."

Andy smiled. "Fine. Now, Dominic, a verse that tells why we need to be saved."

A cross-eyed, dark-skinned boy answered: "For all have sinned and come short of the glory of God." He spoke slowly and clearly.

"Good," smiled Andy. "I see you have been well taught.

Louis, how can we know that we are saved?"

Louis thought a moment. " 'He that believeth on the Son hath everlasting life.' "

"All right, Louis, do you believe?"

"Yes, sir, I do."

"What do you believe?"

"That Jesus Christ is the Son of God and He died for my sins."

"Then what do you have?"

Louis looked puzzled.

"Say that verse over again," directed Andy.

Jan listened carefully with the rest as Louis repeated it: " 'He that believeth on the Son hath everlasting life.' " The boy broke into a smile of surprise. "I have everlasting life," he beamed.

"Then don't you ever do anything wrong, Louis?"

The others snickered at that and Louis turned red, grinned, and poked them in the ribs.

"Sure, I do, sir, but I can go straight to God and tell Him I'm sorry and He has promised to forgive me."

"Oh," said Andy raising his brows, "then you can just go out and sin all you like and God will forgive you. Is that it?"

"Naw!" growled Louis. *"You* know it's not like that You don't *want* to do wrong things when you're born again and think of what He's done fer you. I've found *that* out."

"Yes, you've got something there, brother," answered Andy with a ring in his voice.

Jan, seeing him look so joyous, thought he must have forgotten that his girl friend was sitting alone out in the car glowering.

Just then Andy turned to the blackboard at his back and began to sketch funny little dot-and-line figures of people that seemed to walk and bow and run as he told the age-old story of David and Goliath.

His audience sat breathless and David was just killing Goliath as the door at the back of the room opened and in marched Lucile, just in time to hear Andy shout:

" 'This day will the Lord deliver thee into mine hand; and I will smite thee, and take thine head from thee . . . that all the earth may know that there is a God in Israel.' "

In growing horror Lucile stood transfixed, then putting her hands up to her ears she gave a little scream and ran out of the room slamming the door after her.

Jan, facing the little company, had seen the girl come in. She stifled a giggle and cast a troubled glance toward Andy. But he seemed unperturbed, and carried his story through to its triumphant finish.

There were more songs and then the little meeting closed. Youngsters swarmed like ants up to Doctor Andy, all talking at once, asking how he had made the figures, trying to draw some themselves, pushing and shoving each other to get near the blackboard and the chalk. Some drew shyly toward Jan and put out timorous fingers, patting her arms and looking longingly at the violin case which she had had the foresight to close quickly.

At last they worked their way to the door and Andy turned the key, shooing them all off, promising to come again some time with their regular teacher; and yes, he thought the "violin lady" might be persuaded to come too. Jan smiled assent.

Just as they were nearing the car where Lucile sat in stony indignation, a dirty ragged little girl came running up all out of breath.

She pulled at Andy's sleeve as he stood waving good-bye.

"Please, Mister Teacher," she said, "could you come over to see my mother?" Pitiful tears were making lines in her grimy face that was too thin for such a baby. "She's awful sick and she wants you to make a prayer. She said could the music lady come too? She heard her a-playin' through the winder. My mother ain't goin' ta live, Mister Teacher. The doctor says she may die tonight."

Andy looked at the child in dismay. He had become all too aware of his disgruntled lady in the car and he felt he must hasten to get her back to her own environment, where he could keep his promised date with her. He glanced at her and then at the child. He opened his mouth and closed it again. What should he do?

But Jan stepped up brightly and patted the child's head.

"Of course we'll come, little girlie," she said sympathetically and smiled confidently up at Andy.

Andy wondered how he could have hesitated. He stepped closer to the car and spoke to Lucile in a low tone.

She stared coldly ahead for a moment then suddenly burst out sarcastically:

"Of course, by all means do your ridiculous duty, and leave me here to the mercy of these awful ruffians around here! No, Andrew Hightower," she turned on him, "I'm terrified! You will have to take me home right away!"

Andy glanced back at the little girl and Jan who were already making their way toward a footpath between some trees. He couldn't go back on his promise now.

"Lucile, the woman's dying!" he said desperately. "You are perfectly all right here. I'll leave Danny with you until I return. I will be only a few minutes."

Lucile cast a hateful look at him.

"Danny! As if he was any better than the rest of them!" She stiffened into ice in her seat again as Danny climbed in disapproving silence into the back seat. This woman belonged somehow to his Doctor Andy and so he would guard her as such, but he had no great respect for her, that was plain.

Andy hastened after the two who had disappeared for the moment among the trees.

As he reached them the little girl was just starting across a high bridge of a single plank hung on slender cables across the quarry. It led toward the shack Jan had seen perched on that ridge. The child was apparently used to the frail path suspended in the air, for she ran as lightly onto it as a kitten on a catwalk.

Andy had a feeling of relief that Lucile had decided to remain in the car instead of accompanying them as he had asked her to do. She would have screamed and balked at the bridge.

He saw Jan give a little skip and a delighted cry and start out on the swaying thread after the little child. What a girl! Then he remembered the time so long ago when she had ridden a bicycle across a plank! This bridge would hold no terrors for Jan.

But Jan had never tried a suspension bridge, and when she reached the middle of it, the motion started by the little girl's running, out of rhythm with her own steps, had caused the walk to sway in unpredictable waves. There was a fragile hand cable on either side to grasp but Jan was carrying her violin under one arm and could not reach it on that side. She staggered a little and Andy saw that even she was frightened. There were no sides on the bridge to guard her from falling through. There was only empty space from the footwalk up to the hand cable.

But Andy knew the old bridge from his errant boyhood days and he was aware of its tricks. He measured his own steps to stabilize its swaying and in a few strides he had caught up with Jan and put his arm around her steadyingly. To take her thoughts away from the abyss beneath her he pointed out in a casual voice the low branch of a huge old beech tree that hung far out over the edge of the stone quarry. A scarlet bird sat swinging on its tip and singing a confident little song.

> " 'Be like a bird that, halting in its flight,
>   Rests on a bough too slight.
>   And feeling it give way beneath him, sings,
>   Knowing he hath wings!' "

Andy quoted with a smile.

Jan looked and reveled in the wide empty space, the beauty of the green feathery branch, and the little red dot of life there that seemed so content. The bridge had stopped its wild uneven swing now and it was good to be held in that strong arm. She felt like the little bird herself, in spite of the chasm that stretched away below her with its dark, deep pool lowering at the bottom.

She relaxed in the circle of Andy's arm. "How lovely," she cried. "That little poem, I mean."

Her beautiful face lit up and Andy wondered that he had never noticed before how exquisite she was. She seemed so fragrant and lovely, so vivid and alive. And how sweet of her to be willing to visit a hovel, to use her talent to comfort a poor dying woman whom she had never seen before.

Several moments they stood in breathless wonder. They felt shut in together from all the world. Andy was not intimate in his embrace. He was guarding Jan as he would a precious treasure. Neither of them was conscious for the instant of the furious girl back in the car. They did not know that where they stood they were in full view of her angry eyes.

And neither did they know that Danny was watching them with consternation.

Chapter 19

DANNY HAD WAITED and longed for Jan's homecoming, scarcely able to restrain himself from running away even from his beloved Doctor Andy and the dear home, in order to be there at the station and be the first to greet her and see her dear eyes light up with pleasure when she found him so changed. Of course he had not the right yet to leave the grounds without Andy, and he had had to content himself with the hope that some day when Andy took him in to the boys' club to work, he might happen to see her.

But it had never entered Danny's head that Jan and Doctor Andy might have anything between them more than the merest casual friendship. Danny's heart had been set on Jan for so long that he simply could not conceive of anyone else but himself having first place with her. And in all his strivings to better himself this winter he had had Jan in mind; she was second only to his new Saviour and Master.

But when he saw Doctor Andy look smilingly down into Jan's face, a sword pierced Danny's heart and he could scarcely keep from crying out with the pain of it.

Only after minutes did he become aware of the woman in the seat in front of him. She was looking toward the bridge also, and her lips were shut in a tight hard line, her eyes flashing cold steel.

Then Danny began to come to himself. He recalled that this girl here in the car, not Jan, was Doctor Andy's girl, and because of his faith in Doctor Andy, Danny realized in a flash what must have happened. He drew a free breath again. And strangely enough, he began to feel sorry for that beautiful cold girl in front of him. She didn't know about the sway of the bridge and all. Perhaps he ought to explain. He knew now how she must feel. His own sudden pain had taught him. Anyway he would try to help Doctor Andy. He cleared his throat.

"Ahem!"

The lady did not stir.

"Quite a bridge, that!"

She turned a scornful stare for a fleeting instant.

"It sways a lot. Kinda dangerous," he said and added, "A girl would get scared on that thing easy, you know." Then his heart smote him lest he had made Jan out to be a sissy. It took a good deal to scare Jan, but she might be different now that she had become a lady. Perhaps he had better let well enough alone.

The girl said nothing eloquently.

Danny sighed. Well, he had tried to fix things for Doctor Andy. This sure was a difficult girl. Most women were. All but Jan.

By this time the two on the bridge had moved on. Andy took Jan's violin, freeing her hands. The common rhythm of their footsteps now that the little running girl was off the bridge gave a delightful sensation like a swing. All too soon they were at the other end. The little girl's dress fluttered among the beech trees as she ran ahead to tell her mother they were coming.

As they left the beauty of the woods and emerged into a clearing on the ridge the contrast was awful.

An avenue of trash led to the shanty in the distance. Heap after heap of assorted rubbish crowded the path on either side. Old tin cans lay in piles by the thousand; broken glass seemed to snarl at them with jagged teeth; there were ashes, old plumbing supplies, slate, lumber, iron and broken down furniture.

As they drew nearer to the hovel all of a sudden two fierce bull dogs plunged out growling. Jan drew back and clutched Andy's arm.

He put his other arm about her and led her on.

"See, they're chained," he said reassuringly. "I've heard about this McGarrity family. He's a rag-picker."

A fetid odor of garbage sought them out and they could hear the snorting and grubbing of pigs at the back of the house.

The shack had two rooms and a sort of shed. The shed window had no glass in it, only a burlap curtain. As Jan looked, the burlap moved and a long brown head reached out. The McGarrity horse! He bared his teeth and gave a whinny, like a bitter, disillusioned laugh.

In front of the house a dilapidated sofa crouched on three legs. Its springs showed lumpy under the ragged cover. A goat stood munching at the sofa's entrails. Even the goat looked as if it needed re-upholstering, thought Jan. Altogether it was a dreary scene. Jan had never imagined such conditions. She shuddered. Then she stopped and caught her breath.

There beside the path near the house was a child's ramshackle cot and in it lay a woman, thin and wasted. Her hollow eyes were already glazed and her panting breath came only at intervals as she struggled for more of the filthy air.

"Oh-h-h!" Jan had never seen such misery in her life. Strangely the face bore a resemblance to her Aunt Myra's thin countenance. Jan had the feeling that it was her aunt who lay there dying, and the thought came to her that Aunt Myra's soul was as sickly and stifled as this poor woman's body.

Jan would have knelt impulsively beside the sick woman but Andy held her back.

"You couldn't have helped her," he told her afterward, "and there's no use taking chances, even outdoors. She has T.B. She's had fourteen children and never any care or enough food. Her husband drinks everything up and if the welfare gives the children clothes he takes them away and sells them."

Andy spoke to the woman gently, and she murmured something.

"She wants you to play," he said to Jan.

So Jan played "Nearer, My God, to Thee." Standing there vividly youthful in her fluttering, sunny dress, she made a strange contrast with Death.

The horse looked out again inquiringly. Several children clothed mostly in dirt peered out from behind dump piles, fascinated.

Andy prayed simply and lovingly for the whole household, speaking quite frankly of the fast approaching arrival of this suffering soul in the presence of her Lord.

Then she tried to speak again, and Andy leaned down to catch her words.

"She wants 'Safe in the arms of Jesus,' " he told Jan.

Andy watched Jan's graceful figure as she played. There was wistfulness in his look. He was wishing that his beautiful Lucile had cared as Jan did for the souls of these poor wretches. Would she ever be melted with love for them as this girl seemed to be? For the first time he allowed himself to face the great gulf fixed between himself and Lucile Sommers. Unless she chose to cross that gulf herself, there could never be any fellowship between them. He groaned inwardly.

The sweetness of Jan's music was like a tender voice floating out on the hot summer air. Danny heard it and exulted. But Lucile's heart was hardened with hate.

On the way back across the bridge Andy walked discreetly behind Jan who tripped lightly along, suiting her steps to the swaying of the plank. Now that she had learned how to walk on the bridge she took delight in it. She flung an ecstatic smile back to Andy and in the midst of his heartache it was like a light on his path that seemed just now very dark.

By common consent they slowed their steps as they walked back through the short woods path. Jan looked up with a sweet light in her eyes.

"I think I would rather spend my life doing that kind of playing than to give a command performance before a king!" she said solemnly.

Andy's warm radiant smile broke out.

"I have an idea that that *was* a King's command performance, Jan," he replied. "It was the music that our Lord planned for that poor dear soul to escort her to her heavenly home! I think she will be there before tonight."

"How wonderful," said Jan with tears in her eyes, "to think He'd let *me* do that! Do you know," she said earnestly, pausing in her steps to look up at him, "I have been asking Him to use me somehow in His service!"

"Have you really?" said Andy. "Then He surely will. You know by now what it means to be born again, then?"

"I'm not sure that I understand it all," answered Jan with a troubled frown. "But I've told Him I would like to. I've been longing to ask you more about it."

His face lit up with joy.

"Then we'll have to have a get-together on it. May I stop for you some day this week and take you out to my house again for a little visit? Perhaps your father would come too."

"I'd love it," cried Jan eagerly. But just then they emerged from the woods and there was the car, with Lucile glaring at them in wrath and Danny sitting miserably patient in the back seat.

Lucile gave Jan one long hateful look behind Andy's back as they started and after that she never spoke.

Jan had to cast about in her mind desperately for some subject that would be impersonal. At last she had to resort to the weather and the scenery, and when even that failed they all submitted to Lucile's gloom and only waited for the end of the ride.

Andy let Jan out first as her house was nearest, and then he stopped at the boys' club room, for Danny to finish some preparations for the evening there. Danny's time of probation was nearly up and Andy felt he could trust him.

"I'll be back for you soon," he promised. But there was a troubled frown on his brow as he drove off and left him.

As Jan climbed the dingy stairs at home, she felt a delightful elation. She had a sense that she had been in the very presence of the Almighty and that she had been singled out by Him for special service. How marvelous if He really would

take her music and use it. She hurried to her room and knelt
down beside her bed, pouring out her heart in thankfulness.
Even though the afternoon had turned out so differently from
what she had anticipated, yet it had been a precious time. A few
minutes in Doctor Andy's company seemed a priceless treasure.
Her heart beat fast as she recalled the wonderful feeling of his
strong arm about her. And he had promised to come for her
and take her to his home again! Life looked wonderfully
bright.

"Daddy," she called gaily, "can we have our walk by the
river now? I've had a wonderful time and I want to tell you
all about it."

But somehow she could not bring herself to tell him some
of the most precious things; that moment for instance in the
circle of Doctor Andy's arm and the look in his eyes that she
had glimpsed as she was playing.

"Daddy," Jan began, "I believe we have been missing something all our lives."

Her father looked at her in alarm. Had she grown beyond
him already?

"Yes," she said earnestly, "I remember once you said you
didn't know of any sure way to please God. I think I have
found that there is. He has made the way Himself. He sent
His Son to take our sins and die with them on Him, then He
raised Him from the dead and He gives His own life to whoever will take it. Isn't that wonderful? And it's reasonable to
suppose that He would, knowing we couldn't do anything to
save ourselves."

Jan glanced sidewise at her father. He was not disapproving,
at least.

"Doctor Hightower has taught me a lot, Daddy. He and his
family really *know* God. And I think that is what makes them
so different. Andy knows how to meet things like Death, for
instance. I wish you had been along this afternoon."

Her father wished so too, but he said nothing. He listened
intently as she told him about the scene above the millrace.

"I've asked God to show me how to go the same way as Andy, Daddy," Jan said shyly. "I think He will. Don't you think it sounds wonderful?"

They were leaning on the bridge over the river, looking off at the well-loved forest beyond. John's eyes were misty.

"I wouldn't be surprised," said he uncertainly. "I'm glad you are interested in that sort of thing anyway, girlie."

Jan stole another look at him. Dear old Daddy. She had hoped that he would see as she did and go along with her. But you couldn't hurry Daddy. He would see it in time. It was sweet to be with him again.

They turned back finally and climbed the stairs happily hand in hand. But when they reached their door there lay a yellow envelope addressed to Jan.

Meantime Andrew Hightower was not finding it sweet to be with Lucile.

She sat icily silent, as far away from him as the car seat would allow.

He stole a glance at her several times and sighed. At last he broke the silence.

"If I have offended you, darling," he said gently, "I want to apologize."

She cast him a furious look. The sparks fairly darted from her steely light blue eyes. She was too angry to speak.

"You know," he went on, still in a quiet tone of voice, "I told you I was afraid you might not enjoy that kind of meeting."

"Meeting!" she burst out. "Is *that* all your apology covers! What about you taking me out and insulting me before that uncouth brat of a boy you think so much of? You and your *Christian* preaching! A fine Christian *you* are!" Her voice rose until she was fairly screaming at him. "You court one girl and then as soon as you think you are out of sight you have your arm around another! I suppose you had a lovely time while you dawdled through the woods, too, where you were sure you wouldn't be seen."

Slowing the car Andy stared at Lucile in bewildered horror.

"Oh, you needn't put on your sanctimonious look and make out you don't know what I mean!" she flung at him, her voice discordant in her rage.

"I don't, though," said Andy gently.

"No, of course you don't if it doesn't suit you to. Did you think there was some kind of invisible cloak shielding you on that bridge when you stood there and hugged up that precious slum girl?"

As it slowly dawned on Andy what she meant his eyes filled with trouble, but he smiled amusedly.

"Oh, Lucile!" he cried reaching for her hand. "She is nothing but a child! And she was frightened. I didn't know but she'd lose her balance and fall through that bridge. It's a terribly frightening sensation at first, when the walk gets to swaying under your feet. I'm glad," he laughed, "that is all that is bothering you because truly it was nothing." But even as he spoke Andy began to wonder at the tenderness that stole into his heart at the remembrance of holding that lovely girl in his arms. What ailed him? Had he really been unfaithful in his thoughts to Lucile?

"That certainly is a fine story!" sneered Lucile. "Easy alibi! So she's a child, is she? A child wouldn't look at you the way she did! Well, go ahead and enjoy your slum girls. I knew there must be some other attraction besides your precious gang of boys! You can let me out here, Doctor Hightower. I'll walk up the drive myself. No, I don't care to keep our date now or ever!" she stormed as he started to put his hand out to stay her. "You can keep away from me and my house. I hate your silly old religion and I *hate you!*" She opened the door wildly and Andy, to save her, had to stop the car. The angry tears were raining down her face as she stalked away from him up the driveway.

In heavy silence he sat and watched her go out of his life. She had forbidden him to follow her and somehow he had a feeling of relief when he realized that there was no call for him to do so. But he felt as if he had been struck a heavy blow. The ideal of Lucile that he had built up these past few months was shattered. The hope he had clung to, that some day she would see as he did, was dead now.

As he watched her turn the bend in her driveway, he had the feeling that she was already miles away from him. He bowed his head and spoke aloud.

"Father, I've asked You to save her but she doesn't want to be saved." He groaned inwardly. "If it's not in Your plan that she and I go on together, make my will Yours. And if You want me to walk alone all the days of my life, remind me that my life is not my own. Thy will be done!"

A long moment he sat with his head down, then taking a deep calm breath he started his engine and drove on. His heart had never been so heavy but he was conscious of a peace that he had not experienced for months.

He went straight to the boys' club to pick up Danny.

He was startled to find the door wide open and Danny not in sight. The room was topsy turvy. The chairs were upset and some of them were broken. The ping-pong balls had been mashed flat and the racquets battered. The fresh paint on the walls was smeared and scraped. The floor was filthy.

Andy was aghast. He had expected opposition, but not this. And where was Danny? Had they made off with him? He would not put it past some of those hoodlums to frame Danny with the cops deliberately, knowing that his time of probation was not quite over.

Anxiously he called, at the same time searching the big closet where he had stored a good deal of the equipment he had meant to use. The closet had been ransacked and a lot of the stuff was gone.

Then he heard the cautious turning of a key in the lock of the lavatory off the main room.

Danny peered out, his face pale and ashamed.

"Oh, Doctor Andy!" he cried. "I'm just no good. I shoulda

stayed and tooken care o' things, but when I heared 'em coming I couldn't seem to stand up." In his distress Danny's lately acquired grammar forsook him. "My legs shook and first thing I knew I was in here with the door locked. Doctor Andy, will you forgive me? Oh, you'll never be able to trust me again!"

Greatly relieved, Andy put his arm about the trembling boy. "Don't worry about that, Dan," he comforted him. "Thank God you are safe. I shouldn't have left you here alone yet. We will have to expect this sort of thing, I guess. The kids just can't understand that we love them, that's all. Sometime we'll have a chance to show them. The only thing to do now is clean up the mess and start again. Keep your chin up, Dan. I just don't want them to hurt you, that's all."

In shame and sorrow Danny set about helping put things to rights. Suddenly he gave an exclamation. "Here's a note for you," he called to Andy. It was nailed crudely to the top of a table.

"This is a warning," it read. "You can keep out or else you will be sorry. We are out to get you and that dirty punk with you." The note was signed merely by a crude skull and crossbones.

"That's Pad Hucker's gang," said Danny in a scared voice.

"Yes? Well, our handballs are gone, and the gloves, too," said Andy trying to pass off the threat casually to cheer Danny. "But I guess we'll have to count on replenishing every now and then, anyway."

They managed to get most of the damage repaired by the time the boys came in. So far only a few strays, mostly very young boys, had dared to venture. The older boys still scorned the new project and stayed severely away. The little ones who came reported now and then what the older ones threatened to do if "the doc kept on meddlin'." But up until now the threats had been merely rumors.

Andy made up his mind never to leave Danny alone there again, at least until his probation time was up. By then perhaps they would have won over one or two of the gang's leaders and it might be safer for him.

That evening the little boys showed great interest in the object lesson that Andy gave, and he and Danny were somewhat encouraged.

But Andy slept very little all night. When he did fall into a troubled slumber he kept seeing Lucile's angry back as if retreating from the dishevelled club room. In his dreams he thought she was the one who had caused the disarray. Then he would rouse to his sorrow and go over and over every detail of his association with Lucile trying to find some point where he had failed to act as he should. He tortured himself by thinking if he had done this, or said that, perhaps she would have become more softened. But gradually the bitter truth forced itself upon him that Lucile never had been what he had thought she was. She loved the world with all its pride of life and she had no intention of changing her mind about it. The discovery of this stung Andy more than even her bitter words to him that afternoon.

He paced the floor for hours in anguish of heart until at last, toward morning, he grew ashamed of himself and flinging himself upon his knees he laid the whole matter in the hands of his Lord and left it there.

Chapter 20

JAN OPENED HER telegram with forboding. "It's sure to be from Aunt Myra," she wailed.

But it was from the manager of the hotel where she was to play that summer, asking her to come immediately as the season was opening full blast and he needed her.

Disappointment gripped Jan as she realized that this meant the end of her vacation. There would be no more good times with her father and no chance of that visit with the Hightowers.

She saw the chagrin in her father's eyes, too, as she read the message aloud.

"Oh, Daddy, do I *have* to go? It seems as if I had just got home."

"Yes, I think you ought to," John answered slowly with a heavy sigh, "if you are going to take the work at all."

"I suppose you're right," agreed Jan. "But I had counted on more time here. However, I'll be so proud to be able to send you some money, Daddy! You have always done so much for me."

She flung her arms about him and he held her close, but he trembled at the thought of the long weeks and months when his arms would be empty again.

Jan plunged into preparations for her going and at times seemed excited over the prospect.

"You will be coming up week ends, won't you, Daddy?" she coaxed.

"Oh, I don't belong in a fashionable hotel, girlie," he said. "I don't have the clothes nor the manner for it. You'd be ashamed of me."

"Now, Daddy!" cried Jan. "I'd never be ashamed of you. You

know that. There isn't a girl in the world who has such a wonderful father. I saw some of the fathers of those girls at school and I wouldn't have exchanged you for ten of them with all their money and swank."

John smiled, but the old fear was there. Still he would not keep her. She had her life before her.

So he saw her off as bravely as he could the next day and went back to his lonely apartment again.

When Jan reached the hotel she found awaiting her a cordial letter from Stancel Egbert. The memory of his unwelcome kiss had faded somewhat and she was glad to hear from him. The letter took away the feeling of homesickness that had gripped her when she found herself among entire strangers. She was grateful for his thoughtfulness. There were flowers from him, too, the next evening and a gay little note.

And so her summer of glamor began.

Aunt Myra came up for a week now and then just to bask in Jan's popularity, but Jan dreaded her coming after the first time for she made her feel like an exhibit. She was guilty of feeling relieved when Aunt Myra decided that the mountain altitude was too much for her heart and she stayed at home.

Sometimes Jan tried to steal off by herself for a walk through the woods or down to the shabby little town farther down the mountain. She thought perhaps she could recover some of the sane content that she had felt that day at the mission with Doctor Andy. But almost always she would be overtaken by some admirer and taken possession of, with flattery and fresh plans for passing away the time.

Jan had been at the hotel a month and had begun to wish heartily that the summer was over when one evening just a little before dinner time she saw an elderly couple come slowly into the lobby and seat themselves before the huge fireplace. It was Doctor Andy's father and mother! With a little cry of delight Jan ran over to them.

"How wonderful to find you here!" she exclaimed. "Perhaps you don't remember me, though." She hesitated as they gave her a pleasant, blank smile. "I'm Jan Nielson. Your son brought me out to your house last summer and I stayed for supper. I have never forgotten what a precious time I had with you. I have just longed to see you again."

And then their faces lit up with real welcome and Mrs. Hightower arose and folded the girl in her arms and kissed her.

"You are feeling stronger now?" she asked Doctor Hightower solicitously.

"Yes," he smiled. "At least I have done away with my wheel chair although I'm still not quite up to myself."

Jan gaily took every opportunity to be with the Hightowers. When she discovered that Doctor Andy himself had brought them up to the hotel she could have wept with disappointment that she had missed seeing him. Andy's mother noted her little expression of dismay and wondered.

"Yes, my son insisted on our being here," explained Doctor Hightower, "although I told him that a less expensive place would do very well for us. But he thinks he must treat us like china dolls." He laughed.

"But Andrew knew that you would need special care and rest," urged his hovering wife, "because of your trying to do the Bible teaching down in the town, you know."

"Oh," cried Jan, "are you giving Bible lessons somewhere? How I should love to hear them! I have been just aching for someone to explain a lot of things I've been reading in the Bible."

Both old faces brightened with interest.

"Yes," said Doctor Hightower, "there is a little church down the mountain where the people love the gospel. They fairly turn themselves inside out to get Bible teachers to come and teach them more. My son was apprehensive about my being able to take the meetings, but I feel stronger and it is the work I love best to do." Doctor Hightower looked years younger in his eagerness.

"Could I come and listen?" asked Jan wistfully. "What time are the meetings?"

"There are classes morning, afternoon, and evening every day for two weeks," he said. "I speak in the morning because I feel fresher then."

Jan clapped her hands. "Then I could come?" she cried eagerly.

"Yes indeed," they both answered. "You must ride down with us. Then if you have questions we can talk on the way back."

So Jan, much to the disgust of some of her would-be suitors went off every morning to the plain little church in the valley.

She drank in the truth hungrily and before the first week was over she began to be aware of her old longing to use her music in the service of the Lord.

Every two or three nights she was scheduled to give a short recital in the hotel music room, or play a number or two with other artists. One evening, after she had played a lively gypsy dance and received unusual applause, she stood a moment smiling at her little audience some of whom were around the piano and some standing in the doorways. Then she spoke in a clear voice, announcing her next number.

"I should like to play a selection arranged from one of Mendelssohn's songs," she said. "It was written originally, as you know, as a 'Song Without Words,' but someone has set words to it, and they have come to mean a great deal to me. It seems to me that the words express the longing of many hearts in these days of unrest. May I give them to you before I play?"

Jan smiled sweetly again, and went on to recite,

" 'We would see Jesus, for the shadows lengthen
    Across this little landscape of our life.
We would see Jesus, our weak faith to strengthen
    For the last weariness, the final strife.

We would see Jesus, this is all we're needing;
    Strength, joy and willingness come with the sight.
We would see Jesus, dying, risen, pleading,
    Then welcome, day! And farewell mortal night!' "

In the little awed silence her words brought, Jan played the immortal strains of the Consolation hymn. There were tears on many faces before she finished, and in the pause after her last whispering note died away someone out by the doorway called out, "Play 'Nearer My God to Thee.'"

Jan assented with a smile and putting her violin up to her chin again she played the simple melody through in double-stops, making a rich harmony that filled the big rooms like sweet voices singing. When she had finished there was a deep silence filled with wistfulness. The people in the fashionable hotel seemed to bow a moment in worship as the name of the Lord was proclaimed.

Afterward many came to Jan with tears and thanked her. The manager told her some of his most valued guests had asked if she would lead them in an old-fashioned hymn sing now and then.

Jan absorbed a great deal of Bible knowledge from Doctor Hightower during their two weeks' stay. And she determined that when they left she would continue attending services at the little church down the mountain.

The Hightowers had been overjoyed to re-discover the beautiful girl who so loved the deep things of God. They spoke often of their son's interest in his work among the boys, and told her many little incidents about Danny's life and growth in grace, all of which delighted Jan beyond measure.

The old couple wrote home to Andy about finding his young friend at the hotel, and the day before they were to leave, he came up for them, bringing Danny with him.

Jan was pleased at the quiet dignity that Danny had acquired. He carried himself well, and gave no sign that this was the first time in his life he had ever entered such a place. She greeted him with her old friendliness, and rejoiced to have him one of them.

Danny's heart was in his eyes when he first caught sight of her. They arrived in the evening while she was playing, and Danny thought he had never seen anything so beautiful in

all his life as Jan in her soft white evening gown with a bit
of glitter in her dark hair. His eyes shone, and when Jan threw
him a welcome glance of surprise and pleasure right there before the whole gathering, he felt that his cup of joy was full.

He was so taken up with watching Jan that he did not see
the look on Doctor Andy's face. But Jan did not miss it, and
her heart went to hammering so that she could scarcely keep
her mind on her playing.

When she had finished she almost ran over to their little
group. Danny was nearest and she greeted him first, but when
she put out her hand to Andy he eagerly took it in both of his.

"When we heard that *you* were here," he said looking straight
into her eyes, "we just had to come a day early." The pretty
pink came up in Jan's cheeks. "Dad and Mother have been
writing me all about you," added Andy in a low voice, "and
I've been praising the Lord for you and your testimony here
in this hotel."

The happy tears came into Jan's eyes and she found no words,
her voice was so choked with joy. All she could do was to answer
with her eyes the gladness in his own.

But poor Danny saw their meeting and the color left his face.
It was true, then, as he had suspected on the bridge that day,
that there was more than mere friendship between these two
people whom he loved best in the world. He seemed turned to
stone the rest of the evening.

It was the most natural thing in the world for Jan and Andy
to saunter out for a walk through the moonlit woods after the
concert. It never occurred to either of them that Danny might
have been asked to go along. Andy simply took for granted
that Danny was upstairs on his way to bed.

"We have been promising ourselves this chance to talk for a
long time, haven't we!" Andy said as he drew Jan's arm in his
and steered her down a quiet pine-scented path where they
could hear the faint tinkling of a mountain brook hurrying
along through the night.

Jan looked joyfully up at him in the moonlight. He looked

so dear and comforting beside her. She had not realized how she had been longing to see him.

"Yes, I have been wanting to ask you so many questions," she said. "Ever since that first day—I mean that *awful* day at the big brick house when you saved me so marvelously. I have always wondered, for one thing, whether you had any trouble with the police on my account?"

He laughed.

"I had quite a bit of explaining to do," he said. "But I finally managed to make them believe me. The poor woman died soon after that, and there was no need for any more detective work."

"That's good," said Jan. "I have spent many an anxious thought on you, wondering if you were in trouble on my account."

"That was nice of you," he laughed. "I guess most girls would have been spending more thought on their own troubles than on mine," he said seriously. "But to tell you the truth, I have spent a lot of thought and prayer on you, Jan. I wished so that I might help you. And now Dad and Mother tell me that you are going on wonderfully. I can't tell you how I have rejoiced over it. It isn't often that a girl as lovely as you are, with such a brilliant future, is willing to step away from the path of worldly success and walk with the Lord. If I am delighted, what must He be?"

The wonder and depth of feeling in Andy's tone made Jan thrill again and again. It had never occurred to her that Jesus Christ would take any special notice of her. It was an overwhelming thought.

Andy stopped in the moonlit path and looked down straight into her eyes again. Jan's heart seemed to stop for very joy.

"You know," he said softly, "I feel as if I had some real right to you, because God let me introduce you to Him."

He leaned over and laid his lips reverently on her forehead. "Jan," he said earnestly, "I believe He is going to use you wonderfully in His service some day."

"I wish He would," breathed Jan. "That's what I've asked Him to do."

"You know, Jan," Andy said as they strolled slowly on, "you have grown up a lot since I first met you." There was admiration in his tone and his arm was about her guiding her tenderly between the trees.

"Yes," she said with a little catch in her voice. "It seems years since I was a crazy tomboy in Chester. Well, I passed my eighteenth birthday last month. Of course I'm not so *very* old yet," she laughed with a trill, "but I feel lots older."

All of a sudden they reached a little turn in the path and found themselves near the hotel entrance again.

A young man was standing on the porch looking with annoyance this way and that down through the wooded paths around the building.

His hands were in his pockets and he clinked the change in them in irritation.

"Here, boy!" he called to a trim colored bellboy who passed him. "Haven't you seen Miss Nielson anywhere about? I'm sure she has not retired. I have rung and rung her room. She was expecting me."

"No sir, I ain't seen her since the concert, sir. It seems to me I saw her start out for a walk with some young man but that was a long time ago. Could be she ain't got back yet." The young fellow showed white teeth in a grin which tried to be courteous. He knew better than to show amusement.

Just then two figures emerged into the bright light of the hotel veranda.

"Oh, there you are, Jan!" called Stancel impatiently. "You have been gone a long time. Didn't you get my telegram? I told you I would be here this evening."

"Oh, why—Stan!" exclaimed Jan. In her excitement over seeing Danny and Andy she had forgotten all about the telegram which had arrived at dinner time.

"This is my friend Doctor Hightower, Stan. Andy, this is

Stancel Egbert, the minister of the church in Oak Hill."

The two young men shook hands. Stancel was coolly impersonal but Andy gave the other man a pleasant smile of greeting, adding a word about the delightful weather. Stancel made no response.

As the three walked into the hotel lobby together, Jan wondered why she was so disappointed to have Stan turn up just now. It seemed as if somehow that precious time on the woodpath was desecrated.

It was late and Jan excused herself very soon. So they all retired, for the two young men did not find very much in common except Jan and neither of them cared to discuss her with the other.

Danny was in bed when Andy went up, but he was only pretending to be asleep. After Andy went to sleep he spent a good deal of the night down on his knees, fighting a long hard battle. The next morning Danny the gay young boy was gone. In his place was a grave, serious young man. But on his face was a look of peace and victory.

Chapter 21

DANNY WAS UNUSUALLY quiet on the long trip home. Andy rallied him on it once or twice, but Danny only managed a sad little grin and kept his own counsel. Andy asked him in a low voice so that his father and mother on the back seat might not hear: "What's on your chest, Dan?"

Danny sighed and turned him off with, "Oh, nothing." Then when he saw that he must give some account, he only said, "I was thinking I'd like to get down there to the city and get next to some of the gang. There's quite a few of the fellows would listen, I think, if I can only put it to them right."

"I'm afraid it isn't safe for you, pal," warned Andy. "Remember that note, the time they had the rumpus there?"

"Phooey!" responded Danny doggedly. "Did all those missionaries you've told us about ever stop for that? I tell you what, Doctor Andy, I wish you'd let me have a cot down there in the little room back of your office. You'd be there a good deal of the time, you know. I think it's time I got out and mixed with the gang some. Maybe I'll get somewhere that way."

They had some argument about it but at last Andy consented to let Danny have his way as soon as his probationary time was over.

Andy had arranged for Danny to work short hours at a grocery store. He was taking some courses in the Bible School and that would fill up his time. There had been no more disturbance at the boys' club and although they did not seem to be making much progress Andy and Danny were not too discouraged. Andy had expected that the work would be slow. He had taken rooms for his own office next door to the boys' club room and hung out his shingle. The calls from patients were beginning to come in but they too were slow.

So while the summer sped on Danny prayed and planned, but his heart was back in the mountains with Jan.

Once at "Lookaway" he was sent out to the mailbox to bring in the mail and there, in Jan's handwriting, was a fat letter for Doctor Andy right on top. There was one for him, too, but though he devoured every word of his, the pain never left his heart.

Jan wrote warmly, lovingly, but that was the trouble. She was too ready to love him like a dear old pal. She told him how she had tried to talk about her new Saviour to various young friends of hers up there at the hotel, and how they scoffed at her. She did not mention Stancel Egbert, either to Andy or Danny.

Jan had done her best to interest Stancel in the little church.

"You will surely love it, Stan," she said eagerly. "They are plain people, but so loving and cordial. I feel right at home there already."

"Oh, my dear pious little girl," he scoffed. "Please don't drag me to a country church service! Can't you understand that I've come off here to get a rest from services? Why waste our time in a little country church where the minister likely hasn't even a speaking acquaintance with good English, or modern theology? Do forget your religion, Jan. We are on vacation!"

"Oh, but Stan, you don't realize what you might miss. They have some of the finest Bible scholars of the country there for summer conferences."

"I don't care if the Angel Gabriel is preaching there. I want to spend the time with you!"

At last one Sunday he gave in and went with her. But he made such fun of everything he heard that Jan was sorry she had made him go.

"It was just exactly what I expected," he told her loftily. "What more could you hope for from a little old dump like that? Their religion is as uncomfortable as their old benches,

and as outworn as their hymnbooks! My dear, unless you have
a religion that is geared to the youth of today, by the best minds
of today, you are bound to be classed with the fossils."

Jan looked him steadily in the eye, with a twinkle in her own.

"I have learned that the fossils are a wonderful proof of
the truth of the Word of God!" said she. "I think I shan't mind
being a fossil. And as for comfort, don't you think that it must
have been very uncomfortable for Jesus on the cross?"

Stancel turned crimson with indignation.

"Janette! For heaven's sake, don't go off the deep end with
religion! A lot of young people do just that when they are
carried away with a fancy sounding doctrine. Trust me, my
dear, to help you keep your head. I am thankful that I never
went through that phase of fanaticism. Some people actually
lose their minds over it, you know. And even if they don't go
that far, they become unbalanced."

"Do you think the Spirit of God can become fanatical, Stan?"
Jan asked seriously.

"I'm sure I don't know what you mean!" he replied, ex-
asperated.

"Because," explained Jan, "I think that if individuals would
yield every bit of themselves to Him, so that He filled them,
they couldn't become unbalanced because He isn't. It is only
when they hold back a part of themselves that that could happen."

"Oh my word!" groaned Stancel. "Let's skip this and talk
about something more interesting."

"What is more interesting?" asked Jan.

They were on one of the woodland paths, screened from
view. Stancel glanced about cautiously. "This!" he cried, seiz-
ing her and pressing her close to him, kissing her hair and her
eyes and her mouth passionately.

Jan writhed and twisted in his grasp. She was not a screaming girl; besides, she was not frightened, only angry. When at
last he released her with a hoarse "There! My lovely little
Puritan!" she did not cry out. She simply stood and looked

at him; her scorn spoke louder than words. She stared him down until he became angry, too, and would have seized her again, but she slipped like a wraith from his grasp and fled back through the trees and into the hotel. The next day, to her relief, he was gone.

Aunt Myra did not return to the mountains, even for a week end. Her heart was still in bad condition, her doctor said. The high altitude was too much for her. But she wrote Jan and told her that she was counting on her coming back to Oak Hill that fall.

"I have already arranged for your term at the music school," she wrote. "It is paid in advance and I expect you to be here at the start. Professor Morelli is very anxious that you finish out your studies here and graduate. He feels that this year should mean a great deal to your future success.

"Besides, I need you, child. My health is not good. I can never tell you what it has meant to me to have you here with me, my own sister's daughter. I am afraid you have thought me very hard at times, but I have not intended to be so. It is my nature. You will have to overlook it.

"I shall expect you on the third of September or before, as the school opens the fourth. Do not be late.

"Affectionately,

"Aunt Myra."

That was the nearest to a loving letter Jan had ever received from her aunt. It melted her heart as no amount of money or gifts had ever done. She sent it on to her father and asked him if he did not think she ought to go.

"Of course I had looked forward to being with you again, Daddy, but I can just hear you say that it is her due, as she has done so much for me. It seems as if I have had so many disappointments! But I guess I am getting used to them now. Anyway, I do think this is right."

Once more John Nielson dropped his head sadly in his

hands. He had no hope now of ever having his daughter as his own again. But he could see Jan's viewpoint, and it probably was wise for her to take all the training she could get while it was offered so freely. He felt humiliated to think that he had never been able to give it to her himself. But perhaps this was God's way of providing for her. More and more John had been falling into the habit of taking God into his reckonings, ever since that talk with Jan by the river.

Andrew Hightower had been to see him, too, and he had taken him out to visit his parents one day. John had felt utterly humble but surprisingly at ease with the Hightowers, and it had cheered him greatly to hear their praise of his daughter. Old Doctor Hightower had talked lovingly of what the Lord had meant to him through the years, and John had had the opportunity to have many of his own questions answered.

So the summer sped by and once more Jan was back at Oak Hill.

It was with many misgivings that Andy finally left Danny at his new quarters near the boys' club. He decided that he would do well to sleep as well as work nearby himself. It would be a good thing to be on easy call for his patients in the neighborhood, and also, if he was around to play an occasional game of ball in the street with some of the boys he might win them that much sooner.

So he fitted up another small room next to Danny's. But the night before he moved there he stopped in after a late call at the hospital to make sure that Danny was all right. There was no answer when he knocked. Danny's door was unlocked so he went in.

Danny lay on the floor all but unconscious. His clothes had been stripped from him and torn into ribbons. His face was bloody and one arm lay stretched out abnormally crooked. There were bruises all over him from head to foot.

Andy grabbed a blanket and covered him warmly and then tenderly knelt beside him. He had not realized how very much the boy had come to mean to him.

"Danny boy!" he whispered. "Who was it?"

"It was Pad Hucker and his gang," moaned Danny. "They stomped me. But never mind. I've been prayin' for 'em, an' I'm sure we'll get 'em yet for the Lord, Doctor Andy."

The tears came to Andy's eyes and he choked down a sob.

"It's no more 'n what those folks did to *Him*, back there in the Bible," whispered Danny faintly. "Not near as much. Anyway, I'll mend, Doctor Andy," Danny managed a weak smile.

As gently as he could Andy set the arm and put a splint on it. He picked him up and laid him on the bed. Then he ran into his office, almost afraid to leave Danny for even a moment. He got what supplies he needed and spent the rest of the night there tending him. Except for the broken arm, Danny's hurts were mostly superficial but they were painful and it was some weeks before Danny was able to be about without agony. But he appeared faithfully at each boys' club meeting, and he sent his tormentors various messages of forgiveness by way of the younger boys who were still the only ones to patronize Andy's club room. Andy kept a close watch on Danny. He had wanted to move him out to "Lookaway," but Danny would not hear of it.

"The gang won't do anything more for a while," he assured Andy, "I know how they work. They'll wait to see how I plan to get it back on 'em. An' too, they'll lay low for fear we'll sick the cops on 'em. You let me stay, please, Doctor Andy."

So, reluctantly, Andy had Danny's bed moved into his own room, and hired one of the younger boys who could be trusted, to stay with him when Andy could not be there, warning him to call him instantly if any trouble should arise.

A few weeks after that Doctor Andy had a call in the night. The baby sister of one of Pad Hucker's friends had been left alone in the house and had swallowed the greater part of a bottle of gasoline. Andy worked desperately but there was no use, the fight had been lost even before he was called.

After that Andy learned that the gang was out to "get" him.

All they had been waiting for was some excuse to trump up against him.

Danny put himself quietly on the alert, keeping his ear to the ground for any rumor that trouble was brewing. One or two of the little boys had become faithful attendants and loyal informers, so Danny hoped that he would be warned in time of any fresh disturbance. Each day, morning and evening, Danny would pray with Andy that Pad Hucker might be saved.

"If we get him," Danny said, confidently, "we'll get the rest."

Neither Danny nor Andy told Jan about the details of Danny's beating, although both of them wrote describing the club room and telling of their progress.

They thought that Jan seemed interested, but she did not write often. She was kept constantly on the go, pushed by Aunt Myra and urged on by her music teacher.

Andy had enlisted John Nielson's help with some of the work at the boys' club, teaching the ones who were interested how to make simple engines that would really run. The youngsters who came were fascinated and gradually there was a small nucleus of boys who were beginning to take hold of spiritual truths, also. Now and then a big sister would drop in to watch. Andy suspected that their interest was chiefly in the fact that two young men were in charge, but he welcomed the girls and did his best for them, too.

Christmas was drawing on and Andy had wonderful schemes for a big Christmas party.

"Perhaps we can persuade your daughter to help with the music at Christmas," Andy suggested one day to John. A bright eagerness lit up John's face for an instant and then his usual tired hopeless look returned.

"She hasn't said anything about coming home for Christmas," John said sadly. "I don't know whether she'll be here or not. I don't like to interfere with her work there."

He looked so disheartened that Andy wondered about it. He felt half inclined to write to the lovely girl and tell her that her father was breaking his heart for her, but he decided that was none of his business. She would probably turn out like most beautiful talented girls. She would soon have her head turned and then she'd be interested only in her own career. Andy sighed, remembering the sweet talk they had had in the woods. The thought of Lucile rarely troubled him now. He had not made any attempt to see her again, and she did not appear at the hospital any more. When he did think of her these days it was with wonder that his broken heart was mending, and thanksgiving that he had been kept from making a fatal mistake.

The next day he spoke to Danny about Jan. He thought that since the two had always been such friends, possibly Danny might have some influence with Jan.

"Do you know whether Jan Nielson is going to be back for Christmas?" he asked casually. "It would be great to have her play at the party, wouldn't it?"

He had expected Danny's face to light up with anticipation, but only a deep wistfulness came into Danny's eyes, and then he turned away to hide the pain from his beloved Doctor Andy.

"Sure would," he said. "But I dunno if she is or not." And then he changed the subject.

Andy began to wonder whether there had been some misunderstanding between Jan and her father or Danny. Had she perhaps grown away from them? It might be that the glamor of her life in Oak Hill had already weaned her away. Andy felt a real stab of disappointment at the thought. He planned to write to Jan that night himself.

But he never wrote the letter.

Chapter 22

ANDY AND DANNY with John's help had set up the Christmas tree and trimmed the room with gay balls and branches. It was still a week before Christmas but they had decided to give the boys as long a time for celebration as possible. The festivities and even the pretty decorations seemed to mean a great deal to the youngsters who had never had any real Christmas fun in their lives.

The three took a last satisfied look at the room before they went out for their dinner. There was to be a regular meeting that night, and they were anxious to see the children's faces when they should come in. John had built a make-believe fireplace at the far end of the room, and laid a realistic log fire in it, with the help of a few red electric bulbs.

But after John had left them and Danny and Andy were about to go to a restaurant for their supper one of the little boys appeared out of the dusk and slid into the back seat of Andy's car, crouching down out of sight.

"Drive on," he ordered Andy importantly. Andy started the car and moved slowly down the street.

"The gang's gettin' ready fer a showdown," whispered the child in a scared voice. "It might be tonight er it might be tamorra. Better have the cops on hand. They mean business. Now take me down town an' let me out there. They'll kill me if they find I've squealed."

Andy frowned. It would be like those hoodlums to try to spoil the Christmas party. And he and Danny had so hoped that the party might help to draw them, out of curiosity if for no other reason. He had told the little boys several of the attractions planned, such as a professional magician and games with real prizes. He knew that the news would surely have been thoroughly broadcast in the neighborhood by now.

"I don't think we'll call the cops," he decided. "That might only make more trouble. You kids just keep your eyes and ears open. I guess we can handle things all right."

"But they're out to get *you*, Doctor Andy," warned the child. "I'll tell you one o' the real reasons. I been tellin' my sister all you've taught us, an' she's been a lot diffrunt lately. She won't drink no more ner go places with Pad Hucker, an' he's killin' mad. See? That's why I tole ya." The boy was so deeply in earnest that his voice was choking with fright.

"Oh, don't worry about me," Andy tried to reassure him. "I guess I can handle Pad. But thanks for the warning, kid. We'll be on the lookout."

He let the boy out of the car and he and Danny went on. Danny looked worried.

"If that's true, Doctor Andy, the kid is right," he said wisely. "We ought to tell the cops. I know that gang."

Andy looked surprised.

"You have said yourself, Dan, that cops only mess up the situation."

"Not in a case like this, Doctor Andy," warned Danny.

But Andy still refused to get in touch with the police.

"If we call them, Dan, we might as well quit our work now. We'd never get to first base with any of the boys. You know that, Danny."

Danny said no more, but he excused himself before Andy had finished, saying he wanted to buy a newspaper. He went out of the store and was gone several minutes and when he returned he did not mention what he had been doing.

After a call or two on patients, Andy and Danny returned to the club room. Danny was silent and nervous, and Andy himself was full of apprehension.

They were surprised to find not a boy in sight. There was

usually a little knot of them hanging around, waiting to have the door opened.

They unlocked the door and went in. Andy half expected to find the Christmas decorations spoiled, but everything was in order and the room itself seemed to wear a breathlessly expectant air.

But no sooner was the door closed behind them than six or eight boys burst out from closets and behind furniture. Pad Hucker was in the lead with a snarl on his face. He came straight toward Andy threateningly, and there was an ugly homemade gun in his hand. Danny saw it first. The gang often used them. They called them "Zips."

Danny was about to dart in front of Andy to guard him when his alert eyes caught the gleam of a real gun aimed straight at Pad, in the hand of a policeman at the door. Danny himself had warned the police but Pad mustn't be shot! He wasn't ready to die! With a cry Danny flung himself toward Pad instead of Andy and fell face down as the report of the officer's gun rang out.

There were shouts and sudden uproar in the midst of which the other boys vanished and Pad Hucker was left glaring fiercely in the middle of the room with his wrists in handcuffs. But Danny lay perfectly still, the blood oozing from a wound in his back.

The officer whose gun had shot him was frantic. "I didn't go to do it, Doc, honest I didn't. I was aiming at the Zip in this guy's hand!"

But Andy was down beside Danny, turning him gently. He soon saw that it might be only a matter of minutes before Danny would no longer be with them. His heart was torn with anguish. Then Danny suddenly opened his eyes and saw Pad staring incredulously down at him. A radiant smile lit Danny's face.

"They didn't—get you?" he murmured with relief. "I'm glad! Now maybe you'll—see how I felt—when I found—that Jesus cared enough—to die for me!"

Danny's smile faded and his eyes fluttered shut. Andy thought for a moment that he was gone. He cast an agonized look up at Pad.

Pad stood looking down at Danny, his face working!

Two policemen were guarding Pad, and they watched him closely. Suddenly tears streamed down his face.

"He told the kids that he'd forgave me," blurted Pad, "but I thought he was just tryin' to frame me. He—he *meant* it!" Great sobs shook Pad's big body.

" 's okay, Pad," breathed Danny again. "I guess—there wasn't any other way—to make you understand."

The room was silent. Tears blinded Andy's eyes as he stroked Danny's hand and smoothed his hair.

Then Danny opened his eyes again and looked at Andy.

"Jan—" Andy bent down to catch his words. "Tell her—I loved her—but I'm out—of the way now. She was—yours—anyway. And—you'll get Pad now. God let me—help. I'm—glad!"

Another brilliant light seemed to come over Danny's face and then he was gone and Andy was left struggling with his sorrow, hardly able to believe that the dear loyal soul who had been so close to him lately was in the presence of the Lord whom they had loved and served together.

When Pad took in what had happened he gave a heart-rending cry.

"Officer," he begged, the tears still on his face, "leave me take 'is hand just once. Please, officer!"

Silently the policeman, still distrustful of the boy, knelt with him beside the still form on the floor.

As if it were a solemn rite Pad gripped Danny's lifeless hand, then he bent over and laid his forehead on it a moment.

Andy, in the midst of his heartache, felt a tide of wonder fill him at the change in the boy they had been praying for so long.

As Pad rose to his feet he looked Andy straight in the eyes and said, earnestly, with a break in his voice,

"Doc, you're my boss now. I came here to stomp you but I see I jus' wasn't hep to what Dan here had on his chest. I thought he was just all bugged up an' you had done it. I don't get the gist of it all yet, but I can see this Jesus that Dan talked about must be a big shot for sure. I want ta know that the gang is at your service, even though I—" he glanced down at his wrists, "I'll be outa the picture fer a while. Okay, officer, let's go."

Andy rose to his feet and went over to Pad and gripped the boy's big hamlike hand, bound as it was.

"Okay, Pad," said Andy huskily. "I guess you know this has hit me pretty hard, but I saw what happened and I know Danny wanted it this way. I'll count on you, Pad, and I'll be seeing you. I'll do everything I can for you, brother."

Pad looked into Andy's suffering eyes and saw that he meant what he said.

He nodded in an embarrassed way and went out with the officer.

While the other policeman was at the telephone Andy knelt again beside his beloved friend.

"Danny, Danny!" he moaned. "You've paid such a terrible price! But your prayers are answered, Danny boy, and I know you're rejoicing now! But what will I do without you, boy?"

Then as the realization of his loss came over him like a flood, Andy cried out his heart,

"Lord, I'll need your help. Don't let this offering of Danny's be wasted. Let me make the most of it for Your sake, Lord. Let eternal life come to these boys because of it."

Sorrowfully he arose and set about the innumerable tasks that must be performed. He must tell Danny's father and mother first, then John Nielson, and certainly Jan.

Jan! Would she be utterly brokenhearted? He had not yet taken in what it was that Danny had said about her. Had she loved Danny as Danny loved her? The thought brought a sudden stab, and his heart went out to her. It would be a sad homecoming—if she came home.

With a heavy heart Andy made some arrangements with the officer and the undertaker and then he realized that if Danny's sacrifice were to count for much, he must let the boys come in tonight and have a talk with them while their hearts were softened. So he ordered the two or three young ones who had crept out of hiding to round up the rest, while he went out a few minutes to tell the sad news.

Chapter 23

JAN WAS RESTLESS. It was nearing Christmas and she was fairly flooded with requests to play here and there. Her aunt had accepted many of the engagements without even consulting her.

"But Aunt Myra," objected Jan one morning at breakfast, "if I take that one I'll not get home for Christmas vacation!"

She was almost in tears.

Her aunt opened her mouth and then closed it again. She was canny enough to realize that Jan was near to breaking and the wrong word now might undo all that she had worked so hard to accomplish. For it was through her influence that many of the invitations to play had materialized. If she could manage to make Jan feel that she was indispensable here at Oak Hill and its environs, she felt that she would have won her over for good. So she restrained herself and spoke reasonably.

"It is not easy to build up a reputation, my dear," she argued, setting her prim lips in a tight line and smoothing her immaculate housedress. "Remember you are laying a foundation for your future career, and mere sentiment must not be allowed to interfere. Suppose a man who had a position with a business firm were to absent himself from his office for the mere pleasure of visiting his parents. Do you think he would be a great success?"

"Well, no, of course not," admitted Jan. "But this seems different."

"How is it different?" demanded Aunt Myra.

"Oh—I don't know, it just isn't the same. There is nobody to whom I must account for my time."

"That is just the reason many artists and professional people never make a success of themselves!" Aunt Myra said sharply. She felt that she had won her point sufficiently to snap off her words as she usually did.

Jan simply looked confused.

Aunt Myra studied her a moment and then with an effort she went over to her and put her arm about her shoulders. It was the nearest to a loving gesture that she had ever given Jan.

"My darling girl," she said gently, "you are too young to realize this, but I have seen for a long time that your charm and your talents are too great to be wasted in a little unappreciative place like Chester. Your musical future is assured here, and that is a serious thing to consider. Just supposing you never marry, how else would you expect to support yourself unless by your music? And you have established yourself here. This is a music-loving town and there are more opportunities in our city than in most cities in the country. Do you see what I mean? Don't you realize that this is the obvious place for you?"

Jan gave a hopeless slow nod.

"Then let's not mope over a little disappointment now and then. They come in every life, you know, and you simply must not give in to sentiment when your whole living depends on your sticking close to your work. Now do you understand?"

"I guess so," sighed Jan.

"Then let's get right to work," went on Aunt Myra in her businesslike tone of voice, "and after your morning practice time is over we will go down town and select your new evening gowns for the Christmas engagements."

Reluctantly, with a heart like lead, Jan obediently went off to her work, but she felt as if she had signed her own death warrant.

The doorbell rang and a uniformed boy handed in a yellow envelope addressed to Jan. But Aunt Myra put it aside. She never disturbed Jan during her practice time. And they were so rushed later that she forgot it.

Jan plodded through the day and dropped into bed heartsick

that night. She should have written her father but she felt she simply could not tell him that she would not be home for Christmas.

But Aunt Myra had no such feeling. That very morning she sat down and wrote a short letter telling him plainly that Jan had begun to see that her life would now have to be centered in Oak Hill rather than Chester since her work was here.

"Jan is so busy that she really has not time to write just now but she wanted you to know."

When John Nielson came home the next afternoon that letter was waiting for him. He read it through three times before he could take in its implications, then the paper fell to the floor. It had happened, the thing that he had always feared! It seemed as if his life was just an accumulation of one blow after another. The news last night of Danny's death had gone hard with him. And now this! Danny dead and Jan no longer his. He raised his head dazedly and looked about the little apartment that seemed to have been waiting so many dreary months for the joyous presence of the girl who used to brighten it. A great sob broke from John's very heart. He felt he could not stand it to stay here any longer. He grabbed his coat and rushed out of the building. He walked and walked, frantically at first then more slowly and wearily. At last he found himself down by the river.

It was cold and the streets had been full of slush all day. His feet were sodden and numb. There was a strong biting wind and the slush was freezing fast. John kept on and on, but he could not shake off the feeling that an icy hand had clutched his heart and it was crushing the life out of him.

He stood gazing down into the dark turgid river. Jan had loved the river; but she did not love him any more.

John had forgotten passersby. He raised his head to the threatening skies and groaned aloud,

"Oh, God! When will this life be over?"

In his agony he stepped carelessly on a broken edge of the

river bank that was covered with ice and the next instant he found himself struggling in the icy waters of the relentless river.

Andy could not understand why he did not receive any answer to the telegram he had sent to Jan:

"It breaks my heart to have to tell you that Danny was killed accidentally. Will wait for funeral arrangements till we hear from you."

Andy had thought Jan would telephone or wire that she would be home immediately. But he waited all the day after Danny's death and no word came. He stopped in several times at Severys' where Danny's father and mother sat in stony drink-sodden conference with many relatives and neighbors who had welcomed the opportunity to take a day off and mourn with them. But neither had they received any word from Jan.

Andy called his own home various times thinking that Jan might have tried to get in touch with him there. Finally he decided that she must surely be on her way home without waiting to wire. She would probably arrive on the afternoon train.

But he met the train and Jan was not on it. There was still the possibility that she would come on the evening train, although if she had waited to take that, he could not see why she would not have let him know.

On the way home from the train station he stopped at a drug store for a cup of coffee. The radio was blaring some popular music. Suddenly it stopped and the announcer said: "Anyone knowing the whereabouts of the relatives of John Nielson of Apartment 9, 2341 South Sixteenth Street, please contact the Twenty-fourth Street police station immediately."

In new horror Andy left his coffee untasted and rushed out.

"Yeah," said the officer at the police station laconically, "a guy phoned in that they saw this man fall or else jump in, they couldn't tell which. The rescue squad worked with him a half hour before he come to. He's at Broad Street Hospital right now. We tried to get his home but there was no answer."

"You think he'll live, then?" asked Andy anxiously.

"I dunno. You'll have ta ask the hospital."

On the way there Andy felt as if he was in a tunnel that grew smaller and smaller as he went on.

They told him that John was suffering from shock but that he might pull through.

John couldn't speak to him but Andy thought he knew him. John simply turned hopeless eyes on him and sank into a sort of coma.

Where was Jan? He *must* get in touch with her. He called Oak Hill on the hospital phone. A very cold voice told him that Miss Nielson was out of town indefinitely. Yes, she had left that morning. Then the unfriendly party at the other end of the line hung up abruptly as if unwilling to be questioned further.

There was a possibility that Jan might be on her way home. Andy decided to go to John's apartment. If Jan did come she must be told immediately what had happened to her father. What a homecoming for her, if both Danny and her father were gone!

He was surprised to find John's door unlocked and ajar. The chair by the table was upset as if John had got up in a hurry. On the floor beside the table was a letter.

It was not Andy's way to read other people's letters but he felt as if it was imperative now that he find out what he could. He saw that the postmark was Oak Hill.

As he read in consternation, the conviction grew upon him that John, in brokenhearted misery, had deliberately tried to end his life!

Horror-stricken, Andy tried to think clearly. He found it hard to believe that that lovely girl had deserted her father when he remembered her sweet face as she had looked up at him on that woodland path and told him how she wanted her music to be used in the service of the Lord. Still, he knew what a pull the glamor and admiration of the world could exert.

"Oh Lord, guard her, and bring her back!" he cried in his heart.

He stuffed the letter into his pocket, scribbled a note to Jan telling her the hospital address and enough information to bring her there quickly but not to frighten her too much, and then he went back to the hospital. John must not be left to die alone!

He found John's pulse a little stronger and he opened his eyes once and tried to talk to Andy.

"They should have let me go!" he murmured. Then he fainted again.

It was a half hour before he came to consciousness and during that time Andy argued the whole problem over and over in his mind. It seemed impossible to believe that Jan had actually treated her father so heartlessly that he had tried to take his life. Yet John was not an emotional man, carried away by impulse. There must be something Andy did not know. Still, he could not give up his faith in that clear-eyed girl. It wrenched his heart to think that she might have been playing a part with him. Were all girls faithless? Was Jan no more trustworthy than Lucile? For some time now, when he had thought of girls at all, Jan Nielson had stood out in his mind as the loveliest, sweetest one he knew. Of course she had always seemed like a little girl to him. He remembered her as he had first seen her, in brief plaid shorts, with neat pigtails, her tortured eyes looking up so pleadingly into his. She was grown up now, but there had been that same straightforward earnest look in her face that evening in the woods. Surely she could not have changed in just one winter!

The nurse came in just then to fix her patient for the night. Asking her to call him when she was ready for him to come back, Andy stepped out into the corridor and walked back and forth trying to piece together the puzzle, trying to think of some other place where he could reach Jan. Then as he wheeled once more in his restless pacing, the elevator opened and he came face to face with her!

All the anxiety and sorrow of the past two days were in Andy's face and it shocked Jan. She thought, too, that he wore a stern accusing look. It reminded her of the day of Danny's accident. It cut her to the quick and left her trembling. He had worded the message he left at her apartment so tactfully that she had not been frightened about her father. But now she did not know what to think.

Silently he motioned to her to step into a little waiting room. Her eyes widened in alarm.

Jan had awakened that morning from a restless night with a keen sense that she had done wrong. Could it be that she should not have given in so easily to Aunt Myra's persuasion? She slipped down beside her bed and poured out her bewilderment to her new Master.

"Please show me," she pleaded, "what I should do. You know I *want* to go home, but I'll do whatever You want me to do. Show me whether Aunt Myra is right or not."

As she dressed she found herself laying aside a few garments in a little pile as if she were going on a trip. More and more the certainty grew upon her that she must go home to her father. The engagements that had loomed as so important yesterday while Aunt Myra was talking seemed trivial now. She seemed to hear her own weak little voice agreeing with Aunt Myra in everything she had said. Jan suddenly realized that if she heard any other girl succumbing in that way to another person's will she would despise her.

"Lord," she said aloud, "I'm going home. If You don't want me to, please stop me."

She packed her suitcase swiftly and went downstairs. Aunt Myra was nowhere to be seen. Jan glanced at the clock. It was nearly eleven, for Jan had slept late. If she hurried she could get the train into town that would make connections so that she could get home by evening. The thought of home and father seemed very precious.

She cast a sorrowful glance at her wonderful violin which she was leaving, but she resolutely sat down at Aunt Myra's desk and wrote:

"Dear Aunt Myra: I have thought over carefully all that you said yesterday, but I cannot feel that it is right for me to stay here without seeing my father. I appreciate all you have done for me, but I must go. I shall cancel the engagements of next week myself. If you are too angry with me to want me back I am sorry. Good-bye and thank you for all you have done for me."

Then she called a taxi and was gone.

When she reached home and found Andy's note, she hurried to the hospital. Now she looked up at Andy imploring him with her eyes to tell her what had happened.

Unsmilingly he motioned to her to sit down on a shabby willow settee.

"Your father is out of danger," he told her first.

"Thank God!" she said fervently. "Can I see him?"

"The nurse will call us in a few minutes."

"What was the matter?" she asked anxiously, dreading a heart attack; there were so many these days.

"They found him in the river," Andy stated abruptly giving her a searching look as he handed her Aunt Myra's letter.

Jan's hand trembled as she took the letter and she read with the tears blinding her eyes. Andy, watching, was melted in sympathy for her.

Frantic indignation seized her as she glanced through the cruel words, and she clenched the paper fiercely in her hand. Her tortured eyes looked up to Andy's and she read in his face what he had believed.

"Oh!" she gasped, "you don't think—Daddy didn't—didn't *jump* in, did he?" Her eyes were wide with desperation and her hand clutched her throat.

Andy wished he could reassure her.

"He may have fallen," he said gently. "It was icy. This is terribly hard on you, I know," he soothed.

"But Andy," wailed Jan heartbrokenly, "how *could* Aunt Myra be so cruel as to write all that to Daddy. It's not true! Don't you *know* it's not true? I never said all that! Oh my poor, poor Daddy!" She buried her face in her hands and shook with sobs.

As Andy watched her sorrow a great relief broke the tension he had been under. A number of things began to be clear to him. It seemed as if a dim light were shining through the darkness of the past two days.

"Jan," he said laying his hand on her shoulder gently, "look at me."

She looked up, the agony still in her eyes.

"Janette," said Andy solemnly, "did you get my telegram yesterday?"

She looked puzzled.

"What telegram?" she asked. "Did this happen *yesterday?*" Then it was Andy's turn to be shaken.

"Oh!" he cried, "what has your aunt done! Didn't she tell you that Danny was gone?"

"Gone?" echoed Jan, puzzled. "Gone where? How would she know anything about Danny?"

"Oh, you poor little girl!" Andy took Jan's little cold trembling hands in his. "Jan, I can't bear to give you so much sorrow all at once, but—you'll have to know. Danny has gone Home to the Lord he loved so much."

As Jan took in the truth and saw tenderness again in Andy's face, suddenly she flung herself on his shoulder and let the sobs shake her.

Andy's arms went around her with a strong comforting pressure and he let her cry herself out as he smoothed her soft hair and held her preciously close. His heart ached as he thought how much she must have loved Danny! Why had he not guessed it long ago!

He took out his big clean soft handkerchief and wiped her tears away.

"Dear little girl," he whispered, disregarding the curious glances of a nurse who hurried by, "I'll tell you all about it after while. It was a glorious death, just as he would have wanted it. He gave his life to save Pad Hucker, Jan! Think of that! Only God could work a miracle of love like that! And listen, Jan, Pad is utterly changed. He wants to hear the gospel!"

Jan looked up through her tears in wonder.

"Yes, I was down at the jail this morning and he can't hear enough, he is so eager. Think, Jan, how happy Danny would be over that. I knew you'd want to know, for I know that you loved Danny, Jan!"

Andy choked and had to swallow hard to go on.

"And listen, little girl, Danny loved you! Almost the last word he spoke was your name, Jan. He said—'Tell Jan I loved her'!"

Andy watched the sweet sorrowful face before him, expecting to see a fresh outburst of grief as the girl realized that she had lost her lover. But only a tender smile spread over Jan's face.

"I know he did. Dear Danny!" she said softly. "We have been friends since we were children. He was a loyal pal."

Andy tried again. He was determined to make Danny's message plain to the girl Danny had loved, no matter how much it might wound his own heart.

"No, he meant more than that, Jan. He really *loved* you, didn't you know that?" Andy paused.

Then as the truth dawned on Jan she looked almost frightened for an instant.

"Oh *no!*" she cried. "Not *that* way! Oh, *poor* Danny!"

Gentle tears rained down like dewdrops and Andy thought he had never seen such a sweet expression in all his life as Jan wore now. Her eyes grew bright and she shook her head in wonder.

"Oh, how merciful our Lord was, then, to take him, wasn't He, Andy?"

He gazed back at her in surprise. "You mean—" he began, and hesitated.

Jan nodded tenderly.

"Why yes," she said. "I had no idea that he cared that way, and I just never could have, you know. He always seemed like a dear young brother to me. It would have hurt him so if I had had to tell him." Then she glanced quickly at Andy. "You don't suppose he knew that I—that I didn't, do you?"

With infinite pity and sympathy Andy answered,

"I think he did—dear," he said softly. "Sometime I'll tell you the very last thing he said." He put his arm about Jan and drew her close to him.

Just then the nurse appeared.

"Mr. Nielson is ready to see you now," she said.

"Oh!" cried Jan jumping up and fairly running down the corridor.

Chapter 24

WHEN THEY REACHED John's room his eyes were open. Jan softly dropped beside his bed and kissed his hand eagerly.

"Daddy, dear *precious* Daddy!" she breathed.

Slowly a light began to dawn in his eyes.

He lifted his hand weakly and stroked her hair.

"Did you come, after all, Jan?" he murmured.

"Of *course* I came, Daddy. And I'm here to *stay!* I'm never going back."

Then a great radiance shone in his face.

"Do you want to stay?" he asked incredulously.

"I *want* to stay, Daddy, and I don't want to leave you, ever. I guess I was kind of silly for a while and I let the glamor fool me, just as you said I might. But I'm sorry now. Anyway, that letter that Aunt Myra wrote was all a lie, Daddy. I didn't know she was writing that. Andy just showed it to me. Daddy, you nearly *left* me!" She gave a little wail. "Why didn't you trust me?"

"Trust you, Jan? Oh, little girl! Did you think I would do that on purpose? No, child, I admit I was pretty sad about you, but I was just walking and I slipped. Oh Jan dear, I'm glad you've come!"

Andy had not taken his eyes from Jan since they came into the room. Now he put his finger on John's pulse and smiled.

"You're better already, Mr. Nielson," said Andy with a glad ring in his voice. "Now I guess all you need is a good rest."

John smiled. "And it will be the best sleep I've had in a long time," he answered happily.

After a little they said good night to John and went downstairs. Andy put Jan tenderly into his car to take her home.

"I hate to leave you up in that apartment all alone," he said anxiously as they started off through the evening traffic. "Would you feel like coming out to 'Lookaway' and spending the night with my folks?"

"Oh, I'd love to!" responded Jan wistfully. "You don't know how I've missed them since those wonderful days in the mountains. And it will help," she added sadly, "to have someone to talk to. You all knew Danny so well."

Andy laid his hand over hers and gave a gentle understanding pressure.

"Yes, it's been a tough assignment for you to take. It's not easy to meet so much trouble on your homecoming," he said. "We'll stop on the way out at a little country tea room I know of and get a bite of dinner, shall we?"

Jan snuggled down near him and they drove on in companionable silence for a time until the city's sounds were far behind.

At last Andy broke the silence. He spoke hesitatingly, shyly, "Like a dear little boy," thought Jan looking up at his fine profile in the moonlight.

"Jan?"

"Yes?"

He waited so long that she wondered.

Again he laid his hand over hers and his touch thrilled her.

"May I tell you now what Danny said, about—us?"

Jan nestled her hand in his.

"Of course, Andy. I want to hear it."

"He said—the brave kid!" Andy's voice broke. "He said he'd be 'out of the way' now, that you were—mine!" Andy breathed the last words in a voice deep with emotion.

"Danny said that?" quavered Jan. "Why, how did he know that I—" she stopped in sweet confusion.

"That you what, Jan?" urged Andy eagerly.

"Oh, why, I mean," she stammered, her heart throbbing.

Andy stopped the car. They were on a hill top and the road was fringed with lacy trees. The moonlight glinted down through them in delicate patterns. It seemed as if the whole world were waiting breathlessly for Jan's answer.

Andy turned to Jan, his eyes seeking hers, his arms stretched toward her.

"Do you mean, dear, that Danny was right?"

Jan's eyes were starry as they met his.

"Don't you think he was, dear?" she whispered.

"Oh, I do, my darling. I surely do!" Andy's arms went around her and held her tenderly close and their lips clung to each other speaking words too sweet to utter.

"I love you, love you, love you," breathed Andy thrilling to the softness of her cheek and hair.

"And I think," said Jan in joyous wonder as her hand stole up and pressed his face to hers, "I think I have loved you ever since the day I first saw you. It was Danny who brought us together, wasn't it?"

"Yes, and Danny's love that made us find each other!" exclaimed Andy.

Jan buried her head on his shoulder and let the glad tears come.

"It seems almost heartless to be so happy, with Danny gone," she wailed suddenly.

"I don't believe Danny would think so, darling," Andy said gravely. "It seems as if Danny has wrought more by his death than most people do in a whole lifetime. What a blessing he has been in the short time he has been a Christian, and what a rejoicing will be his when he finds out how God has accepted his offering and multiplied it. Ten of those boys in the gang accepted Christ as their Saviour last night. Think of it!"

"Oh!" breathed Jan. "How wonderful! We do have a wonderful God, don't we! He has done so much for me and now He has given me you!"

Andy's radiant smile broke out and he kissed her again.

"Oh darling! Do you really think you can love me? It's not an easy life I'll ask you to share."

"Beloved, it's *your* life, and that's enough for me. I am not looking for an easy one."

That evening they had a sweet time of fellowship with Andy's father and mother.

"At last I shall have the daughter I've always wanted!" cried Mother Hightower when they told their news. "And you will be married at 'Lookaway,' won't you?" she coaxed.

Jan's eyes shone.

"That would be perfect," she said. "But do tell me what the name means. I've always wondered."

" 'Looking away unto Jesus,' " explained Father Hightower softly.

"Lovely!" smiled Jan. "Yes, this is just the place to be married then, isn't it, dear?" she agreed, meeting Andy's eyes in glad assent.

The next morning they drove back to the city together. The service for Danny was to be at two o'clock. Andy's father was to speak and many of the gang had signified their purpose to be there.

On the way into the city they stopped at the Nielson's apartment and found a letter for Jan. It bore the Oak Hill postmark.

With a heart free from fear at last Jan opened it and read it aloud in awe.

"My dear niece:

"You will be surprised to receive this letter. I am writing because I know that I have not long to stay on this earth. I had a bad heart attack this morning and may have another at any time. You don't need to blame yourself for going home. I can see now that I was wrong.

"I am leaving your violin for you, and most of what I have. I have saved out only enough for your uncle to live on. He doesn't need much, and when he goes it will all be yours.

"There is one more thing I want you to know because I can't

go until I make it right. There is a packet of letters which your mother wrote to your father before you were born. I did wrong in keeping them. They are in my safe at the bank. I wish you would tell your father that I know now that I was wrong.

"Everything has been arranged so that there will be no trouble for you. Good-bye, my precious Janette.

"Aunt Myra."

"Oh Andy!" cried Jan, "and I have been so mean to her! I've actually hated her. Poor Aunt Myra. I'd like to go and tell her that I'm sorry."

"Perhaps we can tomorrow," he promised, holding Jan close to his heart.

"Come, then, let's tell Daddy now. To think of all those letters from my mother! Oh, it will be a joyous Christmas for him. But," Jan added wistfully, "I did so look forward to being home again and having us *all* together. How Danny would have loved to be with us!"

A smile like a soft glow of light lit Andy's face.

"But just think what a Christmas of joy Danny is having, darling," he reminded her. "You wouldn't begrudge him that!"

"Oh, do you think he really knows? I mean can he enjoy things, like we do?" Jan stopped, confused.

"Why, of course!" Andy reassured her. "Do you think that a lover of Jesus would be less happy to be in His presence than to be down here in this sinful old world just waiting for Him?"

"No," answered Jan slowly as the truth dawned on her. "That wouldn't make sense, would it?" She smiled and glad tears came to her eyes. "I'm so glad you told me that! I've wanted to be glad for Danny since I knew he was gone, but I had a feeling it wouldn't be right to rejoice."

"I think it's wonderfully right!"

Andy kissed her tenderly. They were standing at the window looking out at the dear old Mississippi River crack and down at the Severys' dreary kitchen.

Just then a ragged dejected figure lurched into the Severys' back door and the old battle began.

"Oh—h!" cried Jan. "Poor Danny!"

"Poor father, not poor Danny any more, dear!" Andy reminded her. "Down there is part of our work. We're going to carry on where Danny left off."

"Yes," agreed Jan, "we will." Her eyes were misty.

HARVEST HOUSE PUBLISHERS
For The Best In Inspirational Fiction

RUTH LIVINGSTON HILL CLASSICS

Bright Conquest
The Homecoming
The Jeweled Sword

Morning Is For Joy
This Side of Tomorrow
The South Wind Blew Softly

June Masters Bacher
PIONEER ROMANCE NOVELS

Series 1
[1] Love Is a Gentle Stranger
[2] Love's Silent Song

[3] Diary of a Loving Heart
[4] Love Leads Home

Series 2
[1] Journey To Love
[2] Dreams Beyond Tomorrow

[3] Seasons of Love
[4] My Heart's Desire

Series 3
[1] Love's Soft Whisper
[2] Love's Beautiful Dream

[3] When Hearts Awaken
[4] Another Spring

MYSTERY/ROMANCE NOVELS

Echoes From the Past, *Bacher*
Mist Over Morro Bay, *Page/Fell*
Secret of the East Wind, *Page/Fell*
Storm Clouds Over Paradise, *Page/Fell*
Beyond the Windswept Sea, *Page/Fell*
The Legacy of Lillian Parker, *Holden*
The Compton Connection, *Holden*
The Caribbean Conspiracy, *Holden*
The Gift, *Hensley/Miller*

PIONEER ROMANCE NOVELS

Sweetbriar, *Wilbee*
The Sweetbriar Bride, *Wilbee*
The Tender Summer, *Johnson*

Available at your local Christian bookstore

Dear Reader:

We would appreciate hearing from you regarding the **Ruth Livingston Hill Classics**. It will enable us to continue to give you the best in inspirational romance fiction.

Mail to: Ruth Livingston Hill Romance Editors
Harvest House Publishers, 1075 Arrowsmith
Eugene, OR 97402

1. What most influenced you to purchase *The Homecoming*?
   - ☐ The Christian story
   - ☐ Cover
   - ☐ Backcover copy
   - ☐ _____
   - ☐ Recommendations
   - ☐ Other **Ruth Livingston Hill** Classic Romances you've read

2. Where did you purchase *The Homecoming*?
   - ☐ Christian bookstore
   - ☐ General bookstore
   - ☐ Department store
   - ☐ Grocery store
   - ☐ Other

3. Your overall rating of this book:
   - ☐ Excellent ☐ Very good ☐ Good ☐ Fair ☐ Poor

4. How many **Ruth Livingston Hill Romances** have you read altogether?
   (Choose one) ☐ 1 ☐ 2 ☐ 3 ☐ Over 3

5. How likely would you be to purchase other **Ruth Livingston Hill Romances**?
   - ☐ Very likely
   - ☐ Somewhat likely
   - ☐ Not very likely
   - ☐ Not at all

6. Please check the box next to your age group.
   - ☐ Under 18
   - ☐ 18-24
   - ☐ 25-34
   - ☐ 35-39
   - ☐ 40-54
   - ☐ Over 55

Name _____

Address _____

City _____ State _____ Zip _____